AN UNEXPECTED HARVEST

AN UNEXPECTED HARVEST

Sally Stewart

HEADLINE

First published in 2000 by
HEADLINE BOOK PUBLISHING

10 9 8 7 6 5 4 3 2 1

British Library Cataloguing in Publication Data

Stewart, Sally
An Unexpected Harvest
I. Title
823.9'14 [F]

ISBN 0 7472 7144 5

Typeset by CBS
Martlesham Heath, Ipswich, Suffolk

Printed and bound in Great Britain by
Clays Ltd, St Ives plc

HEADLINE BOOK PUBLISHING
A division of the Hodder Headline Group
338 Euston Road
London NW1 3BH
www.headline.co.uk
www.hodderheadline.com

AN UNEXPECTED HARVEST

Chapter 1

Getting through the morning rush-hour traffic seemed much like negotiating rapids in a small canoe, and Georgina Hadley turned out of the noisome river of the Tottenham Court Road with a sigh of relief; Bedford Square seemed peaceful by comparison, a still-elegant backwater left behind by the developers. She let herself into her parents' rented flat, wondering whether departure-chaos this time would be complete or only partial, but a glance at her mother's face confirmed that things were even worse than usual! Tragedy stared out of Olivia Hadley's dark eyes, and trembled in a voice still enriched by Italian inflections after more than twenty-five years of marriage to an Englishman.

'*Cara* . . . I thought you'd never come. Help me before I die of despair!'

She was kissed by her daughter, who managed the feat of looking both sympathetic and cheerful. 'Not as bad as that, surely . . . it never is.'

'Go and look,' said her mother with an operatic gesture in the direction of the bedroom door. 'Every piece of luggage we possess is full, but there are clothes still strewn all over the floor and we must leave in one hour's time. Does your father deal with the crisis? No, he walks along the bookshelves discovering things he thought were in the crates we sent to America.'

Richard Hadley, still indeed prowling along the shelves, turned to smile at his wife. 'I made what I thought were helpful suggestions. When they were spurned, my best course seemed to be to stay out of the way, but I'm ready to do whatever you command me to.'

It was the voice of sweet reason, calculated to goad Olivia into imploring Heaven to tell her why she'd imagined she would enjoy life married to an Englishman. Congenital smoothness had been polished by years as a professional diplomat; he now offered no rough edges at all for an irritated wife to get a grip on. Their married life had been wonderfully happy and she knew it very well, but drama had been lacking; no fights and no great reconciliations to offer a full-blooded Italian proper scope.

Georgina was accustomed to the chronic state of muddle in which her parents normally left London for a fresh posting, and knew by now that nothing would turn them into organised travellers. Even so, gaiety usually broke through in the end, but it was noticeably lacking this morning. She ignored a yelp of pain from her father at the discovery of another book he couldn't live without, and headed in the direction of the bedroom. Olivia trailed after her and collapsed in the only chair that offered space to sit on.

'You see what I mean, dearest!'

Submerged in a sea of tissue-paper and garments for which no home had been found, Georgina indeed saw. Not only had her mother's heart not been in the business of packing, but her mind had been elsewhere as well. On the principle that a start had to be made somewhere, she picked up the suitcase nearest to her and emptied its contents on the bed.

'Desperate times call for desperate remedies,' she announced grimly.

'I was hoping you were going to put things in, not take them out.'

'You may have to do some pressing at the other end, because there isn't time to be careful, but I promise you I'll get everything in.' She worked in silence for a while, and Olivia watched order gradually emerging from chaos.

'English calmness . . . that's what does it.' She sounded torn between pride and regret.

'What does what?' Richard Hadley had come to stand in the doorway in time to hear his wife's remark.

'It's your Anglo-Saxon genes that account for our daughter's lack of muddle. She certainly doesn't get it from me.'

'Never mind, my love. Remember that she doesn't get her beauty from the Hadleys!'

'That is true,' his wife conceded, looking slightly cheered. It was unarguable that Richard's sister looked like a more than usually intelligent horse. He grinned because he'd read her thoughts, then held out a small leather-bound book.

'Just a *little* one, darling. Can you find room for it? I can't think how it came to get left out of the crates.'

Georgina patiently opened the case she'd just closed, while her mother wandered out of the room, murmuring that there was still someone she must say goodbye to.

'Mama seems very low this morning . . . doesn't Washington appeal?'

'Not greatly, I'm afraid, because it's even further from Italy than London by a handsome margin, but unfortunately we tend *not* to be sent back to the place where our careers began.'

2

She stared at her father's preoccupied face and ventured for once on a subject they'd tacitly agreed in the past to leave alone.

'Does it seem to you that she gets *more* homesick for Italy as the years go by, not less?'

'I'm afraid so; it means that when I retire I must take her back to live there.'

'At Poggio?'

Richard Hadley gave a little shrug. 'Perhaps, although getting *me* as well as his daughter might be more than Enrico would bargain for!'

Georgina nodded, aware that he and her grandfather had never quite succeeded in coming to terms with each other – Enrico because he couldn't help resenting a man who'd taken a precious only daughter travelling round the world instead of settling with her in Italy; Richard because the warmth and exuberance he'd loved in *her* were less easy for a reticent Englishman to accept from another man. Georgina loved them both, and wished they could somehow come to love each other.

'Would you mind retirement in Italy?' she asked diffidently. He was the last man to need the retreat of clubs and pubs, but England was in the marrow of his bones. She'd always imagined that when the time came to hang up his hat, he'd find a pleasant country house and enjoy himself introducing Olivia to the oddities of English rural life.

'I don't think retirement in Tuscany would be a hardship. In any case, by then it will be your mother's turn to choose; she's been an uncomplaining exile for most of our married life.' He hesitated a moment before going on. 'It isn't just a matter of geography at the moment; she's worried about things at Poggio. You know the sort of letter your grandmother normally writes – overflowing with news and gossip and enthusiasm. She's written very little lately, but a letter arrived yesterday which was so quiet and uninformative that Olivia's convinced something's wrong. She's been trying to telephone and getting no reply, and that's odd too.'

Georgina didn't pursue the subject because her mother came back into the room, pale-faced, to confirm that she'd still got no reply to her call. She nodded at the question in Richard's face.

'I can't understand it . . . even if they've gone away Maria should be there to answer the telephone.'

'She hates it, don't you remember?' Georgina said quickly. 'I've known her switch things on in the kitchen so that she can say truthfully that she doesn't hear the telephone ring! The children would answer, but they'll be at school.'

3

Olivia nodded. 'I expect I'm worrying about nothing. Lucia would tell me if there was something wrong. It's time to count my blessings and remember how lucky we are to be going to Washington. The poor Williamsons got landed with Moscow this time.'

The sight of the ordered room and neat row of closed luggage even made her smile. '*Meraviglioso, tesoro!* At least we can now travel.'

She was determinedly bright all the way to Heathrow, but sitting in the back with her daughter while Richard drove, her long thin fingers were gripped together in her lap, contradicting the flow of cheerful conversation. When the time came to say goodbye a decision Georgina had scarcely been aware of making announced itself.

'I'll go on ringing Poggio until Maria *has* to answer. If anything should be wrong, my dear William Bird will have to let me take an early holiday to go and see them. But you're *not* to fret. If Lucia's letter sounded miserable, it was probably because Enrico had been prophesying that the European wine lake would ruin them. You know how Gramps relishes a bit of drama!'

It was true enough to make her mother's tragic face relax into a real smile. 'Bad enough contending with the French, he'd say, but with Spain and Portugal in the EU as well . . . ! I'm sure you're right, *tesoro*. But I shall be happier for knowing that you could go and see them. There's Roberto, too! I can't believe you don't want to see him!'

Georgina grinned, but blushed a little as well. 'My childhood hero! I should have to beat a path to him through a bevy of Italian beauties by now, I dare say.'

It was likely, Olivia thought regretfully, but she still nourished the secret hope of seeing her daughter safely married to Roberto Artom in the end. Childhood attachments didn't always last into adult life, but they were perfect when they did. Apart from that, there was bred in her the conviction that neighbouring estates were best linked by marriage. She liked the idea of a considerable chunk of Tuscany being in the hands of some future Artom/Casali descendant. Georgina smiled, knowing that what her mother wanted, Richard Hadley did not, although he wouldn't say so. Even if there wasn't something excessive to another man about Roberto's good looks, he'd still prefer her not to become the wife of an Italian . . . he knew the sadness of a woman torn in two by marriage, uncertain where she really belonged.

She kissed them both and watched them disappear into the departure lounge; an aloof Great Dane padding along beside a beautiful, nervous poodle was how she thought of them when they were out together! Olivia's hankerings for Tuscany apart, theirs had been a wonderfully successful marriage. Richard Hadley was an experienced diplomat, and his present posting to the British Embassy in Washington reflected the fact, but he'd be the first to insist how much his wife had helped his career. One diplomatic couple tended to be much like another, but anyone who met the Hadleys couldn't help remembering them for so piquant a combination.

But on the return journey – on the Underground because her father's hired car had been handed back – Georgina's mind reverted to the subject of Poggio. Her mother had retained some strange telepathic link with her home which separation had intensified, not weakened. If she sensed that something was wrong, then there was a good chance something was, but what sort of problem could it be that Enrico had decided not to share with his daughter? Memory conjured him up in front of her – a small, broad man with a mane of silvered hair and the weathered face of someone constantly out of doors. Eyebrows and luxuriant moustache had remained black, and he wasn't above being pleased that the contrast made him noticeable. He was an Italian, and '*far bella figura*' was the duty of any right-minded Latin male, just as every right-minded woman was required to look as beautiful as possible. They hadn't all, poor things, the natural advantages bestowed on the women in his own family, but at least they must try!

Georgina found his vanity endearing, but loved him for other things – the kindness and good-humour that were constantly winning over small spurts of temper, and the passionate love that he felt for his own land. It was the private grief of his life that there had been no son to inherit Poggio, but at least the instinct to cherish growing things had been passed on to his granddaughter. A patch of London soil outside her ground-floor flat didn't offer much scope to a would-be Gertrude Jekyll, but during the working day the luscious green spread of Kew's Botanic Gardens was her playground. Remembering now the workload in early spring, she couldn't help hoping that it *wouldn't* be necessary to ask if she could take her summer holiday in the middle of March.

She made her first call to Poggio as soon as she got home. The ring echoed along the line, tinnily insistent but still unanswered. By Italian time it was already long past noon. Why were they not indoors, Enrico expectantly awaiting lunch, and her grandmother supervising the cooking of the pasta Maria had made that morning? If they *were* both away, why didn't one of Maria's children answer? Home from school, Alessio normally seized every chance he could to yell '*pronto*' into the telephone.

By mid-afternoon she was beginning to get seriously alarmed, but at last came the little click that indicated someone picking up the telephone. Even then it wasn't Lucia's voice at the other end of the line, and still less the operatic roar with which her grandfather always answered. She had to strain her ears to hear the hoarse whisper, because Maria always held the mouthpiece a foot away in case it bit her.

'No one is here but me,' she said more coherently when she could be made to understand that she knew who was talking to her. 'There is only Maria here.' She always spoke of herself in the third person when she was at a loss, thereby transferring the problem to someone else. Georgina recognised the sign, but persevered.

'Where *is* everyone, Maria? Why is no one at home?'

'This evening, *cara* . . . talk to the signore this evening . . . he will be here then,' she insisted feverishly. Having settled on this formula, she clung to it with peasant obstinacy and offered it as the answer to any question she was tried with. There was nothing to be done but accept defeat and say goodbye.

Georgina spent a tedious hour or two polishing furniture that didn't need polishing, and scrambled eggs she didn't feel like eating, to fill in the time until she could call again. Then suddenly her own telephone rang while she was still waiting. The odd squeaks and whistles coming across the wire signified a foreign call, but she didn't recognise the cool voice that asked her name in English.

'Miss Hadley? I tried your parents' number first, but Maria gave me this one as well.'

If he knew Maria, he was calling from Poggio. Over the dryness in her throat she made herself answer calmly.

'My parents left for America this morning . . . this is Georgina Hadley speaking.'

'My name's Fleming . . . Adam Fleming. I've no telephone of my own; I'm ringing from San Vicenzo.'

She had no idea who Adam Fleming might be, but San Vicenzo was the nearest small town to Poggio. Then a faint memory stirred in her mind; surely long ago her grandmother had mentioned that they were going to rent an empty apartment in the farmhouse on the estate to an English professor? But the crisp cool voice didn't fit her mental image of an elderly academic, and confusion added to the anxiety that now consumed her. She sounded stiff because she was trying so hard not to sound frightened.

'*Why* are you ringing, Mr Fleming? My parents won't be back in London for some time – is there anything I can do for you?'

6

'Not for me personally, but it's time someone did something for your grandparents.'

She thought she could hear a note of accusation in his voice and found herself resenting it. He was a stranger who had no right to meddle in their affairs or pass judgement on people he didn't know. But, dear God, it seemed that something *was* wrong.

'I've been trying and trying to telephone,' she said unsteadily. 'Suppose *you* tell me what's happened.'

'Your grandmother's in hospital, having just had an emergency operation.'

'*Lucia* has? What sort of operation?'

'A stomach ulcer, I gather . . . neglected because she didn't want to worry Enrico, or leave him alone. The surgery has been successful, and she's recovering well now.'

It sounded like her grandmother – a woman who despised illness and reckoned that with no attention paid to it an ailment always went away. She was the rock on which life at Poggio was built, and without her its stability would be lost.

'We had no idea she was ill,' Georgina said slowly. 'Her letters to my mother have been scarce lately, that's all, and sounded as if she might be worried about things in general.'

'That's no surprise; things in general aren't so hot, either.'

It was something else they should have known about, apparently, by second sight or by peering into their crystal ball.

'What else do you know about Poggio?' Trying not to shout her fears out loud, she sounded stiff to the point of rudeness instead, and Adam Fleming told himself he was wasting his time; Maria had been mistaken in assuring him that this was the person his friends needed.

'I know that your grandfather is trying to carry on almost single-handed. Giuseppe cleared out weeks ago.'

'*Giuseppe* did?' She thought she must sound like a feeble-minded parrot echoing everything he said, but his last piece of information was almost impossible to believe. Giuseppe had been at Poggio for as long as she could remember; he was her grandfather's friend, as well as the mainstay of the estate. 'Are you saying that Giuseppe has walked out and left his family?'

She heard a long-suffering sigh at the other end of the line – Mr Fleming was losing patience with her. 'All I can tell you is that Giuseppe *and* his sons have left. Enrico is working alone.'

If she found it hard to believe, he obviously found it hard to accept that

7

she didn't know. But there wasn't room in her mind now for resentment about his attitude; she had too much else to think about. She knew better than any stranger could have done that an estate the size of Poggio couldn't be worked by one man.

Giuseppe's sons, she would have sworn, had grown up in the knowledge that they would carry on where he left off. There'd been occasional fights with Enrico, because Giuseppe had been obstinately convinced that he knew more about the growing of vines than his *padrone* did; but what monumental row could have pushed them both past the point where a climb-down wasn't possible?

'We didn't know about Giuseppe, either,' she had to admit finally. 'But my grandfather has friends there . . . People like the Artoms next door. Are they not helping him for the time being?'

'No one is helping as far as I can see, but my interference in your grandparents' affairs stops at asking why not. I hope it's not too much to suggest that a member of their family takes the trouble to come and find out what's going so badly wrong.'

She thought he sounded less and less like an urbane professor, if that was what he was supposed to be, and more and more coldly disapproving. She'd been judged and found wanting as a granddaughter. But he needn't have bothered to ring at all – there was that in his favour, and his obvious concern for her dear ones.

She quickly made up her mind. 'If I can arrange leave from my job I'll catch Monday morning's flight to Pisa and take the train to Florence from there. With any luck I shall be at Poggio by mid-afternoon.'

'Excellent!'

With gritted teeth she managed to meet smoothness with smoothness. 'Kind of you to trouble to ring. I take it my grandfather doesn't know that you have?'

'Certainly not, and I'd rather he *didn't* know, if you don't mind. He's a proud man who'd probably dislike an outsider barging in.'

Georgina knew that herself, and thought she didn't need it pointed out to her. The outsider in question had a genius for making her feel angry, anxious, and self-reproachful all at the same time; but she acquitted him of a simple desire to meddle – he was concerned about the state of things at Poggio. That thought prompted another question.

'How long are you planning to stay at Poggio, Mr Fleming?'

'I'm here until the end of the summer, at least. It seems likely, therefore, that we may meet.'

He sounded so indifferent to the prospect that she rashly countered with a gush of breathless enthusiasm calculated to irritate him still further.

'How lovely . . . a real live compatriot in the wilds of Tuscany . . . *just* what one always . . .' She hadn't finished before a firm click at the other end told her that Mr Fleming had heard enough and decided to end the conversation. Disagreeable as he'd been she had to feel grateful to him, but now she must concentrate on what to do. A telephone call to her grandfather wouldn't be enough; a visit was unavoidable, and she must find William Bird tomorrow if she was to leave on Monday.

On a Sunday a hard-working man might reasonably be expected to be at home, but having drawn a blank at his flat, she drove to Kew, aware that any day spent away from the Gardens was a day wasted as far as William was concerned.

She found him in the Orchid House, inspecting a specimen that hadn't quite made up its mind whether to live or die. He looked pleased to see her and saw no reason to point out that she wasn't supposed to be there at all.

'What do you make of this? Is it going to go crook on us?' His conversation was loaded with phrases he thought cattle-punchers used, because his only reading matter apart from botanical tracts and plant encyclopaedias was highly coloured accounts of Australian outback life.

She touched the plant with a gentle finger, then shook her head. 'I'm afraid it's going to die.'

'That's what I think too, silly wee bugger.' He was referring to the orchid, she realised, and affronted as usual when a plant refused to thrive under his care.

'William, I've got more bad news for you,' she said quickly before he could move along the row of seedlings. 'I need to take some leave very urgently . . . from tomorrow, in fact. You'll feel like firing me, I'm afraid, but I wouldn't ask if it wasn't so dreadfully important.'

William closed his eyes in anguish and thought of the load of spring-time work all round them waiting to be done. He even toyed with the idea of steeling himself to say she couldn't go, but he reckoned a man would have to be made of iron to withstand Georgina Hadley when she looked at him with huge, entreating eyes.

'Problem of some kind?' he growled, so as not to cave in too quickly.

'My grandmother's sick in hospital, and Gramps seems to have got other troubles as well. I must go and see what's wrong. Mama would normally go herself, but she and Father left for Washington yesterday morning.'

William scratched his chin, remembering that in the three years she'd worked for him she'd never been unreasonable. If she said a thing was urgent, it was. He still recalled with amazement that he'd almost refused to hire her – put off by the sight of hands that looked too delicately formed to coat themselves in wet earth, and an accent that seemed to belong to Sloane Square. Even working out of doors in jeans and sweaters, she always managed to look – 'ritzy' was how William described it to himself; but he understood her better now. She'd inherited the instincts of generations of Italian country people, and for all her outward gloss she belonged to the land.

'You'll have to go,' he agreed at last. 'I suppose it's that funny-sounding place . . . Poggio?'

She nodded, trying to smile at him. 'Poggio a San Vicenzo, to give it its proper name. Poggio means hilltop. My grandfather's land is spread over various hills, and San Vicenzo's the nice little town that sleeps in the sun down below. No claim to fame at all, apart from the fact that it lies at the heart of the Chianti Classico region. Thousands of tourists thunder around Tuscany every summer, but fortunately never even know that it's there.'

'My God, yes . . . those tourists,' William said reflectively. 'I once made the mistake of going to Florence in July. I used to go into the Boboli Gardens just to take the weight off my feet – there was precious little to see there – and got screamed at every time I went near a patch of grass. What sort of a garden is that, I ask you?'

'Not our sort at least!' She stood on tip-toe to plant an unexpected kiss on his cheek. 'Thanks for letting me go, William. I'm very grateful.'

He was confused by the gesture, being a man who seldom if ever got kissed. Even when he was, likely as not it was some maiden aunt who still thought she was pecking the cheek of schoolboy William Bird. Nothing in *that* to make a man's heart beat faster, but Georgina Hadley was a different kettle of fish. William had grown accustomed to being very firm with himself where she was concerned; if anything, he'd made her work harder than his other assistants in case heart was getting the better of head whenever she smiled at him.

'I could stay and do some work now,' she suggested.

'And be tired out when you get to Poggio? I don't think so. Sling your hook, maid, but I shall want to know how you get on, and you're not to get stuck over there, mind, with some fancy Eyetalian!'

He saw her smile and walk away as instructed, and he had to struggle with a sudden shocking urge to call her back and make her promise to remember that she couldn't stay at Poggio because he needed her at Kew.

10

Georgina left the gardens a little more sadly than she expected – she was deserting William at a bad time, but it was more than that. He'd become friend as well as teacher, and beneath their friendship had begun to grow a seam of deep, unspoken affection. She was afraid that he'd consider Roberto Artom a very fancy Eyetalian indeed. Even when last seen six months ago Roberto had been something to catch any woman's eye, and she didn't doubt that he'd become more, not less, desirable.

Her thoughts reverted to him the next morning when the Alitalia flight was skimming over layers of white cloud. All the long summer holidays of childhood that she'd spent at Poggio had been shared with Roberto Artom, the boy on the neighbouring estate. They'd had the usual mixture of squabbles and close companionship, until adolescence had changed the relationship. Subtly, then excitingly, a summer had arrived when casual hugs turned into kisses infinitely more disturbing. It would have been easy enough not to stop there – Roberto had been eager to proceed, and angry with her when she'd managed to insist that she wasn't ready to be made love to. She was too prim, too English, he'd shouted at her. But even at the time she'd known that wasn't true. What she hoped for from Roberto wasn't just the excitement of a passing affair. He was part of her life at Poggio, and she could scarcely imagine it without him. She was aware of Olivia's longing to have him as a son-in-law, and enough of an Italian herself to see the neatness of such an arrangement. But Roberto was still far from wanting her to marry him, and she wasn't even certain that she wanted to become an Italian wife. As much Hadley as Casali, her roots were deep in England, and with the perversity that life sometimes showed she never felt more English than when she was revelling in a summer at Poggio.

Outside the little window beside her the clouds were thinning to reveal a glimpse of sea below; they were crossing the Italian coast over Genoa, and Pisa was not far ahead of them. Time to acknowledge the anxieties that she'd been forcing to the back of her mind. She could understand that her grandmother wouldn't have wanted to worry Olivia just as she was on the point of leaving for Washington, but what could possibly explain Enrico's silence about her illness and about Poggio? No one else had thought to warn them, either, that he was in distress, and it was extraordinary that his friend and neighbour, Dino Artom, hadn't done so. It had been left to a stranger who happened to be spending a few months at Poggio to sound an alarm that she wasn't supposed to mention. Instead, Olivia's anxiety would have to be the reason for her sudden visit; but for the first time in her life she found that she was dreading her arrival at Poggio.

Chapter 2

In London the season had been early spring at its bleakest – scarcely distinguishable from winter. Eight hundred miles to the south and east the sun was shining. As the plane floated down towards Pisa airport there was the usual bird's-eye view of the buildings in the Campo Santo, all looking, she thought, more like toy models carved out of sugar-icing than ever. A few moments later she stepped out of the aircraft into the sudden warmth of a different spring-time. The thinness of her linen jacket and skirt was welcome now, because there was a hot train-ride to Florence in front of her, and an even more crowded bus-ride to San Vicenzo. She was stunned for a moment by the feeling that she'd strayed into the Tower of Babel, then the racket going on around her broke into words she realised she could understand after all. It happened each time she arrived in Italy; she had to reaccustom herself to the fact that here nothing could be done without a great deal of spirited conversation and argument.

Nearly at the door, en route for the train that left almost from the end of the airport runway, she was stopped in her tracks by the sight of her own name written in large black letters on a piece of white cardboard. For no reason that she could think of, the incisive script called to mind the voice of the man who'd telephoned her from San Vicenzo, but behind the piece of cardboard loomed a figure casually dressed in light-coloured slacks and an open-necked shirt. She wasn't very familiar with academics, but nevertheless a precise vision hung in her mind of what she expected: overlong greying hair, a deliberate scruffiness as to collar and tie, and half-moon spectacles over which he would examine her with pernickety distaste. The last item in this inventory was *nearly* true – Mr Fleming wore no spectacles, but he was certainly staring at her as if his worst fears were being realised.

'My name's Hadley . . . you seem to be looking for me,' she said abruptly.

His face, bony to the point of ugliness, registered a small flicker of satisfaction – with himself, she thought, not her. 'Good thing I brought the card. It seemed absurd that I wouldn't be able to recognise Enrico's

13

granddaughter among a plane-load of English tourists, but you're nothing like him after all.'

That he was disappointed, she didn't doubt. Tough for the professor, if that was what he was; he'd been expecting some bosomy, raven-haired beauty like a young Sophia Loren! Her family might look at her with the prejudiced eye of love, but Georgina reckoned herself to be over-thin and rather plain. Setting aside long elegant legs and nice chestnut hair, there wasn't much to brag about. Her green eyes normally sparkled with the amusement that life often seemed to provide, but she was sadly short of things to be amused by now.

'If we're judging by expectations, you don't look very professorial – which is what I seem to think you are,' she pointed out coolly.

'True! I manage to look a bit more impressive in cap and gown, but they don't seem appropriate here.'

He was altogether too cold and colourless ever to be impressive, she thought; a self-satisfied academic whose pale grey glance still lingered on her without a vestige of humour or pleasure. What could have possessed Gramps to allow this killjoy to move in at Poggio? But the thought reminded her that she'd been side-tracked.

'*Were* you looking for me? Is that really why you're here?'

'You said the morning flight to Pisa.'

'I didn't say that I expected you to put yourself to the trouble of coming all this way to meet me.'

She didn't want to be under an obligation to him. The feeling was strong that she wasn't going to get on with the professor, and this unexpected courtesy from him might unfairly cramp her style.

'My car's outside, but if you'd rather struggle home by train and bus I can always wander round Pisa for an hour or two, and pretend it's what I came for.'

She thought he didn't care either way. 'That would be silly,' she said stiffly after a small pause.

'I think so, too,' he agreed with the same perfect gravity as before.

For a moment she was tempted by the extraordinary idea that he might be amused, might be pleasantly human after all; but his face refused to relax into a smile and she realised she'd been mistaken – he was merely pleased to have got his own way. The piece of cardboard he'd brought with him was tossed into the nearest rubbish bin, then he picked up the large suitcase she'd set down, and led the way towards the car park. A dark-green MG, dusty but disdainfully aware of being different from the huddle of Fiats and Renaults parked carelessly, Italian fashion, all round it, bore the GB sign.

The traffic they immediately plunged into required from a foreign motorist nerves of steel and the utmost confidence in the brakes of his car. The professor muttered under his breath at the Vespas and motor-cycles buzzing round them like a swarm of hornets, but she could at least congratulate herself on the fact that no conversation from the passenger was necessary, or even sensible. Only when they were finally clear of the city and out in the comparative peace of the motorway leading towards Florence did she feel obliged to say something.

'I'm grateful to you for coming all this way.' Glancing at him, she saw the pale eyebrow nearest her lift a little.

'Are you? No need to perjure yourself, you know. My first impression was that you weren't grateful at all.'

'I'm going through the motions of being polite,' she said through gritted teeth.

'*That*'s what I thought!'

She would have preferred to sit in silence for the rest of the journey, but the question uppermost in her mind had to be asked. 'How is my grandmother . . . have you heard?'

'Making good progress, I understand. Does Enrico know you're coming?'

'No,' Georgina said briefly. 'I decided to walk in unannounced.'

He said nothing, leaving her to wonder all over again whether it had been the right decision not to warn her grandfather. The nearer they got to Poggio, the worse her worries became, but she kept telling herself that nothing was as bad as imagination running riot; it would be better when she *knew* what was happening.

Half an hour later they were on the outskirts of Florence, and it was clear that the man beside her was familiar enough with the city to be able to avoid driving through the centre of it. But as soon as they'd crossed the Arno, he turned the car along the southern bank of the river and they began to climb one of the steep alley-ways winding up to the Piazza Michelangelo.

'I know the view's marvellous up here, but don't bother to stop; I've seen it many times before,' she said quickly.

'I'm sure you have, but what I had in mind to offer you was food, not the view.'

'Kind of you, but I'd rather get straight on.'

'I wasn't being kind at all, The truth is that I'm extremely hungry.'

She bit her lip in the effort not to scream her impatience at him. He'd spared her a long and tedious journey, but now every second that it took to reach Poggio seemed to count. Anxiety was making her feel sick, and if he insisted on stopping, he'd have to gorge himself alone. The word came to mind but had to be rejected, because his gaunt frame suggested that he hardly bothered to eat at all. She climbed out of the car and trailed after him into a small restaurant on the hilltop, where he was greeted like an old friend. The waiter warmly recommended the lasagne verdi, kissing his fingers to illustrate the treat in store.

'Not for me,' Georgina said at once, trying to smile at the man. 'I'm sure it's all you say, but I'm not hungry – just waiting while my companion eats.'

Fleming smiled at his friend. 'Lasagne verdi for two, and a bottle of Orvieto – very cool.'

She said nothing, and stared out over the panorama of Florence lying below them, tawny-coloured in the sunlight and seemingly more beautiful each time she came back. In the centre of it, hub and heart of the city, the cathedral lifted Brunelleschi's incomparable russet and white dome into a pale-blue sky. It had survived centuries of turmoil and destruction, making nonsense of even her present anxieties, and shaming her into regretting the spiralling ill-temper in which she seemed to be caught up. She was back in Tuscany, Lucia was getting better – this man had said so and she believed him – and she would soon be able to find out what else was wrong at Poggio.

Adam Fleming watched her over the rim of his glass, considering the tense profile that was all he could see of her face. He was betting with himself that she'd refuse to touch the lasagne when it came. In looks she wasn't what he'd expected, though she was highly decorative all the same; but the impression formed from that brief telephone conversation had been the right one. She was cool, indifferent, and only reluctantly fulfilling what even she could see was a family obligation. Her grandparents were misguidedly attached to her, and he'd been a fool to think she would do anything practical to help them. It was surprising that she'd bothered to come at all, but perhaps Tuscany had attractions for her that he didn't know about.

She turned away from the view suddenly enough to catch him still staring at her. The discovery didn't fluster him in the least, and it occurred to her that it would be easy to underrate Adam Fleming. Quiet-voiced and colourless he might seem, but he was unusually self-possessed, and he was certainly rather competent at getting his own way.

He lost his bet with himself, because she began to eat what was put in front of her. 'I suppose you remembered what I'd forgotten: that Maria might be too busy to stop and get me lunch,' she said after a moment. 'Do you make a habit of always being right?'

'We try to cultivate omniscience. It impresses the students,' he explained gently.

She was tempted to smile, but reluctant to capitulate too easily. 'I suppose you're enjoying a sabbatical – from what?'

'Being a don at Oxford. I teach the history of art there.' In spite of himself he was nettled by an expression on her face that he thought he could identify. 'A sinecure, you suppose! No job for an able-bodied man not yet quite in his dotage? I expect your male friends are all out in the great world, making their first fortune by the time they're thirty-one.'

'They're not cloistered academics,' she agreed coolly. 'I don't know whether they've made fortunes or not; I don't ask them.' Her first question had managed to irritate him, apparently; it was too tempting not to try again. 'With a year off from Oxford, what do you do in Florence? Just enjoy the *objets d'art* and soak up the ambience?'

'I suspect you think it's just exactly what I do! However, I can boast one or two small endeavours, like a spring and summer course of lectures at the Uffizi. Apart from that, all I have to do is finish researching and writing a book that's already been commissioned. You might think there's been enough written already on the history of Renaissance art in Italy, but the publishers optimistically hope that mine will be the last word on the subject.'

'Sounds fun!' The mischief was deliberate, but a moment later it occurred to her that she might have tried him too far. The grey eyes she'd decided were cold and expressionless now fairly blazed. The impression of an ineffectual highbrow mooning about in dusty libraries might have to be revised, but she concealed the thought by smiling at the waiter who'd come to clear the table. When he'd disappeared the disconcerting moment was past because the professor had reverted to neutrality again.

'Oh, it's great fun; fills the time nicely. I gather you fill yours by pottering among the flowers at Kew.' His eyes lingered on her hands. 'Not that you look much like a horny-handed daughter of the soil to me.'

The inference was clear, but the frivolous picture of her was so wide of the mark that it amused instead of irritating her.

'Nothing too strenuous,' she agreed with a sweet smile.

It seemed to leave them roughly where they'd begun, two people completely at odds with one another. They finished lunch and drove the rest of the way to Poggio almost in silence. It was a relief to be running through San Vicenzo, shuttered and silent during the mid-afternoon siesta. Then there was only the stony lane leading out of the town to be climbed, and the knowledge that this home-coming to Poggio was sadly different from all previous ones. By now, normally, Gramps and Lucia would be out on the terrace looking for her, and Maria's small son Alessio would be halfway down the, lane, determined to get the first glimpse. This time Lucia wasn't even there, and Enrico would be taken by surprise. Perhaps it *hadn't* been a good idea to come unannounced, after all.

They were on Casali land now, but she was too deep in thought to look around her and that wasn't normally how her arrival was, either. The stone house that sprawled over the top of the hill seemed wrapped in the same slumber as San Vicenzo. Fleming switched off the car engine and there wasn't a sound in the world except the distant clucking of Maria's chickens foraging for the corn Alessio always threw down for them in the orchard. Then, echoing forlornly across the garden, a cuckoo's voice floated from the oak tree at the far end of the lawn.

'I'm sorry it's not a very merry arrival,' Fleming's voice said quietly.

She turned her head to stare at him, ready to assume that as well as sensing her dismay he was privately enjoying it; but she had to admit that it wasn't so. There was no trace of malice in his face, and instead she had the sudden, strange certainty that he shared her grief for whatever was wrong at Poggio; it was the very reason he'd telephoned, to seek help for something he valued.

'Thanks,' she murmured at last, 'and thank you again for fetching me – meant this time, not a polite form of words.'

He nodded but said nothing, merely leaned across to open the car door and then got out himself to deal with her luggage in the boot. She was halfway up the steps when the front door opened and a woman stood there, transfixed by the shock of seeing someone who should have been in an unimaginable place called Londra.

'Maria, it's *me*,' she said, forcing herself to smile when her only inclination was to burst into tears.

'*Santa Virgine . . . signorina . . . cara, cara . . .*' Maria, still wearing the morning's working overall that wouldn't have been permitted if Lucia had been there, promptly did burst into tears and flung herself into Georgina's arms. Over the maid's dark head, the professor's little salute suggested that he was tactfully going to leave them alone, but his gesture towards the flat at the far end of the farmhouse said also that he would be there if they needed him. She nodded and watched him walk away, aware that she had no right to feel abandoned. The passing kindness he'd offered was one thing, but getting involved in Poggio's problems was quite another, and she could think of no reason why a man who was there to think about fifteenth-century Medicis should be expected to prop up late-twentieth-century Casalis.

She patted Maria's still-heaving shoulders and suggested that it was time the weeping stopped. 'I know Granny's sick, but where is my grandfather?' she asked gently.

'An *appuntamento* in Siena, *cara* . . . that's what he said. He'll be back in time to visit the hospital this evening.' She had no curiosity about how Georgina came to be there; once the shock of seeing her was over, it was as if she'd never been away.

'Tell me about Granny. How did nobody know she was ill?'

Maria wrung the end of her overall in her hands. 'You know how the signora is . . . always calm and strong. I could see that she suffered, but she wouldn't give in. Then, suddenly, one morning she collapsed in the kitchen . . . *Madre di Dio*, imagine it, *cara* . . . she as white and silent as the grave, the signore red and shouting . . .'

Maria's description was as graphic as it was simple, and the scene could be imagined, exactly as it must have been. 'But she is getting better,' the housekeeper quickly added. 'Our prayers have been answered.'

That was said simply too, and summed up Maria's philosophy; life was as Heaven willed, and for good or ill mortals had no choice but to accept the fact. Georgina nodded, on the point of asking why Giuseppe and his family were missing, but before the question could be uttered a whoop of joy behind them announced the arrival of Alessio home from school. A small whirlwind took the steps up to the terrace in two enormous bounds and flung itself at her.

'Mamma didn't say . . . she *didn't* tell us you were coming.'

'Mamma didn't know. I just decided I couldn't do without seeing you all a moment longer.'

She bent down for the customary kiss on both cheeks, smiling wholeheartedly for the first time since she'd arrived in Italy. It was impossible to look at Alessio's small brown face and not smile. 'You've grown since last summer.'

'Five centimetres,' he agreed with touching exactitude. 'We measure every week, Caterina and me.'

His sister, collaborator in the measuring business, was coming up the steps behind him – a girl of fifteen who had not only grown as well, but grown into self-confident attractiveness. With her mother's sturdy build, she might become plump in ten years' time, but at the moment she was well proportioned, and her dark hair and eyes were beautiful. She had to be kissed as well, while Alessio hauled at the luggage the professor had left just inside the porch. He was anxious to be helpful, but he was also not without experience in the matter of the signorina's luggage. On past showing there was a good chance that it contained more than clothes for herself. He waited with his black head cocked like an expectant bird, and she rendered private thanks to Heaven for the cache of birthday presents that would normally have been sent that she'd remembered to bring with her. He would have forgiven her if she'd come empty-handed, but she'd have missed the blinding smile that greeted the odd-shaped package she handed him. He thought he could guess from the feel of it what it might just contain – surely roller-skates, that few of his friends in San Vicenzo had. There was a soft lambswool sweater for Maria, because even Tuscany didn't escape cold days in winter, and she held it against her cheek while Georgina rummaged in her bag again for Caterina's present. Also something to wear, of course, but for a fifteen-year-old it was a pale-green top and matching skirt, plain except for the enormous golden sunflower embroidered on it. The delighted girl shook out the folds and held it against herself while she danced round the room.

'It's beautiful . . . I shall put it on now, this minute . . . I want to show it to Adam.'

Adam? Georgina blinked as she waltzed out of the room, and Alessio tore after her, parcel clutched in his arms like treasure. Something else to be displayed to the professor?

'We have an English gentleman staying here,' Maria explained after they'd gone. '*Molto gentile* he is; so kind to everybody, but especially to the children.'

'He gave me a lift up here, so we've introduced ourselves,' Georgina said, leaving the improbability of the meeting unexplained.

She stared at Maria's smiling face and changed her mind about asking any more questions. The person to ask about Giuseppe was her grandfather.

'I'll go and unpack, and then I shall feel at home again. *Ciao*, Maria!'

She climbed the wide uncarpeted stairs to the room Lucia always called hers. It felt all wrong not to have her grandmother there to talk to her while she hung up clothes and set out books and photographs. Olivia's silver-framed face reminded her that she must soon telephone Washington, but first she needed to know the details that her mother would ask for. She must see for herself that Lucia was recovering, but what else had been happening at Poggio would take longer to discover – except that Professor

Fleming had obviously made an impression on Caterina. That was something odd and unexpected; not only more than twice her age, he must seem almost invisible among the colourful Italian men he was surrounded by. Georgina's conclusion was that an impressionable girl saw him as a father figure – a replacement for the man who'd walked out on Maria just before Alessio was born. He had, unmistakeably, an air of authority about him, and no doubt this was what the children found comforting.

With everything stowed away in her room, she opened the casement wide and leaned out to stare at the garden. The cuckoo was still calling, and sunlight lay over a landscape that was vividly green after the rainy weeks of early spring. Tuscany was all about her – fold upon gentle fold of wooded hills losing form in the hazy blue of the horizon; the background to every Renaissance painting in the Uffizi, unchanged in essence for five hundred years. Nearer at hand the hillsides were striped a brighter green where the vines were beginning to come into leaf again. Here, they were allowed to grow into small intertwining trees, not spread horizontally over frames as they were further north, or kept in low individual bushes as in France. She preferred the Tuscan way – it seemed more natural and more beautiful. Staring out at the quiet landscape, she realised how lovely it was to be back. Perhaps it wouldn't be the wrench she'd always feared to part company with Kew and her home in London if she ever decided to spend the rest of her life here.

The thought inevitably brought William to mind; she could imagine his long, earnest face bent over a sick plant, while he willed it to recover. For a disconcerting moment she found herself looking at Poggio with his eyes, knowing that he wouldn't have been satisfied with what he saw. The garden was beautiful because it was full of growing things, but it was downright unkempt. The kitchen garden that lay on one side of the house was normally her grandmother's pride and joy; by now it should be dug and raked and planted with the vegetable seeds that would feed them for another year. Instead, it was a wilderness of weeds, growing with spring-time abundance. With three men gone, and without Maria's help in the garden, it was easy to understand why everything looked so untended, but why her grandfather hadn't replaced his workers immediately was a worrying mystery. Anxiety was back, nibbling at her heart again. Enrico had the male attitude typical of his generation: home and children were a woman's proper concern; everything else must be left to the head of the family. Even Lucia had been obliged to go along with such antiquated nonsense, and breaking it to him that his emancipated granddaughter had

different ideas was only the first of the problems that she could see looming ahead of her.

Chapter 3

Enrico stared at the face of the young man sitting opposite him, and found his mind wandering from the urgent matter in hand. How could someone he'd known from childhood suddenly seem so unfamiliar? Even *more* odd, how could Roberto Artom, brought up to run wild about the vineyards and olive groves of Tuscany, somehow have become a city man? A successful city man, Enrico amended silently; even he recognised a silk shirt and handmade Gucci shoes as symbols of success, but there were other things, too, that spoke of a self-confidence as potent in the air as Roberto's expensive after-shave lotion.

'It's a better than fair offer, Enrico. You won't get a more generous one.'

The casual use of the Christian name to a man old enough to be his father underlined something else: Roberto was in charge of the discussion, and Enrico had been summoned to see *him*. His office in Siena was elegantly furnished; above it in an old and beautiful house overlooking the Campo was his equally elegant home. Their talk was easy, as between friends; but this was a matter of business all the same. Roberto put down the silver paper-knife he was playing with and smiled at his father's neighbour.

'The offer is generous, but not open-ended. If not Poggio, then we must look elsewhere. I'm sorry to press you now, when the signora is ill, but decisions like this can't wait on individual convenience. I hope you understand that a matter of such importance can't be shelved.'

Enrico knew he wasn't a slick young businessman, but he wasn't a fool of a country bumpkin, either, with more hair than wit. In the midst of much else besides, he was conscious of a sharp jab of resentment. Of course he could see for himself that some matters were more urgent than others, and that *this* was one of them. Resentment made him continue the farce that he was confronted by a choice.

'I shall let you know quickly, of course,' he said loftily, 'but I must have a *little* time to consider – a week, Roberto. After the weekend you will have my decision.'

His host saw him courteously to the door, willing to grant the week Enrico had asked for because he knew already what the decision would be. Waiting on the hall table, as a sign that here was a man capable of thinking of everything, was an exquisitely arranged posy of flowers protected by cellophane.

'For the signora, with all my good wishes,' he said gently. Then an afterthought occurred to him, just as Enrico was on the point of leaving. 'What news of Georgina?'

'No news. It seems too long since we saw her, but how can life in London not be exciting for a girl like my granddaughter? We can't expect her to remember Poggio when she is away from it.'

Roberto's little shrug conveyed the fact that his question had arisen out of nothing more than courtesy, and confirmed what Enrico had long suspected – that in this one matter his Lucia, normally so infallible when it came to judgements about other human beings, was mistaken. She had continued to insist, against all the evidence, that Roberto hankered after their girl as his wife. Nothing of the kind. Gina was simply the half-English companion who'd shared the holidays of childhood and adolescence, and was remembered now with amused affection. There was nothing in that to help them and ease the trap they were caught in.

Back at Poggio, he left the car on the gravel drive below the house and walked round to the steps leading up to the terrace. Georgina watched him, shocked not only by the sharp physical change in someone who'd always been ebullient and full of life, but by the air of defeat that hung about him. He walked heavily, with his eyes fixed on the ground; an old man, suddenly, burdened by too many anxieties, It was unfair not to let him know at once that she was there, watching him.

'Gramps,' she called out, 'I thought I'd give you a little surprise.' But for a dreadful moment she wasn't even sure that the surprise was a pleasant one; his face looked blank, unwelcoming even.

'Gina love . . . I'm not dreaming, am I? I was thinking about you on the drive home . . .' His voice wavered, suddenly on the edge of tears, and again she was made aware of the heart-aching difference of *this* arrival at Poggio. No Lucia, and this tired, sad, old man instead of the rumbustious host who would normally have been showering her with questions and kisses.

When he kissed her at last her own face was wet with tears. 'I came because Mama was worried . . . sensed something was wrong; if it had been possible, she'd have come herself. Maria swears that Granny is getting better. Is it true?'

'God be thanked, she's recovering,' Enrico said simply. 'It's been terrible, *cara*, but she is mending now.'

'You *should* have told us. Mama would have got here somehow, or I'd have come sooner.'

'She hoped you wouldn't have to know at all. *I* wasn't told until she got to the point of collapse, and even then she made me promise not to tell. She had no intention of dying, she said, so what was the point of making a lot of fuss?'

Georgina smiled at last. It sounded exactly like her grandmother, and when Lucia did finally give in to dying, she would see that that, too, was done with the minimum amount of fuss.

'Can I go and see her?'

'This evening, *cara*; we'll drive to Florence together. Having you here will do her more good than all the doctors' medicine.'

'I can stay a month, Gramps; that's all the leave I have. It should be time enough to get her fit and well again.'

He nodded but still, she thought, looked less than overjoyed. She couldn't believe for an instant that he didn't want her there; it was simply that there were other matters weighing on his mind. He became almost himself again over the early supper that Maria had ready for them, but kept the conversation geared to her own life in London or to her parents. Once, she asked about someone on the estate, but the question was turned aside immediately and for the moment she was content to take the hint. Enrico's glance skimmed her face, noting in it a resemblance to Richard Hadley that seemed stronger than usual. In feature she took after her grandmother, and the likeness to her father was a matter mostly of expression. But in character she was Richard's daughter and, greatly as he loved her, Enrico found himself wishing that she hadn't chosen this of all moments to come to Poggio.

She asked to be allowed to drive the car in to Florence, suggesting that she needed practice in driving on the right again. The truth was that Enrico, in charge of a car, always seemed uncertain whether he was riding tractor or horse, and the evening traffic in Florence didn't favour a motorist who couldn't make up his mind.

Lucia was sitting up in bed when they arrived, still mistress of herself despite surroundings she didn't care for, still elegant despite the indignities of hospital life. Her silver hair was drawn back in its usual severe knot, and her skin still looked brown against the whiteness of the pillows. But she'd grown very thin, and at the unexpected sight of Georgina walking down the ward behind Enrico weakness betrayed her into tears that overflowed and trickled down her cheeks.

'*Tesoro* . . . how lovely,' she whispered, 'but how do you come to be here? Your grandfather promised . . . !'

'He didn't breathe a word, poor man. Mama just got the feeling something was going on that she didn't know about.' She kissed her grandmother's face, gently mopped its tears, and then sat down beside the bed. 'I won't nag until you're stronger, but you must promise never to keep us in the dark again.'

Lucia looked faintly ashamed of herself. 'Olivia would have insisted on coming – I know that; but her place was with Richard. First impressions are important, and he needed his wife with *him*, not nurse-maiding me.'

Georgina didn't challenge the idea that her self-sufficient father couldn't have managed on his own for a few days. 'I've no doubt she's taking the Capitol by storm; at least, she will when I telephone her and say that she can stop worrying about *you*. What does the doctor say?'

'That I may come home in ten days' time provided I'm sensible. They are all very kind here, *cara*, but I *long* to be at home.'

'Well, we can guarantee that you'll be sensible. If you should look like being difficult, we can always tie you to a chair! Gramps knows already that I can stay for a month.'

Lucia tried to smile, but it went awry, and this time it was Enrico who patted her face with the tenderness that a man and a woman share who have lived long and happily together. 'A gift from Heaven is it not, *amore*, to have her here?' he asked gently, and then walked away to leave them alone.

Lucia smiled more resolutely. 'You'll find a change at Poggio, *cara*.' Georgina thought she was about to hear at last what had happened to Giuseppe, but apparently it was another change her grandmother had in mind. 'You'll find an English professor staying there. His name is Adam Fleming.'

'I've met him already.' The dryness in her granddaughter's voice caught Lucia's ear, but she decided to ignore it.

'He isn't what we expected, and he's so good at laughing with a serious face! Everybody loves him, especially Maria,'

Not to mention Maria's daughter, Georgina thought but decided not to point out. She also remembered a moment when he might have been privately amused, but didn't refer to that either. 'I gather he only emerges occasionally from the fifteenth century; the chances are that we shall never meet at all.'

'Maria will at least expect you to notice the improvement in Alessio.

Adam emerges often enough to take *him* in hand. The child isn't backward at learning at all, which is what his poor mother has been led to believe for years. He just hadn't bothered because he wasn't interested. All changed now, and Maria bursts into tears of joy whenever she thinks about it!'

'Well, the professor's got some competition on his hands now – I brought Alessio a pair of rather splendid skates!'

She said goodnight to her grandmother, and was sitting in the car waiting when Enrico appeared five minutes later. He seemed disinclined to talk for once and Georgina herself was suddenly aware of overwhelming tiredness. She seemed to have left London days ago, instead of just that morning. A hard slog at Kew would have left her less drained than she felt now after being buffeted by the day's emotions.

That night, slipping over the edge between awareness and sleep, one last puzzle about the day jerked her awake again. No one during the course of it had mentioned the Artom family; even Roberto's delicate posy had been accepted by Lucia without any comment whatsoever. It was all part of the general oddity of things that she must begin to grapple with tomorrow.

She began at first light, determined to make a tour of the estate before anyone else was about, The world was cool and quiet, only shared with Lucia's prize cockerel self-importantly waking up his harem, and the swallows who chattered to each other as they made their early-morning, aerial circuits of the garden.

On the surface nothing much had changed; the old stone house lay among its sheltering ring of trees, rose-hung almost to its beautiful pantiled roof. The fig tree beside the steps was already breaking into leaf, and the wild narcissus drifted like snow down the slope to the olive orchard, filling the air with sweetness. Across the lawn another house already caught the first of the morning sunlight – the original farmhouse, converted into two now that farm animals no longer occupied the ground floor. In the larger part of it Giuseppe and his family had always lived; the other part now presumably housed the professor.

She walked over Poggio land for the next hour, becoming more and more disheartened. The tell-tale signs of neglect that were visible near the house itself were bad enough, but in the vineyards and orchards they spoke not only of lack of care but of a frightening lack of interest. The vines and olives provided her grandfather's income. He was the last man in the world to make himself rich: what he had he enjoyed, shared, and often gave away to anyone who needed help. But even if he'd saved more than she supposed and had decided to take life easily, in the past at least he would never have contemplated neglecting precious land. It was he who'd taught a small girl to love the Tuscan countryside, explained to her why it was different from a dozen other old and beautiful landscapes. Its soil and its climate still combined to produce the two most vital symbols of mediterranean life – the vine and the olive – because the land had been worked with loving care by generations of men like himself.

She went slowly back to the house, wondering what her chances were of getting to the root of Poggio's problems. If her grandfather decided to retreat behind a wall of male dignity, neither guile nor frankness would help her very much in persuading him to set aside the masculine habits of a lifetime.

She was halfway across the lawn when the door of the farmhouse opposite was thrown open. Adam Fleming walked down the steps, trying to disentangle himself from what turned out to be two tortoiseshell kittens.

'Good morning, Miss Hadley.' She looked different from the aloof and slightly hostile girl he'd collected the day before – it had something to do with the faded jeans she now wore, the shabby sweater, and the sandals on her bare feet, but the change was more fundamental than that. He decided with a feeling of surprise that she looked like a woman in her natural habitat, but she'd also, in the moment of being come upon, looked deeply worried.

'Friends of yours?' she asked, gesturing to the kittens now trying to swarm up his legs.

'They think I'm their best hope of food, so they try never to let me out of their sight.' He bent down and picked them up, glanced at her again to see the expression on her face.

'You think I'm misguided – or worse! Why delude a couple of rather unwanted kittens into thinking they're valued after all?'

'The life of Riley for as long as you're here, then it's back to fending for themselves; it will come rather hard by then,' she felt obliged to point out.

'But at least they'll be bigger and better equipped than they are now.' While it was occurring to her that perhaps exactly the same principle explained his interest in Alessio, the professor decided to change the subject of conversation.

'How was your grandmother last night?'

'Much better. Making such good progress that we can bring her home in ten days' time provided she promises to behave herself.'

'Will you be here long enough to see that she does?'

'I hope so.'

The courtesies had now been observed, and she was free to walk away, but instead she found herself asking the question that still beat unanswered in her mind. 'I've been out walking,' she said abruptly. 'You mentioned on the telephone that Giuseppe and his family had left; do you have any idea why?' The expression on Fleming's face impelled her to say something else. 'I shall ask my grandfather, of course, but there hasn't been much chance so far, and he has a slightly Victorian attitude when it comes to the things that women should properly concern themselves with.'

A faint smile warmed the professor's eyes. 'I can imagine! Well, all I can tell you is what Enrico told me: that Giuseppe was becoming too demanding and impertinent.'

'Giuseppe? Impertinent?' She sounded so incredulous and troubled that he knew he would have to change his first impression of her. Whatever else might be lacking, her concern for Poggio was real, and what became of it mattered intensely to her.

'I've told you what Enrico said,' he reminded her. 'There might have been some other reason he saw no need to share with me.'

She considered this in silence for a moment. 'Of course Giuseppe was free to go if he wanted to, but he'd worked here happily for years . . . His sons grew up at Poggio and I imagined they'd spend the rest of their lives here.'

'Attitudes are changing, even in this charmed place,' Fleming pointed out gently. 'Young men grow up expecting to work less hard than their fathers did. Giuseppe was offered a job at Greve on a bigger, more easily worked estate; but I understand from Caterina that his sons decided to leave the land altogether. Jobs in Florence beckoned.'

'Tourist jobs, no doubt,' Georgina said with a sudden flash of anger that took him by surprise. 'More and more people are sucked into the business of providing for them in one way or another, and fewer and fewer are left to preserve what attracted the tourists in the first place.'

'It's a powerful argument, I agree, but it isn't the only way of looking at things. I'd advance a different theory if I thought you had the slightest interest in listening to it.'

'Another time, perhaps, Professor! At the moment there's enough to think about right here. Everywhere I look there's work crying out to be done, and I can't believe that it's impossible to find someone to do it even now. Why hasn't my grandfather tried?'

Fleming suspected that he knew the reason, but hesitated to say so. She misread his expression and was tempted into battle again.

'You look as if you think I'm mad! It comes of being trained to take the long historical view, I suppose. What happens now doesn't matter, because life's measured in centuries, not seasons. It's a very comforting philosophy if you can make yourself believe in it.'

'It's not one I'm actually claiming,' he said with sudden sharpness. '*You* insist on tying a label to me which reads "booby intellectual"! I don't know much about working the land, but even I can see that Poggio's being dangerously neglected, and I can regret the fact as much as you do.'

She realised that she could scarcely deny it when his telephone call to London was the reason she was there at all.

'I'm sorry. And I don't think I thanked you properly for troubling to alert me,' she mumbled reluctantly.

He was angry enough not to let her off. 'You didn't thank me at all; you resented my interference instead.'

'Yes . . . well, I do thank you now. I should have come anyway eventually, but it might have been too late by then.'

'Humble pie so early in the morning?'

She nodded, with a rueful twinkle lighting her eyes to beauty. 'And very indigestible it is! I shall take the taste out of my mouth by asking Maria for some breakfast.'

She nodded and walked away towards the house, leaving Fleming still deep in thought, until squeaks of protest from the balls of fur in his hands reminded him that his friends also had hopes of breakfast.

The kitchen was still empty when Georgina went in, but welcoming after the coolness outside. Maria's rounds of dough left to rise the previous evening sat on top of the stove, and the room was scented with the drying herbs hanging in bunches from the rafters, and the coffee beans that were always being ground. Lucia's cherished collection of copper pans glowed on the wall, and Maria's marble-topped table stood awaiting the pasta she would make and roll out on it that morning.

Georgina was making coffee when she came bustling in, looking flustered to find someone already there.

'*Cara!* I'd have come sooner if I'd known.'

'No need; I went out early. Alessio not about this morning?'

'He's gone to feed the chickens on his new skates, of course!'

As always at any mention of her children, Maria's heavy face brightened into something that was nearly handsome, a reminder of the girl who'd been seduced at nineteen, married to the man who'd fathered Caterina, and then abandoned by him just before Alessio was born. It was Lucia who'd offered her a home and work where she could keep the children with her, and they had all been at Poggio ever since. What Maria felt about her missing husband no one knew. She simply got on with the job of bringing up her children and working with a passionate devotion for the woman who'd taken them in. No task about the house seemed beyond her, and she was just as happy to whitewash the kitchen walls as prepare lunch for a dozen people.

'Granny says Alessio's beginning to make great strides,' said Georgina, smiling at her.

'Yes, God and the professor be thanked! My boy's doing well now.'

The heartfelt statement reflected her awareness that times had changed. The days were gone when peasants working the land were not expected to be able to read or write. Education was the key to success: everybody knew that now, including Maria. 'Professor Fleming is kind, with a kindness that comes from the heart.'

It was hard not to remember him flanked by a couple of kittens that were luckier than some of the farm cat's frequent progeny. Even without that clue to his heart, it would have been stupid to deny the conviction in Maria's voice. With no education at all to speak of, her reaction to people was instinctive, not rational. But when instinct told her to value people, value them she did, come Hell or high water. The rest the Devil could take, and welcome. Georgina sipped coffee, watching her shape the dough into round loaves ready for the oven.

'I've been out walking,' she said at last. 'Tell me what's been going on, Maria. Why did Giuseppe leave?'

The heavy, gentle face opposite her looked troubled. What she knew was one thing, what she felt free to talk about, even to the *padrone*'s granddaughter, needed thinking about. But she'd known this girl since she was a small child; even then there'd been little hope of deflecting her from something she'd set her mind on being told.

'I . . . I think money came into it,' she murmured reluctantly. 'He was offered more to go to another estate the other side of Siena. Emma persuaded him in the end.'

Georgina looked unconvinced. Something more than his wife's nagging would have been needed to uproot someone as stubbornly fixed in his ways as Giuseppe. 'The boys got tired of life at Poggio, too, I gather?'

Maria seemed even more unhappy, but felt obliged to be fair. 'There was some . . . some gossip, *cara* . . . talk about the vines not being replaced. They had the idea that there wasn't any future for them here.'

'But that's rubbish,' she was told fiercely. 'Can you imagine there not being vineyards at Poggio?'

31

'I'm only telling you what Emma said. I know nothing about it. You'll have to ask the signore.'

It was perfectly true. There was no one else *to* ask, except perhaps the Artoms, but she disliked the idea of airing Poggio's problems round the countryside. She wanted to see Roberto again, but only for reasons that concerned themselves. Mindful of the local bush telegraph which operated almost faster than the speed of sound, she promised herself a telephone call to his office in Siena immediately after breakfast.

But the call hadn't been made by the time she drove down to San Vicenzo to get supplies Maria needed, and there the first person she met in the town square happened to be Roberto's mother, Erica Artom. Groomed to the last eyelash as always and dressed in a linen jacket and trousers cut by a master hand, the signora was first surprised to see her, then coolly welcoming.

'Gina, my dear, *no one* told us you were coming, I'm sure. Naughty of you to slip in so secretly, but of course you've come to see Lucia. How is the poor darling?'

'Making great strides.' That at least could be said cheerfully. 'It was a spur of the moment decision to come, so nobody knew; but I *was* going to ring Roberto later this morning.'

'He'll be overjoyed. You must come to lunch on Sunday – bring Enrico, too. Where's dear Olivia at the moment?'

'Just setting up house in Washington, and wishing it wasn't quite so far away from Italy!'

'Your mother is mad, you realise! She's given Washington – and yearns to be here, instead! It's a good thing we love her anyway. Until Sunday, *cara.*'

Georgina watched her drift away, aware that what had just been said was untrue. Two girls growing up on neighbouring estates might have learned to love one another, but not this one and Olivia. Erica had been glad to marry Dino Artom, a clever, hard-working, thrusting lawyer who was bound to succeed. Succeed he certainly had, and his wealth had transformed her family's rundown estate at Casagrande. If her husband hadn't been born quite a gentleman, her son undoubtedly was, and all the signs were that he was going to be even more successful than Dino had been. The only real rub had been Olivia, scooping Richard Hadley. She hadn't deserved the glamour of being a diplomat's wife, and it was very hard that her husband should have in abundance that quality of style that Erica prized so greatly. No one could accuse Dino Artom of having style.

Georgina also suspected the signora of hoping that her son wasn't seriously interested in someone who'd inherited too many of the Casalis' strange ideas. There'd been a still-remembered day when Erica had sneered at Lucia's habit of letting Maria and her children sit down at table with them for Sunday lunch. Roberto had had to soften the disagreement by making a joke about it when Georgina had flown to her grandmother's defence. But she knew she would probably still find herself just as much at odds with Signora Artom on every other issue that wasn't trivial. She finished her shopping, and drove home wishing that she'd been able to speak to Roberto before she'd encountered his mother.

Chapter 4

Enrico excused himself so sharply from Sunday's lunch invitation that she didn't argue, supposing that he blamed the Artoms for not helping him as they might have done. Idly studying a viniculturist's catalogue, he seemed a man with nothing on his mind in the middle of a working morning except, apparently, a little light reading. Frustration and despair welled up, pushing Georgina into words more abrupt than she meant them to be.

'Gramps, can we talk, please?'

'I'm busy, *cara*. Why not take the car and drive into Florence . . . or what about your special place, San Gimignano?'

'I can always think of somewhere to go, but I came here to help, not go jaunting about the countryside.'

He managed to smile at her. 'Of course you'll help – when Lucia comes home.'

'Poggio needs help *now*.' The words were left to echo in a long silence that hung stiflingly in the air between them.

'Poggio needn't concern you,' he said at last. 'It isn't for you to worry about.'

'I can't help worrying,' she insisted quietly. 'I've been walking around outside. It was *you* who taught me to love it; you can't expect me not to notice that something's wrong.'

'I repeat that it doesn't concern you. We can't work miracles, and miracles are what we need for the times we live in. Two hard winters have damaged the olives, and the return on wine has been hopelessly low. There are too many growers everywhere, making too much wine, good or bad.'

'By the look of things outside, we shall be lucky to produce anything at all. Poggio can't manage without help. If Giuseppe has really gone for good, why don't we find someone to take his place?'

'Don't interfere, *cara*. It's my decision whether or not we replace Giuseppe.' It was almost impossible to believe that her grandfather should be shouting at her, but suddenly he was, and his face was suffused with anger that was real and dangerous. 'You know nothing about it: leave Poggio to me.'

She'd expected, at the worst, a smiling reminder that women weren't supposed to bother their poor little heads with such matters; not to be glared at by an inimical stranger.

'I was hoping to help, not interfere. You've been worried to death about Granny . . . had to think about her instead of Poggio . . .'

'That's *enough*, Georgina; leave Poggio to me!' His rage was so terrible that she could risk pushing him no further. A seizure or a stroke would be the only result.

'Very well,' she said finally. 'If you won't let me share the problems I can't make you; but whether you like it or not I'm going to do something about the gardens outside. I refuse to let Granny come home and see them in the mess they're in now.'

She stood facing him, tall and straight and quite as angry as he was himself. He was reminded of Richard Hadley confronting him after announcing courteously that he wished to marry Olivia. Enrico's objections had been listened to with the utmost politeness and done not a particle of good in the end. Their girl had married him anyway, and her parents had been forced to look happy about a son-in-law who would drag their precious only child over the face of the earth like a wanderer for the rest of his working life. After that, it would be England probably. Without any surprise Enrico saw in his granddaughter now the self-same quiet obstinacy that he'd recognised in Richard Hadley.

'Do what you like with the gardens,' he shouted. 'I don't care.'

She watched him stalk out of the door, and shivered in spite of the sunlight flooding into the room. More was wrong even than she'd feared, but she didn't know how she was ever to find out. Enrico might just agree to discuss things with Olivia, but that meant ringing Washington again and confessing that there was much more to worry about than Lucia's health. She decided in the end to wait a little while. He wasn't a man who could hold on to ill-temper for very long; when he'd had time to cool down, she would have one more try. Meanwhile, she'd laid claim to a job however little she felt like doing it, and must make a start.

When she went outside, the professor's MG was parked by the farmhouse door, He appeared a moment later, and the formal collar and tie, and a pile of books under one arm, suggested that it was a day for lecturing at the Uffizi.

'Students in Florence all agog, I trust,' she said politely.

'As do I! Would you care to enrol in the class?'

'Thank you, but I've got other work to do. In any case, I should be ashamed for you to discover that I can scarcely tell Giotto from Ghirlandaio.'

'Miss Hadley jests, I suspect. In any case, at least she knows their names.'

She smiled faintly, but he thought her face looked pale and strained. He was instrumental in bringing her here, and suddenly felt that he'd been unfair. Poggio wasn't a responsibility that ought to have been dumped on a girl's shoulders, but in the usual way of wilful doers of good he'd salvaged his own peace of mind at the expense of hers. He opened the car door, then turned round to look at her again.

'Will you keep an eye on the kittens for me? They're hell-bent on getting into the *cantina* to drown themselves in a butt of Chianti!'

She was still smiling at the idea when he drove away, cheered in spite of herself by a light-hearted scrap of conversation with someone who not only spoke her own language but thought the fate of a couple of farmyard kittens mattered in the scheme of things; no one else around Poggio was likely to, such creatures being expected to live or die by themselves.

By the end of the morning she was hot and tired, but already there was some progress to be seen. The lawn below the terrace had been mown, the lavender border neatly clipped. After lunch she would make a start on the overgrown bed that curved all round the edge of the lawn; the geranium and petunia seedlings that had miraculously escaped death by neglect in the greenhouse would soon need to be set out. The urns that lined the terrace steps normally cascaded blossom in the summer-time, but if something wasn't done about planting them, it would soon be too late.

Enrico stared at her flushed face when she appeared at the lunch table, but merely said that he had an afternoon appointment in Florence and would go straight to the hospital from there. With no car of her own, she couldn't visit Lucia unless he invited her to go with him, but umbrage clearly hadn't subsided yet and she wouldn't beg him to take her.

'Give Granny my love,' she said simply, and went on forcing herself to eat the spaghetti Maria had put in front of her.

By late afternoon she knew that it was time to call a halt, and trailed wearily indoors to soak away the day's aches and pains in a hot bath. She was still there when Maria thumped on the bathroom door to say that Signor Roberto wanted her on the telephone. Draped in a towel, she padded downstairs and picked up the receiver.

'Gina, darling, welcome back! My mother told me that you were here, and I'll forgive you for not letting me know yourself if you agree to help me entertain some important people this evening.'

'I would have rung you, but I bumped into Signora Artom first. You'd do better to let me off this evening; I've been working hard and my sparkle value at the moment is definitely low!'

'I don't believe it – but, if so, you need the Artom cure: soft lights, sweet music, and *me, tesoro*!'

She smiled at a possibility that could well be true. His special brand of infectious gaiety was exactly what she needed at the moment. Depression couldn't live in his company, and she'd allowed herself to despair unnecessarily.

'I'm recovering already, just talking to you,' she admitted. 'You may rely on me this evening, provided the dancing isn't too strenuous; I've been toiling in the garden all day.'

'Nightclub stuff, darling, not Highland reels! I'll pick you up at eight o'clock.'

She put down the telephone, then realised she'd forgotten to ask who the 'important' people they were entertaining were. For a certainty, though, Roberto's guests would be of a sophisticated kind because he didn't waste time on the dull and dowdy. Her travelling wardrobe offered no choice in the matter of what to wear, but fortunately included one dress in which she felt ready to go anywhere – a tunic of jade silk jersey, as simply pleated as the drapery on a Greek statue. She coiled her hair and fastened it with a gold clasp, and made up her face more carefully than usual. Unless Roberto's other women guests were in the supermodel league, at least she wouldn't let him down.

His smiling face confirmed as much when he arrived. 'You get *more* beautiful every time I see you. Do you know what you remind me of? One of those woodland nymphs who entice poor mortals into fairyland: lovely, but very dangerous!'

As tributes went, she thought it couldn't fail to get the evening off to a good start. Any true-born Italian could turn a pretty compliment and make it sound sincere, but Roberto managed to do more than that. His eyes now said that he hadn't seen her for far too long; it was a state of affairs he wouldn't let happen again. None of the Englishmen she knew could cram that amount of appreciation into a single glance, and the most she'd ever wrung out of William Bird in the way of a compliment was the admission that she didn't look at all bad! She might, in a calmer moment, stop and consider which she preferred – Roberto's charming all-out assault on her defences, or the inarticulate warmth that lay beneath William's surface gruffness. But her English friend was far away, and

Roberto was beside her, offering the comfort she needed.

'You were away when I was here last – I missed you,' she said truthfully. 'For the first time now Poggio begins to feel like itself again.'

His handsome face looked sympathetic, but he made a gesture of pushing problems aside. 'It's a pity about the Kramers – I think we could spend the evening more profitably by ourselves; but duty calls, *amore*. We shall have to talk about Poggio another time.'

Reassured by the knowledge that here, at last, was someone who *would* talk to her, she smiled and followed him out to his car.

John Kramer III was the son of an American hotel magnate, with business interests that obviously coincided with Roberto's. His wife Karen's interests even more obviously coincided with Roberto himself as the evening wore on. Dressed lavishly in fuchsia-coloured satin, she monopolised her host on the dance floor, and after one purgatorial gallop with John III, Georgina could quite see why; he had the drive of a charging rhinoceros and the grace of a man with two left feet. It was safer just to let him talk, and she sat listening, wide-eyed and inattentive, while he took her on a reminiscent tour of every Italian hotel he'd stayed in. They'd got to the Danieli in Venice, and she was clenching her jaw to stop it yawning, when Roberto pleaded exhaustion and dragged his partner back to the table. Georgina carefully avoided catching his eye, and after a brief gulp of champagne John was off again, halfway across the Lagoon, to a promising hostelry he'd discovered on Torcello, that only needed the Kramer touch to put it on the discerning traveller's map.

By one am even he was ready to throw in the towel, but Karen insisted on a rendezvous with Roberto the following morning: the sights of Florence and a long, slow lunch would fill the day very nicely, she thought. Roberto threw an anguished glance at her husband but no help was forthcoming.

'Don't worry about me,' said John Kramer kindly, thankful to be spared the museums he hadn't escaped in Rome. 'You go right ahead; I want to study all those papers you left with me. By the time you and Karen get back, I'll be ready to talk business.'

They said goodnight at last and Georgina and Roberto walked back to his car.

'Busy day ahead of you,' she said thoughtfully, 'what with the sights, and all!'

He turned to glance at her, saw the mischief in her face, and began to smile. In another moment they were both helpless with laughter, clutching each other as tears rolled down their cheeks. Then Roberto sobered up sufficiently to kiss her laughing mouth into stillness, and when he let her go she knew that some boundary in their awareness of each other had finally been crossed. The friendship and fights of adolescence must now be transmuted into a different relationship that would reshape their lives or have to be regretfully put aside as an enticing, heartbreaking near-miss. But the near-miss was beginning to look less and less likely. There was, for a moment, the echo of William Bird's voice in her ear, warning her against fancy 'Eyetalians', but that was because he'd wanted her back at Kew.

'What an evening,' Roberto murmured, 'but I can't complain if it ends like this. You should have come back sooner, *amore*.' His mouth brushed hers again. 'Of course, the evening really ought to lead to something else – me taking you back to Siena, but I have the feeling you still wouldn't agree to that. Am I right?'

'Yes. But only because I'd like us to be sure that what we do is . . . meaningful; not just what any couple might fall into after an evening out together,' she said after a moment. If he tried to persuade her or, worse, took it for granted that she could be overruled simply because he was in charge of the car, she would know she had been mistaken in thinking that something important was happening. But he did neither of those things. Instead, a brilliant smile seemed to acknowledge the truth of what she'd just said, then he let go of her and put the car into gear.

'Poggio, in that case, before resolution weakens and I change my mind.'

'Tell me about the Kramers,' she suggested, once he'd threaded his way out of the centre of the city. 'Why are you concerned with them?'

'I'm concerned with *him*, appearances to the contrary! In fact, I've been stalking him for a long time. We've got a big development project on hand, just the sort of thing that interests him, but people are offering him such projects all the time, and I couldn't be certain of hooking him. But I think he's caught now.'

'What's the project? Restoring more dilapidated buildings that would otherwise be pulled down?'

'Something like that . . . but I still have a superstitious feeling that if I talk about it too much it will disappear into thin air! I'll tell you about it when I know it's going to happen.'

She smiled and obligingly changed the conversation. It hadn't occurred to her before that his self-confidence, which seemed impregnable, might be the armour he wore against disappointment or failure. The discovery made him more vulnerable, even though she thought he was worrying unnecessarily. John Kramer would concern himself in Roberto's project not least because his wife would see to it that he did. She thought of saying so, then decided against it; their new relationship might not stand up yet to teasing.

'Your mother invited us to lunch on Sunday,' she said instead. 'Will you be at Casagrande?'

'Most certainly, if you're going to be there. I hope that's what you *want* me to say?'

'Of course, I'd like you to be there.' She hesitated a moment, then added an honest afterthought. 'I also want a chance to talk to you about Poggio but it's much too late to start now.'

Roberto had expected the request, sensing in her some strain that had nothing to do with an evening spent with not very congenial strangers. He felt certain that Enrico wouldn't bring himself to confide in her and that she would seek information elsewhere, but he hadn't made up his mind yet what to say to her. There would be time enough before Sunday to decide how much she should know about his own entanglement in Poggio's affairs. He left her with a lingering goodnight kiss that insisted again how serious his claims were, and she finally went indoors with the knowledge that her moment of truth had crept appreciably nearer. Soon she might have to make her choice, as Olivia had done – the dear, known life in London, working with William, or something different altogether.

Next morning at breakfast Enrico was untalkative, but she had the impression that he was silent because he was abstracted, not angry; whatever weighed on his mind had little or nothing to do with her. When she asked if she could go with him to the hospital that evening, his smile was affectionate again, and slightly shame-faced.

'Of course, *tesoro*. Lucia wanted to know where you were. I didn't say we'd had a little difference of opinion!'

Georgina clung to the hope that he would eventually begin to talk to her of his own accord, simply because it would be a relief to share his worries, and on her way out of the room kissed him to help restore good relations. But while she waited for him to recover, the kitchen garden cried out for attention, and she must neglect the flower garden while she concentrated on it. Prowling up and down, she discovered that the neglect was recent; Giuseppe had obviously sown his seeds as usual, because small vegetable seedlings were struggling for life under a choking carpet of weeds.

She was easing a row of carrot seedlings into the light of day when a voice spoke behind her.

41

'You're tugging at that wretched plant as if you hated it.' It was Adam Fleming standing there, watching her.

'It's bindweed, and I do hate it,' she muttered. 'Filthy encroaching stuff.'

He looked at the sea of greenery all round them, and then at the flushed, set face of the girl in front of him. 'I won't say a word about the labours of Hercules, just ask if I can lend a hand?'

She straightened her back, glad of an excuse to stop bending double for a moment. 'You, Professor? Shouldn't you be at your desk, poring over some quaint medieval text or other?'

'I do quite a lot of that,' he agreed pleasantly. 'It doesn't stop me doing other things from time to time.'

'Well, it's kind of you to offer, but I don't think I should drag you back to the real world. It's much more tiring, for one thing, than looking at painted landscapes on gallery walls.'

The derisive drawl, which she regretted but couldn't alter, was born of too much anxiety. Even the task of clearing the vegetable garden looked hopeless, and it mirrored the near-despair about Poggio that was overtaking her altogether. But she forgot that the man in front of her had no way of knowing that. In the act of bending over the carrot row again, imagining that the conversation was over, she was dragged upright by hands that bit painfully through the thinness of her shirt. The anaemic-looking academic was angry. She'd offered him one thoughtless jibe too many, and if she'd written him off as a bloodless intellectual, she was wrong about that as well.

'Shall we clear the air once and for all? I'm tired of being your whipping boy when you're displeased with the rest of the world. Agreed that I spend time looking at things you appear to despise, but I don't understand *why* you despise them. If you find the masterpieces that permit us to call ourselves civilised only good for a cheap sneer, then I despair of you.'

The flame in his eyes was nicely balanced by the ice in his voice and, taken together, the result was akin to being flayed alive. What made matters worse was the knowledge that she deserved it. His hands had let go of her, but she was still held in the grip of a personality that must, she thought, set students alight with the sheer force of his own conviction.

'I jeered once too often, I'm afraid,' she conceded stiffly. 'You were right to slay me.'

'That wasn't slaying . . . I thought I was being very gentle!'

'Then I hope I'm not around when you really start to lay about you.' Her smile was faint, but it showed him how strained she'd looked before.

Tiresome and hostile she might be, but perhaps it was a better response to her worries than the hopelessness another girl might have sunk into. This one was at least fighting the damn weeds. His voice had lost its edge when he spoke again.

'The apology was handsome and I accept it if you'll let me conduct you to some painted landscapes one day. Jeer at *me* if it allows you to let off steam, but grant what matchless genius has left behind; it isn't as if we come anywhere near equalling it nowadays.'

'I don't want to jeer at you at all, but I'm afraid you'll have to let me off the conducted tour. There's far too much to be done here.'

She spoke lightly but he couldn't miss the effort it cost her. Whatever was going on was working up to some crisis that she both dreaded and wished to precipitate because the present state of tension was even worse. He had no right to interfere, and felt certain that she'd reject an offer of help the moment it was made. All he could do was insist on taking some physical strain off her shoulders – such slender shoulders, too. He could still feel them under his hands.

'I can see what there is to do out here, which is where this conversation began. I'm no horticulturalist, but if you'll tell me what to do I can promise to go on doing it until you tell me to stop.'

'Stop when you want to,' she capitulated with a real smile. 'If you insist on helping, I'll leave the carrots to you – no expertise is needed to tell them from weeds; they're these pretty ferny things.'

She watched him for a moment or two until it seemed safe to leave him on his own, then moved to the other end of the plot. They worked for the rest of the morning without exchanging more than a friendly smile when one or other of them stood up to stretch a tired back, but rather to her surprise he returned after lunch. By late afternoon he'd not only fought and won his battle with the carrot rows, but scythed all the grass paths that intersected the vegetable garden as well. She reckoned he must be blistered of hand by now, as well as aching of back, but he seemed quietly determined not to give in until she did. It was a relief to see Alessio, released from school for the Easter holidays, come dancing along, anxious for his usual reading lesson with the professor.

'You've worked miracles, and I'm very grateful,' she said to Adam, 'but it's time to knock off now.'

'What about you?'

'Me as well. I must get ready to visit Lucia. I wasn't allowed to go yesterday because Gramps and I had what he calls a "little difference of opinion", but I think we're friends again now.'

43

She smiled again as she spoke but he couldn't help feeling that the difference of opinion hadn't been a slight one, and he was conscious once more of having involved her in problems that were too big for her. She mostly remained a mystery to him, but there were two things that he now knew about her for certain – she didn't 'potter' when it came to gardening, and her commitment to Poggio was far from being the dutiful affection she might be expected to feel for her grandparents' home,

'If what Enrico objects to is seeing you slave away all day out here, I'm not surprised,' he commented quietly.

Georgina shook her head. 'It wasn't that: women are expected to work hard in Italy! My sin was doing something they're *not* supposed to do – interfere in matters that don't concern them!'

She was astonished to see the professor smiling at her with a rueful sweetness that made his face look unexpectedly pleasant. 'I feel responsible, bullying you into coming out here. My intentions were good, of course, but that's what the road to hell is supposed to be paved with!'

'No need to feel responsible; I should have come anyway.'

Bored by a conversation in English he couldn't understand, Alessio gave Adam's hand a little tug as a reminder that he was still there.

'A pupil who insists on being taught!' she pointed out. 'It seems to say something for the teacher.'

'In this case it says more for the pupil. My friend here only needed someone to take a little interest in him.'

They walked away together, the tall thin man and the small boy hopping by his side, already deep in conversation. 'A little interest' didn't make much of a claim, but he had his own work to do and she couldn't help wondering how many other Oxford dons would have bothered to concern themselves with a backward ten-year-old. Maria had insisted that Adam Fleming had a kindness that came from the heart and as usual, when it came to instinctive wisdom about people, she seemed to be quite right.

Georgina cleaned her tools, gave a last look around a garden which still depressed her by the amount of work that remained to be done, and found that she was being watched by Caterina, who'd come to stand behind her, unsmiling and looking tense.

'Mamma says Adam's been out here all day,' she said accusingly. 'He's supposed to be writing a great book, not working like a peasant.'

The word on her lips sounded bitter, and her eyes were full of wounded rage. Georgina noted the danger signals, sighing inwardly at yet another complication, another problem that she felt incompetent to deal with. Without Lucia's firm control the entire household seemed to be falling to pieces, She'd noticed a change in Caterina the moment she arrived, but told herself that a schoolgirl was bound to attach importance to any man who treated her for the first time with charming adult courtesy. A father-figure fixation wasn't likely to do much harm, especially given the gentleness with which Fleming would probably handle the situation; but a mixture of calf-love and hero-worship combined made for something much more combustible and painful. The strange thing was that the professor seemed an unlikely candidate for the focus of an impressionable adolescent's heart. She didn't suppose that Caterina had managed to needle him into honest-to-goodness rage, so all she would have seen was a kind but colourless man who looked invisible against the vivid backcloth of daily Italian life. It was downright unfair of the man to cause more trouble by having such an unexpected effect; but unfair or not, the pangs of jealousy now had to be dealt with.

'Professor Fleming offered to help today because there's so much to do out here,' she said finally. 'He won't make a habit of it, and you needn't fear that his own work will be neglected.'

'He'll come if he feels sorry for you. I don't want him to see you working out here.'

Maria's children were allowed licence at Poggio but Georgina thought her grandmother would say that it was time to be firm. '*Cara*, now you're being silly. Work *must* be done, and I can't crawl around the garden in the dark.'

Caterina stared at the half-smiling face of the *padrona*'s granddaughter – so coolly beautiful in a way that an Englishman might be expected to appreciate, so hard to compete with. Anguish drove her into wanting to inflict hurt as well as suffer it, because her own pain wasn't being taken seriously.

'What's the point of slaving out here? Everyone knows Poggio's finished.'

The sudden tension in the air between them was frightening, but the words were out now and couldn't be taken back.

'Who is "everyone"? And what precisely do they think they know?'

Caterina managed a shrug, unwilling to admit that she hadn't any very clear idea.

'Answer me!' Georgina cried in a voice the girl had never heard her use before.

'Find out yourself! I don't care. I hate this place!' With tears beginning to stream down her face, Caterina launched herself across the lawn in a wild dash for the safety of the house. Georgina looked down at her own hands, gripped until they were white on the fork she'd been cleaning. She relaxed her frantic hold on it, put it away with the rest of the tools, and walked slowly indoors herself.

Chapter 5

The long and tiring day at least ended cheerfully; they found Lucia so much stronger that she was being promised she'd be allowed home within the space of a week. She even *sounded* herself again, and the various searching questions fired at them made it clear that the reins of the household were practically back in her hands again.

'I'm a bossy old woman,' she said apologetically. 'Can't bear not to know what's going on.'

Georgina edited out of her report certain items that were better not mentioned, and entertained both grandparents with the story of her meeting with the Kramers. Then it was Enrico's turn to provide information for his wife.

'A surprise, *amore*: Paolo and his family are coming back to Siena.'

Lucia stared at him in astonishment. 'You mean your nephew, Paolo? I thought nothing would prise him away from Rome.'

'I had a letter from him this morning; his law firm is to open a branch in Siena – who better to run it than a man who grew up there? Filippo has now qualified, too, and he will help his father. It will be nice to have them nearby again.'

On the drive home Enrico relapsed into silence again, and Georgina was aware that his mind was riveted on some problem that had had to be set aside while he visited the hospital. When she stopped the car at the foot of the terrace steps he gave a little sigh. Something, perhaps, had been decided, but his face looked sad and she knew that the decision he had come to gave him no pleasure.

'*Cara*, forgive me for shouting at you yesterday,' he said gently, 'but I don't want you to ask me those questions again. There is nothing to be talked about until I have had a meeting with . . . with someone on Monday. After that I promise I shall tell you what is happening.'

She wanted him to talk to her *before* his decision was taken, but there was nothing to be done except kiss him goodnight and accept the warning hidden in the apology. More questions were useless because he simply wouldn't answer them.

Next morning it was something to be thankful for that Adam Fleming didn't appear in the garden again to upset Caterina. Georgina saw him drive away and hoped that Maria's daughter had noticed the fact as well. The professor was going about his proper affairs and the Great Work wasn't being neglected. Even better from a jealous teenager's point of view, he wasn't being exposed to the wiles of a woman who had the unfair advantage of being ten years older than herself.

She saw nothing of him at all until a few days later when she was in her room changing for Erica Artom's Sunday lunch-party. The signora's entertaining was formal and guests didn't arrive for her parties dressed in jeans and a cotton shirt. Hesitating over how formal she needed to be, Georgina was drawn to the window by shrieks of laughter coming from outside. The professor was being given a lesson for a change, but every time he lost his balance on the skates Alessio hugged himself with the pleasure of it and Caterina patiently explained to her hero yet again what it was that he must do. She was still looking out when a showy white Alfa Romeo nosed its way along the drive and stopped with a swish of tyres on the gravel. Quite unnecessarily, Roberto had arrived to escort her to Casagrande.

The morning was warm and spring-like and he was rigged accordingly, in faultless white trousers and a blue and white striped silk shirt. A gold chain glinted against the brown skin of his throat but even that couldn't make him seem effeminate, because he looked superbly fit, and as lithe as a panther. She watched him being introduced to Adam Fleming, and felt a twinge of pity for the Englishman. Roberto's male beauty couldn't be missed, any more than could that of the young David, sculpted by Donatello. Beside him most Anglo-Saxons would have suffered by comparison, but the professor's case was worse than most; his fair hair had been bleached almost to colourlessness now by the bright sun, and his pale skin had resisted the smallest hint of a tan. Roberto shook hands with him with careless grace, then strapped on the skates himself, not reluctant to show what a natural athlete could do. It was an elegant performance, but Georgina suspected that Alessio got more fun out of watching the professor fall off than seeing Roberto stay on.

When she finally went outside, dressed in cool cream linen belted with green to match the sandals on her bare feet, Roberto at once abandoned the rest of the company. He kissed her hand and then her mouth, and the gestures were deliberate, she thought – intended to make a statement they were all to understand. Perhaps she wasn't quite ready to be so publicly claimed, but it was impossible *not* to feel more alive simply because he was there, and more beautiful simply because his eyes said that he found her so. But she was aware of something else as well – Alessio and Caterina had ranged themselves beside the professor; she suspected all three of them of looking forward to the moment when she and Roberto went away.

As they set off along the lane he waved aside the excuse offered for Enrico's absence and made a laughing reference instead to the man they'd just left.

'I caught a glimpse of your strange lodger in Florence the other day – happened to be passing the Pitti Palace when he came out with a bunch of students. Bored to tears, I should think, poor things! Some of the girls were beautiful, and if the boys with them preferred to look at bits of painted canvas, then Heaven help the human race!'

Georgina surprised herself with a faint desire to be perverse; she would have liked to say that Adam Fleming wasn't strange, just his own man in a way that happened to be totally different from Roberto's swashbuckling persona.

'The students have presumably been sent here for that purpose – to keep their minds on what the professor shows them. There'll be plenty of time later for them to laugh and gambol in the hay!'

'Time for them, but I'm afraid Fleming is beyond saving. No doubt he feels safe going into raptures over Botticelli's painted ladies. Put a real live woman in his arms and I'm afraid he'd probably die of embarrassment.'

Georgina found herself wondering if he would. 'He invited me to go with him one morning,' she felt obliged to point out.

'Purely for the sake of improving your mind, *amore*. Any other man living at Poggio and I should be jealous,' Roberto said, putting a hand on her knee. 'With *this* one there's no need!'

It was true, of course, and after a slight struggle with herself she admitted as much. Then she asked if they could stop for ten minutes before getting to Casagrande.

'So that I can kiss you properly?'

'No – I need for *us* to talk about Poggio, please, because Gramps will do nothing but refuse, and fly into a rage. Please tell me if you know why Giuseppe left, and why we're in such a mess.'

He took so long to answer that she wondered whether he was going to refuse as well, but finally he spoke. 'The answer's obvious, my dear: a simple shortage of cash.'

She stared at him in astonishment. 'But . . . that's not possible. Poggio's always been prosperous.'

Roberto shook his head. 'It's always *seemed* so; there's a difference, I'm afraid. Can you really see Enrico as a prudent man, investing the proceeds of good years to tide him over the bad ones?'

She knew as well as Roberto what her grandfather's philosophy had been: another year, another harvest, so why not enjoy what we have and share it with others.

'He *said* there have been some bad years,' she admitted, 'but even so, that's what banks are for, surely, to help people out of temporary difficulties.'

'His difficulties are not temporary, and the banks know that. These days businesses have to be shrewdly and vigorously managed to stay alive; Enrico is old, tired, and he has no one to succeed him. Why should a bank feel helpful?'

'Don't talk as if Poggio is just a business,' she flared suddenly. 'It's a way of life.'

'To your grandfather, possibly, but it's a way of life that Italians in large numbers are abandoning as fast as they can. Labouring from dawn to dusk for a reward that can be wiped out overnight has lost its appeal. Look at Giuseppe's sons.'

There was a long pause before Georgina spoke again. 'It's hard to see what we can do next,' she said slowly. 'If we can't get help, or can't afford it even if we can get it, Poggio will die.'

Roberto hesitated himself, choosing his next comment with care. 'Enrico was given help – by my own company.'

'You mean *you* lent the money the bank wouldn't offer?' He nodded and her face glowed beautifully with sudden gratitude. 'Oh, Roberto, that was very good of you. But why is Gramps still in difficulties in that case?'

He gave a little shrug. 'We come back to Enrico himself, *cara*. I'm afraid the truth is that today's conditions, which are not easy, are too much for him. Viniculturalists have to move with the times to survive; your grandfather is still using outworn stock, outworn methods. A man of his age and temperament doesn't take kindly to change, and change is what survival is all about.'

Despair, beginning to choke hope to death, weighted down her next question. 'Then what is Poggio to do? How are Gramps and Lucia to manage?'

'*Amore*, don't look so desperate. There *is* a solution, but I can't discuss it with you yet, because I'm waiting for Enrico's decision; all I can tell you is that I'm prepared to go on helping.'

Her eyes pricked with sudden tears. In the past she'd been attracted to

Roberto for a number of reasons, but disinterested kindness had never figured in her assessment of him. How wrong she'd been, she now realised. 'What would he have done without you? I'm so grateful,' she murmured unsteadily.

'I haven't told you to make you feel grateful. I'm a businessman, *tesoro*, and it's a business offer.' But his smile reassured her. It was much more than that; he would go on helping her grandfather because he understood the value of what Poggio represented, saw not just a stubborn refusal to move with the times but a stubborn fight for continuity and precious tradition. Her hand touched his cheek in a little gesture of thankfulness, and he caught it in his own and kissed it.

'We've had fun in the past, but I have the feeling that fun soon isn't going to be enough,' he murmured softly. 'Say you agree with me, please.'

His eyes held her own, and she didn't look away, knowing that the moment was too important for anything but candour between them. 'I think I do agree,' she admitted, 'but forgive me if I say this doesn't seem quite the moment to be thinking of our own affairs.'

'It's *always* the moment for our own affairs!' His confidence made her smile, but his face was full of tenderness as well, assuring her that with her future in his hands, she would have nothing to fear. Anxiety for her grandfather, even some small, faint regret for what might have been a different future, seemed unnecessary now. Together she and Roberto would save Poggio, and together they might build a rich, exciting life there.

She lifted his hand to her mouth in a fleeting gesture, but tried to sound firm. 'Right now it's the moment for us to appear at your mother's lunch-table! I can remember times enough in the past when we were in trouble with her for being late for meals.'

He accepted the hint – not only that they shouldn't be late, but also that she wasn't to be pressured unduly; their relationship had changed and she was as aware of it as he was. He'd be content with that for the moment, knowing that she shared his own growing certainty of what the future held. He could sense it in her, feel an excitement and desire to match his own that would make life ideal. He was accustomed now to having his plans go well, but her return to Poggio – *not* foreseen, he had to admit, and certainly not expected – put the final perfect gloss on things.

Her own happiness only dimmed when they turned on to Artom land and she saw its contrast with Poggio. No sign of neglect or bad management here, and no evidence that this professionally-run estate was suffering from having too little olive oil to sell and too much wine. Roberto stopped the car in the courtyard behind the house, built

51

traditionally of stone, like Poggio. It was less old and, in her view, much less beautiful – everything at Casagrande was opulently luxurious – but she couldn't deny its well-tended, nurtured air. The elegant figure of her hostess detached itself from a group of people clustered on the terrace and came towards them.

'Bad creatures! You've been dawdling! Now, Gina dear, who don't you know? A distant cousin of mine, perhaps, Contessa Clara Giordana?'

The countess was thin as a greyhound, and dressed in a clashing medley of colours that unexpectedly achieved style because total self-confidence denied that she could ever achieve anything less. She was sharp-tongued and funny, and not at any pains to include the new guest in a conversation that was mostly about people in Siena. It wasn't courteous behaviour, but Georgina was content to let her shine. Roberto's eyes could meet hers occasionally, agreeing that they must put up with a boring lunch-party for his mother's sake; it had very little to do with them! There was her host to talk to as well. Dino Artom was a small volcano of a man Georgina liked much better than his wife. Native roughness hadn't quite been polished out of existence, and when a party was in progress and his own wine was flowing, he reverted to the rumbustious man who could still embarrass his wife by laughing too loudly and talking too much. Georgina suspected him of being a hard driver of business bargains, but the warmth and gaiety she prized in Roberto had come from Dino, not Erica.

Sunday lunch at Casagrande tended to spread itself across the entire afternoon, but finally she murmured that she must return home in time to leave for the hospital with Enrico. Clara Giordana overheard, and suggested that she would keep Roberto company on the return journey to Casagrande. She saw Georgina smile calmly at the suggestion, and couldn't make up her mind whether to despise or pity her. There were certain ground rules to be observed between women stalking the same man; the *inglese* was either very sure of herself or didn't appear to understand them at all.

She wasn't to know that the *inglese*'s mind was on other things. In the middle of her conversation with Dino an idea – a tiny candle of hope – had been lit, which her thoughts were busy sheltering against stray draughts of doubt and uncertainty. The little flame grew steadily brighter in her mind, while she sat in the back of the car, not even listening to the flow of provocative small-talk directed at the driver. Roberto sensed that she'd withdrawn from them, and drew her attention back to himself by kissing her very deliberately when she parted company with them at Poggio. He didn't feel entirely sure of her yet, and the sensation was both disagreeable and exciting.

'*Ciao, amore*. Spare a thought for me – for *us* – occasionally, as well as for Poggio,' he suggested.

'You *and* Poggio – certainly as much as I can cope with!' she agreed, smiling at him.

'When you look at me like that I can even bear to share you with Enrico and Lucia; in fact, I can do anything at all . . . climb mountains, work miracles!'

Her eyes lit with amusement. 'Your first miracle will be to get back to Casagrande unscathed.'

'At least you noticed that I was being pursued; I was afraid you hadn't!' He dropped another light kiss on her mouth and then returned to the car and a rather taut-faced contessa, while Georgina walked up the steps wondering whether she could contain her great idea until after their evening visit to the hospital.

In the end she did, because Maria appeared, dressed in her Sunday finery for the visit to the signora that Enrico had promised her. It wasn't until they were back at home again, sitting over a late supper, that it was time to take a deep breath and fire her opening salvo.

'Gramps, I haven't forgotten what you said – that I wasn't to ask questions until you'd had a meeting with someone – but I can't help feeling that what I want to say might affect the way you make up your mind about whatever it is that worries you.'

Her hand touched his where it lay on the table, mutely begging him to listen. After a moment he looked at her and nodded.

'Say what you want to say, *cara*.'

'You reminded me that I know almost nothing about Poggio, and it's true, but there are certain things that see themselves, as Maria likes to say. Poggio is in difficulties for the moment. It needs help with all the work that's crying out to be done, and a breathing space to enable it to survive until times get better. But help and breathing space require money that it hasn't got. Roberto mentioned that his company had helped once before, but he said he couldn't discuss with me some new offer you were still considering.'

'All that is true,' Enrico said heavily. 'That is the position.'

'The new offer presumably means a further loan. It's tremendously kind of him, but it simply puts us deeper in debt, and borrowing other people's money is wasteful if we don't have to. I've got a much better idea.' Her face was suddenly so luminous with the beauty of it that he knew he couldn't end *this* conversation by whipping himself into a rage that would enable him to stalk out of the room.

'Roberto didn't tell you what his offer was?' When she shook her head he went on. 'Well, the details are not clear, *cara*, but if Poggio were no longer to be short of money, it'd be likely not to need Enrico Casali either. I think Roberto was being vague to be kind, but I got the impression that his company would buy the estate, in effect, and put in a young, energetic manager – I can't say that's unreasonable.'

It came as no surprise, remembering Roberto's estimate of her grandfather. She looked at Enrico's bowed head, tried to imagine him anywhere but where his whole life had been spent, and knew that what Roberto was suggesting couldn't be allowed to happen.

'Gramps . . . you haven't heard my idea yet. Listen! I have a flat in London, bought with money my father insisted I should have when I needed it, not much later in life when I might not need it at all. My idea is to sell the flat and invest the proceeds in Poggio.'

'*Tesoro*, you don't know what you're saying,' he murmured unsteadily. 'It's madness! What would your father say to such a scheme?'

'He'd say that I'm twenty-six – quite old enough to make up my own mind. The inheritance he gave me was for me to use as I wanted to. At that time I decided to buy a home with it, but I'm almost sure that I'm not going to need it much longer.'

'Because you would stay here?'

'Well, certainly for the moment if you'd have me, but my feeling is that I shall end up marrying Roberto! Nothing's fixed yet, Gramps, but we're . . . we're feeling our way towards it. I think we both know that we'd like to share life in future. Can you imagine how pleased Mama would be? She's tried not to make it too obvious, but she's been yearning for years for just this thing to happen!'

There was no yearning in her grandfather's face that Georgina could see; she might even have admitted to herself that she was disappointed in a reaction that was decidedly unenthusiastic.

'Are you sure, *cara*? I know the two of you have always seemed to belong together, but it's a big step for a girl who's enjoyed a very independent, different sort of life. Marrying Roberto would deprive you of that, and of England as well.'

'I know – but you can't expect to get something precious without paying a price for it.' Her face broke into a radiant smile. 'If I'm counting my chickens before they're hatched and Roberto decides that he *doesn't* want to marry me, then you'll have to let me live a rejected spinster at Poggio.'

Enrico shook his head. 'I don't think you fear rejection, *tesoro*. I've listened to your idea, but I haven't accepted it – I can't possibly do so.'

She got up and walked round the table to his side. 'Give me one good reason why not. Convince me that Poggio is finished, that nothing we can do will make it thrive again, that we'd simply be throwing good money after bad. If you *can't* say that and believe it, then you've got to let me help – because I love it as much as you and Granny do.'

There was a long silence, while Enrico chewed his lip and stared again at a future away from Poggio that had seemed unavoidable half an hour ago. For himself, he hoped he could have survived it – been resolute enough to turn down his granddaughter's offer; for Lucia, though, it was another matter. He wasn't resolute enough for that.

'Dearest, do you realise the risks involved?' he asked at last. 'With money to invest, I believe that Poggio *can* survive, but I can't be certain that you won't lose your inheritance. I must explain all that to your father, and he must agree with what you propose to do. Otherwise I shall accept Roberto's offer tomorrow.'

'Then there's nothing more to worry about,' she said with great content. 'Oh, Gramps, I was so terribly afraid you'd turn me down!'

'*Tesoro!*' His arms enfolded her in a hug that told her what his private anguish had been. For the first time since getting to Italy she could see the real Enrico Casali: open and warm and natural. His eyes were full of tears when he kissed her own wet cheek, but optimism was reviving; her grandfather was almost himself again.

'We'll ring Washington straightaway,' she insisted. 'Then you can give me my first lesson in the making of Chianti. I rather fancy myself as a lady viniculturist!'

'You won't be here long enough to learn. Roberto will realise that he must marry you before some other man with a grain of sense steals you away from him,' Enrico said regretfully.

Chapter 6

Enrico set off early next morning. He smiled so cheerfully at the professor, encountered on a post-breakfast stroll, that Adam wondered what had happened to transform him from the taciturn stranger of the past few weeks.

'Business meeting,' he shouted cheerfully. 'Then I must hurry back . . . lot to do here.'

Something had changed, because the *padrone* was even driving with all his old dangerous gusto. Adam grinned as he watched the car roar off along the drive, but hoped that business wasn't taking the old man anywhere near the centre of Florence where Heaven's intervention would certainly be needed to get him through the traffic unscathed.

Half an hour later Enrico reached Siena safely and walked into Roberto's office wondering whether a purely business meeting should include the slightest hint that he was aware of talking to someone who was probably going to become his granddaughter's husband. In the end he decided with rare self-restraint that he would leave Roberto to set the tone of the conversation, but it became apparent the moment he stepped inside the elegant reception office that his decision hadn't been required because Roberto wasn't there. A beautiful, brisk young woman, wearing a skirt only just on the hither side of decency in Enrico's opinion, apologised for the fact that Signor Artom was even then airborne on a sudden and unexpected visit to Geneva.

'We had an appointment this morning, a matter of some urgency to discuss.'

She smiled kindly, came near – he noted with irritation – to patting his ancient head. 'Everything has been attended to, signore. Roberto made sure that the papers would be ready for you. Only your signature is needed, and the rest can be attended to as soon as he gets back.'

Automatically he took the documents she held out to him, registering Roberto's obvious certainty that his offer would be accepted. Without Georgina's help, it would have been. Dear God in Heaven, how thankful he was to be able to refuse.

'A piece of writing paper, if you please, signorina,' he asked.

'No letter is needed – just your signature.' She still smiled, but impatience was beginning to fray the edges of her not very impregnable courtesy. No doubt she was driven hard by a demanding boss; even so, Enrico resented being made to feel like a bumbling old fool, whose only part in the proceedings was to be told what to do.

'I shall not be signing the documents,' he explained with dignity. 'My note to Signor Artom will explain why. Now may I have a sheet of paper?'

She was disconcerted but sensible enough not to comment on a situation that Roberto had clearly not foreseen. Fifteen minutes later, with his letter written and a courtly bow offered to the signorina, Enrico was outside in the sunlit Campo again, breathing in great lungfuls of air and freedom. Poggio still wasn't safe, and God alone knew whether he and his granddaughter would live to regret what had just been done; but all the same he thought he knew what a condemned prisoner felt at the very moment of being reprieved.

He got home to find Georgina already hard at work in the garden and, at the other end of the vegetable plot, the professor earthing up rows of potatoes with calm concentration. Adam had presented himself as soon as Georgina went outside herself, and she'd been warned by the sounds of the travelling escort that accompanied him across the garden – assorted chickens, guinea fowl, and Maria's current batch of baby turkeys, all curious and all apparently determined to investigate the slightest move he made.

'Gardener's lad, third class, reporting for duty,' Adam said, smiling at her from the middle of his attendant flock.

'Reporting with bodyguard, what's more!'

'Ridiculous, isn't it, but the moment I set foot out of doors, they insist on coming too. They're as unsnubbably inquisitive as the ladies of the village at home!'

She registered the fact that 'home' wasn't some peaceful ivy-smothered retreat overlooking a college garden, but there was more to think about than that. Immediately she must find a way of refusing his offer that wouldn't provoke another disagreement between them; there'd been enough of those already, and she wasn't feeling belligerent this morning.

'It's very kind of you to offer to help,' she said finally, 'but sabbaticals don't go on for ever and your time is precious. Caterina rightly ticked me off the other day for dragging you away from your own work.'

'You didn't drag; I volunteered.'

She hesitated about what to say next, and he decided to help her. 'Our

58

young friend has a touching faith in me, not to mention a misplaced trust in my book that would gladden the heart of any publisher.'

The ice was getting thin beneath her feet, because she wanted not to give Caterina's secret away, but still a little more had to be said.

'I'm sure you're right about both faith and trust; like the rest of the Pizzone family, she has the "professor's" interests very close to her heart.'

His grey eyes watched her with a hint of amusement. 'It's quite a treat to see you walking more delicately than Agag! But at the risk of sounding inordinately pleased with myself, I *had* noticed a slight attack of hero-worship. It's nothing to worry about; just a temporary condition. Soon enough some dashing young Italian will illustrate the difference between us and I shall become just an elderly gent she's mildly fond of!'

Georgina couldn't help smiling at the idea, even though she thought he underestimated the severity of poor Caterina's attack. Then it occurred to her that perhaps the problem of having a lovesick maiden on his hands wasn't new to him.

'Occupational hazard?' she asked, more to herself than to him. 'The life of a university don is more exciting than I'd imagined.'

He grinned but refused to be led up so provocative a by-way. 'You still haven't given me my assignment for today.'

She decided to accept that deflecting him from something he'd made up his mind to do was about as rewarding as tugging a bulldog in the opposite direction to the one it had decided to take. Given that he was such a quiet-spoken man, he had an unexpected capacity for sheer cussedness.

She capitulated with a little shrug. 'If you insist on doing something, the potatoes need attention. That means earthing them up, like this. Left as they are, the light will get in and turn the tubers green. Then they'll be inedible, poisonous in fact.'

Isolated from him at the other end of the garden, where not even Caterina could accuse her of distracting him from the job in hand, she slowly freed rows of young spinach from the surrounding jungle. There were times when the Tuscan soil could be too fertile, but although she muttered to herself about it, the truth was that she was feeling very content. She could see Enrico already back from Siena, prowling among the olive trees, inspecting them for signs of damage. He looked different, purposeful again, with the air of hopelessness that had surrounded him like a cloud dissolved in a new sense of optimism. She could have danced for the joy of seeing him busy again, but if she wanted to be truthful with herself, she must also admit that the vegetable garden felt less lonely when she could see the professor at the other end of it diligently earthing up potatoes.

There only remained one hurdle to tackle. She couldn't put off talking to William Bird. She knew how little she wanted to do so, but still kept skirting round the obstacle in her mind. She loved Poggio more than anywhere else on earth – no difficulty about acknowledging that; she had no regret at all about surrendering her London flat – no problem there, either. She was deeply happy to have become so necessary to Roberto, without whose help Poggio would have foundered before she got there. All in all, the future looked bright with promise, and only the thought of William Bird rubbed the bloom off her new happiness. She was letting down a man whose good opinion had been her greatest pleasure in the past. Facing the whole truth, she acknowledged to herself that she would miss *him* as he would miss her in the future.

With that accepted at last, she went resolutely back to work until Maria called that lunch was ready. She expected to see Adam head in the direction of his own apartment, but Enrico came to insist that those who worked must be fed. The professor was obliged to sit down to the enormous helping of saffron rice that Maria put in front of him, and be told that he was overthin and obviously undernourished. Maria had made up her mind to put flesh on his bones before he left Poggio, seeing it as a challenge she couldn't resist.

The wine Enrico poured came from the estate, and it led naturally enough to a discussion that Adam was intent on starting.

'Last year's, or earlier? I have no idea how long you let the ageing process last.'

'This was bottled last summer, having spent three years in the cask. Our method is different from the French, who generally let their wine mature after it has been bottled. Chianti Classico ages in the cask; once bottled, it is ready to drink – *should* be drunk, I think.'

Adam sipped what he'd been offered and smiled appreciatively. 'Not much like the Chianti that's sent to England, The straw overcoats it used to arrive in looked very fancy but the wine was dreadful, and it's not much better even now. Is Classico a definition of quality?'

'It's a definition of quality, and of geography to the extent that Chianti Classico comes from a comparatively small region between Florence and Siena. But mostly it relates to the way the wine is made, and only those vineyards that follow the method laid down by Baron Ricasoli a hundred years ago are entitled to carry the distinctive mark of the black cock on their bottles. The Sangiovese grape is the backbone of the wine, but three others are used as well, and we add more unfermented grapes that have been left to dry in the sun when the usual fermentation is dying down. This gives the slight sparkle that you find in good Chiantis. They vary, of course, from vintage to vintage, but there's no reason why the best of them – the Riservas – shouldn't be the equal of very good French wine.'

Enrico made the claim proudly. The next best thing to making wine was talking about it to an interested audience, and Georgina accepted without resentment the fact that an interested male was better than a mere girl any day.

'I'm an ignorant Englishman,' Adam admitted. 'You'll have to tell me where Casali wine comes in the league.'

They were getting on dangerous ground, and it occurred to her now that they were there because he'd planned it that way; the professor was deliberately leading the conversation to a point that Enrico couldn't retreat from.

'Poggio's like every other vineyard – it moves up and down. We've made some of the very best Chianti and, in a bad season, no doubt some of the worst!'

Adam glanced at the girl watching him across the table, unable to decide whether her expression implored or forbade him to go on with the most delicate question of all; he thought it was too late to stop now.

'What's happening in *this* year of grace?'

Enrico gave a little shrug. 'We still suffer from a mistaken decision in the past. Like a lot of other growers, we went for quantity. It seemed the right thing to do, but since then countries like Spain and Portugal have stepped up their production enormously as well, and the newcomers – Australia, Chile, Argentina – have been very successful. Poggio's too small and too hilly to take advantage of mass production. What we *should* have done – what we must do now – is concentrate on quality, which means high labour costs, and investment in new vines. At one time it didn't seem worthwhile, but with our dear Georgina involved now everything is changed.'

Adam hesitated to ask what her involvement meant but, although Enrico stopped short of confessing that she was going to provide the necessary capital, he saw no reason not to mention that her future was going to be in Italy.

'At Poggio?' Adam queried.

'No, but the next best thing: as the wife of our neighbour's son – Roberto Artom.'

61

Georgina looked reproachfully at her grandfather. '*Nothing's* settled yet. I wouldn't have mentioned the subject at all if I thought you were going to shout it from the roof-top!'

'Was I shouting?' he enquired of Adam with dignity. 'I thought I was merely mentioning what I shall *not* discuss with anyone else, and nor will he.'

'Naturally not,' the professor agreed, looking supremely uninterested in the eventual fate of Georgina Hadley. He was no more interested in Roberto Artom, either, his expression seemed to say, and she thought this understandable – no two men were ever less likely to appreciate one another.

After lunch they all went back to work, and she forgot about Adam Fleming. Her most pressing need was to think out what she was going to say to William that evening.

She telephoned him at home after supper, and suddenly felt homesick at the sound of his unemotional London voice answering her call.

'William! It's me, Georgina.'

'Extravagant wench! Do I guess this is to warn me that you can't get back by the end of the month after all?'

It was worse even than she'd imagined it would be. She clutched the telephone in a damp hand and forced herself to say what needed to be said. 'It's worse than that,' she admitted baldly. 'I'm about to say that I can't come back at all.'

There was silence at the other end of the line, her dear friend William apparently being oblivious for once of the fact that telephone time cost money. At last his voice came hesitatingly along the wire. 'You promised me, girl. You said you'd come back unattached.'

She'd expected him to be justifiably irritated, but hadn't bargained for what sounded like a devastating sense of loss. She didn't know how he'd spent the last week, missing her painfully and crossing off the days. Now the whole future had to be faced without her, and he'd been the fool who'd agreed that she could go. 'Think again if you're about to do something you'll end up regretting,' he insisted sadly.

It wasn't the moment to drag Roberto into the conversation; instead she did her best to explain about Poggio, certain that this was something he, of all men, would understand. By the time she'd reached the end and apologised with unmistakable distress for leaving him in the lurch, he'd got himself in hand again, could tell her not to be daft. It was obvious that a place like Poggio couldn't be left to rot.

'I shall have to come back to sell my flat,' she told him, 'because we need the proceeds from that to keep us going. We can't afford the labour we desperately need until we can get some working capital.'

'No job for a girl, selling flats,' William said morosely. 'You won't ask half enough for it. Much better leave it to me. You can come back when you need to, to clear the place out.'

Being in Italy was making her very emotional, she feared, because now she was strongly inclined to burst into tears, overcome by many emotions but most of all by his goodness of heart.

'Oh, William! I know we're told to return good for evil, but this is ridiculously generous of you. It would be the most tremendous help if you *could* just start things moving with an estate agent.'

She sounded so overwrought that he wanted to say that he'd come out himself and help dig the bloody place over for her; but he had problems of his own at Kew, and finding a replacement in a hurry for the best assistant he'd ever had would certainly be one of them.

'I'll make a start on selling it; then you'll have to authorise me to handle it with your solicitor.'

'You're a lovely, good man, William.'

'And you're a forward hussy, but I shall miss you. Give me your number there, and I'll ring when I've got some news.'

He said goodbye, and she put down the telephone with the sad and overwhelming knowledge that her boats were burned. She couldn't *not* do what she was doing, and of course Roberto and Poggio were infinitely worth what she was giving up; but William and her job at Kew had meant even more to her than she'd realised, and a little ache settled round her heart that she thought might never quite go away.

She got up the next morning still feeling oppressed, but blamed it on a change in the weather that ruled out the slightest chance of doing any work out of doors, because the rain had the sort of steady persistence about it that said it intended to go on falling all day. Enrico went off after breakfast in search of replacements for Giuseppe and his family, while Georgina hung about the kitchen waiting to be given a task to do.

'Why not drive in to Florence, *cara*?' Maria suggested. 'You said you had shopping to do.'

It was true that the clothes she'd brought with her were inadequate for a long-term stay, and she could usefully spend a wet day in Florence whereas she couldn't afford to waste a fine one there. She nodded and went to fetch mac and handbag. By the time she came downstairs again, Maria was deep in conversation with Adam Fleming.

'The *caro professore* came to ask if we needed anything in Florence. I said you were going anyway.'

'Silly to take two cars?' he enquired neutrally. 'We could do our bit to reduce congestion on the road and pollution in the air.'

'No doubt, but I'd rather be independent.' She thought she was probably becoming paranoid about avoiding him in order to be able to look Caterina in the eye, but apart from that she felt unsociable and disinclined to make small-talk all the way to Florence and back.

'I'm prepared to play chauffeur . . . await instructions,' he insisted gently.

She shrugged and gave in, making a mental note of the fact that if she didn't soon refuse to let him have his own way, he'd get into the habit of expecting it. They ran through the downpour to his car and travelled in silence while he steered them through the torrent now hurling itself down the steep track towards San Vicenzo. She stared out of the window beside her, almost content with a veiling of raindrops resembling tears that exactly suited the lowness of spirits her conversation with William had left behind. She roused herself to say something only when the car was turned on to the tarmac road leading through the town.

'You aren't dressed for lecturing. Have you got something else to do in Florence?'

He neatly thwarted an Italian lorry's desire to wrap itself round the MG before answering her. 'Yes: I thought I'd make a start on your education.'

The time for asserting herself had arrived even sooner than she'd thought, and here and now she must put him straight. 'I'm afraid you'll have to think again. Kind of you to bother with a Philistine like me, but I've come with the simple idea of shopping in mind. I'll meet you when you're ready to leave.'

'I thought we'd start at the Uffizi,' he murmured, as if she hadn't spoken at all. 'Chronologically we should begin in Siena, but there isn't time for that today. Still, you can get a glimpse of fourteenth-century painting here, and what came even before that.'

She fought with herself not to endanger the car by doing violence to its driver, took a deep breath, and tried again. 'I hope *you* have a lovely day at the Uffizi; I myself am going to the Via Tornabuoni.'

There was a silence in the car while he threaded his way through a swarm of scooter-riders apparently bent on suicide.

'You're in need of what the French call "chuchoter-ing". Maria said it in her own words, of course, but I could see what she meant. I shan't dare look her in the eye when we get back if I haven't *chuchoté*-ed you sufficiently.'

Still cross, but unfortunately curious as well, Georgina felt obliged to enquire what the ridiculous word meant.

'Literally, whispered to. In practice, gentled; taken care of a little.'

His quiet voice made nothing of the explanation, and she knew that she must certainly make nothing of it herself. This self-contained but compassionate man simply felt required to put other people together again when he saw them falling apart. There was no need for her heart to miss a beat as though she'd stepped on a stair that wasn't there.

'And a . . . gallop round the Uffizi is your idea of a . . . a little gentling?' she enquired faintly.

'Considering the possibilities open to me, yes,' he agreed with the hint of a smile. 'So, which is it to be – the Via Tornabuoni or what I think would do you more good?'

They were stuck in yet another traffic-jam and she hesitated between the desire to teach him a much-needed lesson and the knowledge that she wasn't anxious for a day of her own company. There was also the fact that she was curious about him. He glanced at her undecided face and began to murmur to himself:

> The Centipede was happy quite
> Until the Toad in fun
> Said 'Pray which leg goes after which?'
> And worked her mind to such a pitch
> She lay distracted in the ditch
> Considering how to run.

She gripped her lower lip firmly between her teeth until it seemed safe to trust her voice again. 'I can't have you quailing before Maria, and it's obviously going to rain all day, so I suppose it might as well be the Uffizi.'

'Just as well,' he agreed gently.

She went back to looking out of the window and made the discovery that magic had been at work on the raindrops. Nothing like tears now, they resembled tiny droplets of laughter, golden and irresistible. The car itself was full of lightness, so buoyant that she wouldn't have been surprised to see it sail up over the queue of earth-bound Fiats in front of them and float down into the forecourt of the Uffizi. The change was very puzzling, but she was prepared to accept it as one of the gifts a beneficent Heaven occasionally provided when they were needed most.

65

They began at the beginning, as Adam had promised, with the gravely beautiful Byzantine Madonnas of Cimabue and Duccio, forever enthroned in a mysterious world where cherubs swung upside down in a blue, star-sprinkled Heaven, immune to the laws of gravity. Then, the whole stupendous flowering of Florentine painting: Giotto, Masaccio and Uccello, between them solving for all the artists who came after them the mysteries of perspective, so that the ranks of angels no longer seemed to be standing on each others' heads; the delicate loveliness of Filippo Lippi, then Botticelli's spring-time magic; Raphael, Michelangelo, Leonardo da Vinci; the rollcall was endless and spellbinding. Georgina looked where she was bidden, listened, and knew that she was privileged. The man by her side was an expert, sharing with her the accumulated knowledge of a lifetime; but also he loved what he shared, and that made the gift very great indeed. She was aware of a sharp sense of loss when he stopped talking and announced that the lesson was over.

'Why? There's masses more to see,' she said wistfully.

'I know; we've only just begun. But any more now and you'll get indigestion. I shouldn't want you to feel like one feminist American visitor who'd obviously overdone things. She swore she'd just seen her one hundred and fiftieth painting of the Madonna and Child, and couldn't understand why in every one of them the Child had had to be a boy!'

Still chuckling, they walked to a small restaurant in the shadow of Santa Croce where, quietly in charge of the expedition, Adam ordered golden Frascati to drink while they were waiting for their food to arrive. She obediently sipped, then risked a question that Adam Fleming would probably turn aside because it trespassed on ground he considered private.

'Out of everything we saw this morning I have the feeling that the Botticellis mean most of all to you. Am I right?'

'I hear the note of surprise in your voice! Is that because you think they're the most hackneyed? Or the most romantic, and therefore the most unlikely?'

She picked on hackneyed as being the safest adjective. 'Well, awful reproductions do rather abound – you can even see them in any array of greetings cards.'

'And why? Simply because the artist's vision is so irresistible; a man holding his own breath at the wonder of the created world! As you say, bad reproductions are everywhere, but that's exactly why I like to watch the average tourist confronted with the originals for the first time. You can't mistake the moment when he or she catches sight of "Primavera" and says to himself, "Oh, God, so this is what it *really* looks like."'

She remembered Roberto, laughingly predicting boredom for the professor's students. That forecast was surely wide of the mark; they wouldn't find anything but delight in his company. She could also see the two men would never appreciate each other. Roberto's gift was to make people vividly aware of *him*; Adam Fleming's ambition was to make them relish the world around them in all its varied beauty and dottiness.

'You don't think people try to look impressed, reverent even, in front of some great work of art because they feel it's expected of them?' She saw him frown, and added hastily, 'I meant it as a serious question, not a sneer.'

'Of course some do, and some set out in the first place with no greater ambition than to wipe the eye of the Joneses next door by saying that they've *been* to Florence, or wherever. But in the end even *they* are impressed; they can't help themselves.'

He was staring into the depths of his glass, intent on the discussion, and it was safe to look at him: a quiet, colourless, unheroic man, easily passed over in a crowd because that was the way he wanted it to be. The difference between him and her Italian lover brought Roberto vividly to mind. She could conjure up a mental picture of him without the slightest difficulty, but it was harder to feel secure when he wasn't there. They hadn't had enough time together yet, hadn't got used to a future that still needed spelling out. Enrico had reported that he'd gone away. He'd gone without telling her, because their changed relationship was new for him as well. They still had much to learn.

Unaware of having been so deep in thought, she scarcely heard Adam Fleming's quiet question. 'You were sad when we set out, then recovered a little. Now you're looking anxious again. Is the problem something you don't want to talk about?'

Reluctant to discuss Roberto, she mentioned someone else instead. 'A slight attack of looking over my shoulder, which is always a stupid thing to do! I spoke last night to the man I worked for at Kew – had to tell him I wouldn't be going back. It's a wrench, because I loved my job and I've realised that, in a funny sort of way, I even loved William, although he might be horrified to hear me say it!'

'Not a ladies' man, I take it?'

The idea was enough to make her laugh outright. 'Hardly! William's one of Nature's gentlemen – *not* at home in the salon or the bedchamber! For him passion is about growing things, not about women. He feels for plants what you feel for paintings.'

Adam nodded. 'He sounds nice; I can understand you don't want to part company with him.'

'He's up to his neck in work, and now short-handed as well, but even so he's offered to take care of selling my flat for me. That's William.'

The professor's grey eyes met hers suddenly in a glance that was full of speculation. 'I didn't realise your separation from London was going to be as complete as that.'

She gave a little shrug, not prepared to give away the reason for it. 'I've made up my mind to stay here. What's the point of keeping a flat at Chiswick?'

'Of course – I was forgetting what we're not supposed to mention! I've only met Roberto Artom once, and that very briefly, but it wasn't difficult to see that he's got a bright future ahead of him. You and he together will make a very good pair.'

The professor delivered his opinion calmly, and then poured more wine far them both – a man, she thought, on whom passion was as unlikely to settle as on William Bird. She was suddenly propelled into wanting to find out about *him*.

'You seem to have got remarkably entangled in Poggio's affairs, but we know nothing about you, except that you teach at Oxford. I'm not much acquainted with university professors; are there many around like you?'

Amusement gleamed in his face when he looked at her. 'Another serious question, I hope, not a sneer! I suppose you mean, are there any more oddities, like me? The answer's probably yes – Oxford seems to breed them. It's a danger of the place – we all cultivate our eccentricities too much in the end!'

'Shall you stay there always?'

'Probably not, beautiful though it is. Teachers get stale if they stay in the same place for too long. I enjoy writing, but my chief pleasure is in teaching. Most of us work our way up the scale, imagining that the more advanced students are the rewarding ones. With my usual perversity, I shall probably travel the other way. Teaching a child of Alessio's age has been a discovery, as exciting as tackling a beautiful clean blackboard with a new piece of chalk!'

It was revealing in its way but told her nothing about his private life, but she suspected that he hadn't intended to do that anyway.

By the time they left the restaurant the rain clouds had drifted away. Colour was seeping back into the world, and the white-ribbed, russet-coloured curve of the cathedral dome in front of them was now outlined against a pale-blue sky. She gave a little sigh of contentment at the sight of it.

He heard it and turned to smile at her. 'I get the feeling that *that* means something special to you.'

'Yes, although I doubt if I could tell you why. All I know is that I've loved it since I was a small child, and I still defy anyone to look at it and not be comforted.'

He said nothing for a moment because they were about to plunge through the river of traffic swirling around the square. Safely on the pavement on the other side, he didn't let go of her hand immediately.

'You're a fraud, you know, pretending to need things to be explained to you. The truth is that you feel them instead, and that's the heart of the matter.'

She had the strange sensation that they were isolated from the rest of the world: two people seeing one another for the first time through a clearing fog of misunderstandings. The moment was illuminating but brief; noise intruded again, and the curious stares of people who looked at them standing there. Now she must go home and pick up the burden of Poggio's anxieties again.

It was only on the drive back that she remembered she had nothing to show for a day's shopping in Florence. Maria might not notice, but if Lucia had been there she most certainly would have done.

Chapter 7

As the end of the week approached Roberto was still away and she was becoming anxious to see him; it seemed necessary, before she could be comfortable again, to know that he understood the reason for their refusal of another loan. That uncertainty seemed to be the only small cloud on the horizon, because Lucia was coming home and Poggio would have its lynch-pin back again. It was true that Enrico hadn't yet been able to track down extra help, but at least they now knew he could go looking for it in the confidence that they would be able to pay for it. William's telephone call the evening before had announced a buyer for her flat, and she still smiled whenever she remembered the conversation.

'Cousin of mine, as it happens,' he'd confessed. 'Needs to shift back to London after being stuck in some godforsaken town in Yorkshire, and he couldn't believe his luck when I said I knew just the place. Told him there was to be no haggling about the price, but he wouldn't want to – he's a bachelor and loaded! Won't be ready to move in, he says, till the end of the summer, so you haven't to come rushing back.'

'William, it sounds perfect. I'm so very grateful to you. I'll present Kew with the most beautiful young sapling that ever was, by way of saying thank you.'

He named the figure he'd asked for the flat and she murmured faintly, 'One sapling? I'll make it an entire copse! I had what I thought was a reasonable figure in mind. Are you sure you haven't charged the poor man too much?'

'Estate agent's price, not mine. Today's going rate, not a penny more. We'll tie up legal ends as soon as you authorise your solicitor to let me act.'

'I'll go and break the good news to Gramps in a minute, but first of all I want to know how things are with you. Have you found someone to fill my job?'

'Think so,' William confirmed unenthusiastically. 'Keen young chap just out of college who knows all there is to know, apparently – he'll be telling *me* what to do inside a week. Even when you thought you knew better than me, at least you didn't make the mistake of saying so.' He was silent for a moment and she thought he was preparing to ring off. Then he managed the question he most wanted to ask. 'What about you, girl – are you going to be happy there? I know you love your grandparents, but they aren't quite in your age-group.'

She answered after a moment's thought. 'I've got friends here, dear friends I've known since childhood.'

'Well, that's all right then. Just thought I'd ask.'

She smiled into the telephone as if he could see her do it, and then thought of something herself. 'William, don't make any holiday plans – come out and see Poggio. Come at the end of the summer and enjoy the grape harvest – we'd all love you to.'

He seemed to consider the idea, then sounded cautiously pleased by it. 'I might just do that. Poggio sounds the sort of place I'd like.'

She said goodbye to him and replaced the receiver, asking herself why she'd spoken of 'friends', instead of mentioning Roberto. The answer had to be, of course, that it would have seemed like rubbing salt in the wound she'd undoubtedly dealt William.

The next morning, in search of Enrico, she found him in his office, drafting an advertisement for various newspapers. The frown on his face cleared when she went in, but he was inwardly depressed by the lack of local interest in his offers of work. What he wanted were men he knew, but none of them seemed interested in a job at Poggio. If they were any good, they were already employed on other estates and, although filching wasn't unknown, they listened to his offer so carelessly that he had the impression they didn't take him seriously. Men he'd known all his life couldn't quite bring themselves to laugh at him, Enrico Casali, while he was standing in front of them, but the heart-sickening feeling was growing in him that they were laughing at him behind his back. Instead of admitting it to Georgina, he explained now that they must make wider enquiries than in San Vicenzo – hence the advertisements.

'I know Giuseppe's gone further south,' she said thoughtfully, 'but is there any chance that his sons might come back? I caught a glimpse of the younger one working in the vegetable market in Florence, He looked so miserable that I wondered if he was missing Poggio.'

'Missing his mother's cooking, more likely. She spoiled him, and his elder brother even more because Pietro was the one she doted on. Months before they went it was obvious that they were losing interest here; there's easier money to be earned elsewhere. We need men who still believe in our way of doing things.' He sounded depressed again, and she was suddenly seized by a new fear. She had wanted, even more than keeping Poggio safe, not to see *him* beaten. But perhaps after all that had been unfair; perhaps he was tired of struggling, swimming against the tide as it must now seem, in an age when young men wanted an easier life than the one their fathers had taken for granted. She walked round behind him and wound her arms about his neck.

'Tell me the truth, please. Have I pushed you into going on when all the time you were sick and tired of the battle? Have you and Granny had enough of hard work and uncertainty? It's the only thing that matters – what you and she really want.'

He pulled her round to face him, and tried not to shout. 'What we want is to stay here! Of course we must still work – what else? Can you see your grandmother happy to sip cocktails and change her dress three times a day like Erica Artom? What am I to do instead – take up golf, or learn to pass the time sitting in city cafés? Of course Poggio will be taken over eventually, because you and Roberto will combine it with Casagrande, but then it will be Artom-Casali. Nothing wrong with that!'

She nodded, smiling at him. 'On we go then; bloody, bold and resolute, as an English poet once said!'

On the point of walking out of the room she suddenly stopped to look at him. 'I wish we could hear from Roberto. He hasn't been in touch with *you*, I suppose?'

'No, although I'd have expected him to try to make me change my mind about his offer, because he seemed so anxious for me to accept. But the poor boy seems to lead a terrible life, half of it spent in aeroplanes.'

There wasn't time to worry about Roberto's silence. Lucia was due home in twenty-four hours, and the house and gardens must be looking their best for her. While Maria and her daughter scrubbed and polished indoors, Georgina toiled outside with Enrico. On the hillsides the vineyards were erupting into a vivid mass of spring green, untended, and still unsprayed, but close at hand Poggio was looking cared for again.

Georgina had seen nothing of Adam Fleming since their visit to Florence but he drove up just as she finished mowing the lawn below the terrace.

'Either we're getting a visit from the Queen, or Lucia's coming home.'

'Tomorrow! Poggio will seem like itself again.'

'Who's going to fetch her . . . by which I mean, who's going to be in charge of the car?'

'Gramps, of course! It's too important an occasion to be left to a female driver!'

But she thought it should have come as no surprise the following morning to see Enrico's car waiting outside, and the professor installed behind the steering wheel.

'Adam suggested driving so that I could be free to keep my eye on Lucia. It's a good idea, don't you think so, *cara*?' 'Excellent,' she agreed without batting an eyelid.

In fact, on the journey home she and her grandmother shared the back of the car, while Enrico directed operations from the seat beside the driver, in case any bump or stone along the way should escape his notice.

Maria, waiting with the door open, burst into tears when Lucia was helped up the steps, and Alessio hurled aside every item of furniture that might be thought to constitute a hazard to an invalid. Torn between tears and laughter, Lucia allowed herself to be escorted inside and introduced to Poggio's latest arrival: a small black puppy that Alessio had been permitted to save from destruction. He'd assured Georgina that it was going to grow into an English retriever, but she suspected that its parentage was considerably more mixed than he allowed for. Nevertheless boy and dog were already so inseparable that it wouldn't matter at all what mixture of breeds his Nero finally turned out to be.

Tired by the journey home and the excitement, Lucia agreed to rest on the sofa in the drawing-room. When he'd finally convinced himself that she could come to no harm there, Enrico agreed to leave her with her granddaughter and take himself back to work. It was the moment Lucia had been waiting for.

'I was going to scold you, *tesoro*, for using up all your holiday here; there was no need – I could have managed with Maria's help. But Enrico tells me we can expect to keep you in Italy. Are you sure, child? You know how much I love your father, so it won't hurt you if I say you seem more like him than Olivia.'

Georgina smiled at her, telling herself that she imagined a slight hesitancy in her grandmother's manner. 'Of course you can manage without me, but I'm staying for my own benefit, not yours!'

'And selling your flat for the same reason, I suppose? Dearest, your grandfather told me. He's been so desperately worried for months – to see him now, almost himself again, it's like some kind of miracle. But I don't think I could have let him agree if you hadn't been going to marry Roberto.'

'He's convinced himself of that though I keep trying to point out that poor Roberto hasn't actually asked me yet! We have a sort of understanding, it's true. Well, I suppose it's more than that – we both know we want to be together in future.'

Lucia nodded, accepting that the matter was settled. 'We must ask the Artoms to lunch on Sunday, just a quiet family party.'

'To celebrate having you home again. Nothing more than that, or I refuse to come.'

'Of course, *tesoro*, and to thank Erica and Dino. You know they sent me flowers and fruit every day, and more magazines than I should be able to read in a life-time. All that I must thank them for.'

Georgina was sent to the telephone and the signora, caught on the wing between social engagements, agreed that she and her husband could attend Lucia's lunch-party on Sunday. 'But for Roberto I cannot answer, *cara*. He leads a terrible life these days. From Geneva he suddenly flew to New York. The price of success is very high.'

She sounded complacent about it all the same, as if his failure would have been much harder to accept than the demands of being successful.

Roberto returned sooner than his mother anticipated because late on Friday afternoon, summoned indoors to the telephone by Maria, Georgina heard his voice at the other end of the line.

'Darling, I've just got back, and I can't wait to see you. You've got to have dinner with me here this evening. I've still some work to get through, but I could collect you after that.'

'I'd love to come, but you must let me drive myself in,' she insisted. 'There's no need to drag you out here, and you sound tired already. Just tell me where to meet you.'

He named a restaurant she knew, and she put down the telephone trying to decide what else he'd sounded, apart from tired – tense, impatient? If he'd been offended by their rejection of his offer to help, she must make him understand this evening that saving Poggio was a matter for Enrico and his family.

She dressed with care, knowing that no amount of tiredness or anxiety would excuse slovenliness in the eyes of a man who thought appearances counted for a great deal. In Roberto's philosophy outward signs of muddle simply reflected a lack of order and self-control within, and on the whole she felt bound to agree with him. Her black and white print dress was crisp and cool, and with hair caught back in a bow of black velvet ribbon she looked neat enough; inner uncertainties were at least safely hidden from view.

He was late, which gave him the opportunity to be escorted to the table

75

where she sat with a flurry of attentiveness that signalled to everyone else present the arrival of a client the *padrone* valued. He kissed her hand and then her mouth with slightly theatrical grace, and she felt a twinge of amusement at the performance they were offering the other diners. When they were allowed to sink into privacy again, she smiled warmly at him.

'It's lovely to have you back, but I wish you didn't look so tired. Must you work as hard as you do?'

'It's been an exceptional week, and I hate long air journeys, especially on top of the Americans' idea of hospitality.'

'Karen Kramer's idea of hospitality, by any chance?'

His face relaxed in a smile at last. 'Hers included, certainly, but there's no need to be jealous, *amore*.'

While they ate they talked only about his visit, and she admired the self-discipline which enabled him to ignore the weariness and strain she sensed in him. Even Adam Fleming, not generous with praise, had formed a high opinion of him, and she must learn to help him as much as she could in future. It wasn't until coffee was on the table and the waiter had finally disappeared that they approached what she felt was the real purpose of the evening.

'Enrico's decision was passed on to me while I was away. Tell me what it's all about. I can't spare the time to *persuade* him to accept the money he clearly needs!'

'Didn't *he* explain?' she asked cautiously.

'He left a muddled note about being able to carry on after all because "funds" had suddenly become available. *What* funds, for God's sake? It's going to take more than a small windfall to get Poggio out of the mess it's in.'

He sounded contemptuous, but she tried not to be irritated. They probably couldn't help seeming amateurish and vacillating to a man working and living on his nerves. 'The windfall isn't small,' she pointed out calmly. 'It should be enough to get Poggio on an even keel again, so that it can survive this bad patch.'

Roberto's dark eyebrow climbed. 'It's still got to survive Enrico, *cara*.'

The sneer at her grandfather angered her but she knew that she must stay calm; Roberto could be persuaded, reasoned with, but not won over by an all-out fight, and a public scene in a restaurant would be anathema to both of them. This wasn't the moment to explain that *her* money was keeping Poggio afloat – it would make their rejection of *his* more hurtful, and there was a much worse thing to think about as well. She'd sold her flat, he might think, so as to give him no choice but to marry her.

76

It took time to work all this out, and finally Roberto himself broke the silence, smiling at her almost ruefully.

'*Tesoro*, forgive me – I shouldn't have spoken like that of your grandfather. But you must believe me when I say that Poggio can't be saved by half-measures, or a small investment of cash.'

She was grateful for his change of tone, and anxious to remember how much they already owed him; but still something had to be said. She asked her question with a directness he remembered from the past.

'Enrico seemed to think that your plan would have been to install a new, young manager. *Was* that your idea? If so, I have to say my grandfather couldn't have agreed to it. Leaving aside himself, there's Lucia to think of, as well as all that makes Poggio precious. It's never just been a means of making money, and mustn't be that in the future.'

She expected Roberto to get angry, but instead he managed to speak with the exaggerated patience of a man condemned to talk kindly to an idiot because he loved her.

'Listen, *tesoro*. Enrico has passed the age when most men are grateful to retire, and Lucia is weakened by ill-health. *Is* it so stupid to suggest that they should give up now, while they can still enjoy life together? They wouldn't be destitute, you know – I'd have made sure of that. And the truth you're reluctant to face is that by Enrico's traditional methods Poggio can *never* yield him a profit in future.'

Georgina stared at the handsome face of the man opposite her, knowing that there *was* truth in what he said. Because of it she couldn't be angry with him now, but something else had just been made clear as well. She remembered a different conversation on the subject of what men felt passionate about – William only wanted to grow things; Adam Fleming was intent on preserving created beauty; for Roberto, she now saw, what mattered was turning failure into success. It wasn't an ignoble ambition, just a different one from any she'd encountered before.

'Roberto, now it's your turn to listen,' she said gently. 'I did think about my grandparents' life, and I know something you don't know. They would *never* see comfort, and even freedom from all anxiety, as a worthwhile exchange for Poggio. They'll be content if they can do no better than make sure they can stay there for the rest of their lives, but they *might* even go on to prosper as well.'

'With whose help, may I ask? The ghosts of long-dead Casalis? It's pie in the sky, *cara*. All they'll do is throw good money after bad.' He made a tremendous effort to control the anger that still unsteadied him, and gave her a strained smile. 'Admit that if you can and tell Enrico to come and see me tomorrow.' His eyes were fixed on her face, willing her to accept that he knew what was best for them. 'I can't wait any longer than that.'

'I'll give him your message, but he won't change his mind,' she said steadily. 'And I should never try to persuade him, Roberto, because I think he's right to want to go on.'

Nothing had changed, the man opposite her realised, except that she'd grown beautiful and desirable. Underneath, she was still the girl who'd fought him and inflamed him from childhood up; she was stubbornly half-English, and tiresomely, maddeningly resistant to pressure of any kind. But he couldn't afford to lose her now – he wanted her too badly.

'I'm tired out of my mind,' he said at last, 'and *you* must go home. Let's leave things as they are for the moment.'

She nodded and got up to leave. 'Lunch is with us on Sunday – Lucia's welcome home. Will you be able to come?'

'Perhaps, but I'm not sure.' He saw her to the car, and kissed her goodnight, then watched her drive away. Things would work out in the end, he told himself; it was just tiredness and the night air making him feel that a ghost had walked over his grave.

Georgina informed her grandmother hesitantly next morning that Roberto had seemed exhausted, and disappointed with them, the night before.

'Of course,' Lucia agreed with her usual serenity. 'I expect he thinks we ought to listen to his excellent advice.'

'Well, yes, he does.' Georgina was brought to a halt again, then went slowly on. 'He doesn't know where Poggio's new money is coming from. It didn't seem the time or place to tell him then.'

Her grandmother, pearl among women, accepted even this as well. 'You know best, *tesoro* – we shall leave it to you.' She was kissed and given a grateful smile, and it became easy to explain that Roberto might be too busy to join their lunch-party on Sunday.

Erica and Dino duly arrived the following day – his jolly cheerfulness concealing her lack of warmth – and the party was helped along by Lucia's inclusion of the professor, who arrived looking unusually neat in blazer and college tie. He perceived at once that his task was to keep Signora Artom happy, and could well have succeeded without even trying, Georgina decided wryly. Erica liked cool English style and gentle manners, and Adam Fleming was wonderfully endowed with both.

When lunch was nearly over the conversation turned to the subject of the Palio, and Dino mentioned with pride that Roberto would be riding in it. 'You know about it, of course, *professore*?' he asked, hopeful that Adam would say no.

'A little . . . tell me more, though.'

'Well, the race has been run twice each summer since medieval times. All seventeen districts of Siena – *contrade* we call them – compete in the heats, but only ten of them take part in the two final races. It's the double high spot of the year for us – everyone packed into the Campo, flags, music, processions and then, when excitement is at fever pitch, the running of the race itself in honour of Our Lady. You mustn't miss it.'

'It's beautiful and exciting as you say, Dino,' Lucia put in quietly. 'But it's also murderously dangerous – bareback, and no holds barred. I can't think why anyone should want to get elected as the jockey of a *contrada*.'

'You're forgetting the *honour*, *cara*,' he explained with a forgiving smile. 'And there's something else a woman finds it hard to understand. The sheer risk is exactly what makes it exciting for someone like my son!'

'The honour of winning may have to be fought for with a Casali this year,' Enrico announced surprisingly to his guests. 'You probably don't remember my brother's son, Paolo; he and his family have spent the last fifteen years in Rome. They are all back in Siena now, and Paolo tells me that *his* son, Filippo, is offering himself as the Ostrich jockey; it's the *contrada* that our family have always been associated with.'

Georgina had the strange but strong impression that life was becoming more and more like a runaway horse at the Palio, three parts out of control. Relations between the two families were delicate enough at the moment without adding the strain of a public contest that was notorious for the passions it aroused. She shivered suddenly, touched by some cold breath of fear that she couldn't reason away, and looked up to find Adam Fleming watching her. Then there was a crash of cutlery being dropped against china, and the noise directed her to Caterina, present to help her mother serve lunch. The professor's glance had been noticed, and Caterina's eyes were so full of wounded disapproval that Georgina sighed inwardly; life in Italy was definitely getting to be too much for her. It was hard to believe that she'd been back at Poggio so short a time. There'd been more onslaughts of emotion in these last weeks than she'd known for whole years of her uneventful life in England.

When lunch was finally over she did what her grandmother expected she would do, and took herself off for a calming walk, but her mind still fretted over the thought of Roberto and Filippo riding against each other in the Palio. She remembered Roberto as she'd seen him last, exhausted, irritated with her no doubt, but just as aware as she was of the pull of attraction between them. She didn't know yet whether what drew them together would prove stronger than the problems that might drive them apart. But she was certain of one thing, and strangely comforted by it. This time in Tuscany had been ordained for her by whatever forces controlled the fate of puny human beings like herself. She was where she was meant to be, and whatever else had already been worked into the pattern would also have to take its course.

Chapter 8

Easter, later than usual, arrived with the return of perfect spring weather. They went down the hill to early Mass on Easter morning through a sunlit world quite beautiful enough to reaffirm that yes, Christ was risen indeed. Enrico drove Lucia and Maria in the car, but Georgina and Alessio walked down the track ahead of them, with Caterina and the professor bringing up the rear. Alessio was unusually subdued, and his companion assumed it was because he'd lost a battle with his mother over whether Nero should be allowed to accompany them to church.

'He can stay outside,' he'd offered generously.

'And wail like a lost soul all through Mass because you're inside? He stays here, Alessio.'

They walked in silence for a time, until Georgina decided it was the moment to offer comfort. 'Nero will forgive you for leaving him at home.' The small boy's grin still didn't come and she realised she hadn't got to the heart of the trouble. 'Something else bothering you?'

The quiet question took him by surprise, jerking out of him an anxiety he hadn't wanted to talk about. 'Gina, when we can't stay at Poggio any more, where shall we go?'

His voice shook suddenly with desperate uncertainty, and the knowledge that they were different from other families. His mother and sister needed him to take care of them as a man should, but he was still too young. She looked down at him, resisting the temptation to give him a hug; male dignity was unpredictable, and there were times when a ten-year-old was prepared to be kissed, times when he was not.

'You don't have to go anywhere,' she said as calmly as possible. 'Caterina may not always want to stay, but we hope *you* will, with your mother.'

His eyes were fixed on her face in a painful effort to decide whether what she'd just said was the truth.

'It's not what Caterina says,' he muttered after a moment. 'She thinks we must all leave Poggio – go and live in a town. Nero wouldn't like that, nor would Mamma.'

81

'Caterina's been listening to gossip, *caro*. People talk stupidly, without knowing what they're talking about. Poggio will be here for as long as you need it, so there's no need to worry.'

He had perfect faith in her. If she said he could stop worrying, that was what he would do. The burden of worry that had been weighing him down slipped from his shoulders, and he gave her the blinding grin that had been missing lately.

'Girls,' he said largely. 'Trust them to get things wrong.' It came as no surprise that his sister didn't know what she was talking about; she was a trial altogether at the moment – moody and cross most of the time, and always trying to hog Adam's attention just when *he* had something to discuss with him. Georgina sympathised when this was put into words, but thought it wouldn't hurt to remind him that his sister had problems of her own.

'Caterina's a bit further on with the business of growing up than you are. It's quite difficult at times, as you'll find out for yourself, so don't get irritated with her if she seems unreasonable!'

'Well, I'll try, but she's silly about Adam – thinks he's just *her* friend.'

'That's the most difficult thing of all, sharing friends. I expect she misses Giuseppe's family; probably you do, too.'

'I didn't like Pietro, but I'm sorry Franco left,' Alessio admitted after a moment's thought. 'Will the *padrone* find someone else soon?'

'As soon as he can,' she agreed, 'but it's not easy to find people who want to work the land nowadays. They'd rather live in towns.'

'Then they're *stupido*,' the small boy said with scorn, '*molto stupido*.'

When Mass was over they stood outside in the sunlight while Lucia was greeted by friends, but she began to look tired and Enrico asked Adam to drive her home because he had people to see in San Vicenzo.

Maria bustled away to the kitchen as soon as they got back to Poggio, but after seeing Lucia ensconced in her favourite chair on the terrace, Adam asked if he might keep her company until Georgina and the children came in. 'It's too lovely to be shut away indoors at my desk,' he suggested, smiling at her.

'You like to offer kindness and pretend it's the other way round! In any case, we expect you to share Easter Day lunch with us. Maria is preparing it, but she will sit down when the time comes and Georgina and Caterina will share the serving. That's why Erica Artom disapproves of me: she has a theory about keeping servants in their place!'

'You mean she can't tell the difference between servants and friends?'

Lucia nodded and put the subject aside. 'Enrico's talking to old friends in the town – he hopes they'll tell him why men aren't willing to work here. He can't understand it.'

'You sound as if you *do* understand it.'

She gave a tired little shrug. 'People talk, Adam. In a small town it's one of their chief pleasures. The fact that an estate is in difficulties soon becomes common knowledge, and then no one wants to be involved with it.'

'Help is crucial, I take it?' Adam asked after a moment.

'Yes. Enrico couldn't manage on his own even if he were twenty years younger and the vineyards were in good shape; but they're not.' Her dark eyes stared at him, full of despair. 'It's Georgina I worry about most – her home in London and her job there gone. We should never have allowed her to sell her apartment and invest the proceeds in Poggio.'

Adam was silent for a moment, thinking how little he'd understood Georgina Hadley; then he tried to deal with Lucia's anxiety.

'If worrying about her is destroying your peace of mind, she might well regret what she's done,' he said calmly. 'She knows the risks. Why not accept the fact that she's made her choice with her eyes open?'

'English common sense! You put me greatly in mind of my dear son-in-law. We shall miss you when you go home, Adam.'

His hand touched her thin one for a moment before he spoke again, with more diffidence than usual. 'At the risk of interfering unpardonably, will you let me say one more thing? I think Enrico should explain the situation to Maria. There *has* been gossip in the town, and the children have caught echoes of it, so they're feeling rather unsettled at the moment. I believe it would be much better to let them know how things stand.'

She thought about what he'd just said, then nodded. 'You're right, of course. Maria deserves to be told the truth. Enrico hoped to hide it from her, but she's been with us too long not to have sensed for months past that he was in difficulties. I shall suggest it's time he confided in her.'

Lunch went smoothly apart from Caterina's tendency to blush vividly whenever Adam glanced her way, but he refused to be embarrassed and after a while she even managed to hear what anyone else said to her. When the meal was over and only he was left at the table with Georgina and her grandparents, Lucia thought it time to admit that they couldn't help noticing Caterina's state of painful rapture.

'It's difficult, being fifteen. Even I can remember it – not being sure from one minute to the next whether I wanted to die at once because life was hopeless, or live for ever!'

Adam's bony face was transformed by a reminiscent grin. 'I doubt if

83

boys suffer in quite that way, but a sister of mine certainly caused us endless embarrassment. She *would* prance about, trying to be supermodel and film star rolled into one, and convinced that my more disreputable schoolfriends would fall in love with her.'

'Did they? Was she pretty?' Georgina wanted to know.

'At that age she wasn't pretty at all, and they weren't a bit interested. But I'm bound to say she finished up quite well.'

'Spoken like a true brother! Did she marry one of the disreputable friends in the end?'

'No – strangely enough, my starchy elder sister did that! Amanda became a nurse and went out to Africa to work among refugees. She finally married a French doctor out there doing the same thing. They live in Paris now, and have three very French sons who utterly mystify my mother when they go to stay with her. She loves them dearly but hopes that by feeding them porridge for breakfast she'll make them less foreign in time!'

His grave face broke into a grin, and Georgina wondered how she could have begun their acquaintance thinking that his eyes were cold and colourless. When he smiled it was no wonder that Caterina, accustomed to the raw young men she saw in San Vicenzo, was in the state she was in.

Lucia's conversation with her husband later in the day, suggesting that Maria should be told the truth about Poggio, had one unexpected result. When Georgina went outside after breakfast next morning to start work, she found that a labour force consisting of herself and her grandfather had been strengthened by two new recruits spared from school by the Easter holidays. Caterina and Alessio were there, wearing businesslike shorts and T-shirts, and Nero was present as well, wearing the usual expression of surprise conferred on him by a small patch of white fur above one eye. Enrico thanked them for coming, and explained that nothing could be done with the vines until expert help arrived, but they *could* make a start on the olive trees.

Poggio oil was famous, but the trees had been damaged by a harsher winter than usual. To make matters worse, rampant undergrowth was now choking the trees and taking precious moisture from the soil. While Georgina and the children made a beginning on the jungle around them, Enrico worked his way from tree to tree, expertly pruning the old dead wood and removing twigs that had been killed by the frost. She wasn't aware that a fresh reinforcement had arrived until the smile lighting Caterina's face told her so. The professor solemnly offered to work alongside the children so that he could beat them if they showed signs of flagging, but Georgina thought they were more likely to need restraining from killing themselves with enthusiasm for his benefit. She smiled and left them with the cheerful announcement that she would start at the other end of the orchard and hope one day to meet them somewhere in the middle.

It was a good morning's work, cheered on by the sight of Lucia making her first solo stroll outside to watch progress. A wetter than usual spring had left the ground still soft and workable, and every leaf and flower looked as if newly dipped in colour. The air was sweetly pungent because herbs grew wild as freely as the weeds, and the scent of crushed mint, rosemary and fennel was all about them as they worked. Georgina hacked and swore at what lay near at hand, afraid to let her eyes wander further afield in case despair should set in. Beyond the orchard stretched acre upon acre of vines – lovely in their spring greenness, but all of them unsprayed, unweeded, and unkempt. The children couldn't be expected to spend the summer labouring for Poggio, and Adam Fleming still less; but the truth was that she and Enrico could work until they dropped and still make no impression on what needed to be done.

Maria's delicious lasagne was shared among them on the terrace, but then Enrico insisted that he wished to see none of his fellow workers until the following morning; for the moment they had done enough. Caterina looked faintly relieved, and Alessio admitted that it was time for Nero's training session.

'Adam says he must be taught to obey,' he said proudly. 'It is the English way for dogs to be obedient.'

'And does he realise this?' Georgina asked, resisting Nero's fond attempt to eat her sandals.

'*Poco a poco!*'

'Then try it the English way,' she suggested. 'Shout, "Heel, boy," and see what happens.'

After lunch, as a change from bending over weeds, she offered to walk down to San Vicenzo for Maria. It was a trip to town like any other – a quick dash in and out of shops, interrupted by frequent requests for news of Lucia's health or Olivia's whereabouts. Nothing about the visit, and no pricking in her thumbs, warned her that they were on the very edge of a momentous change.

She set off towards home, slightly surprised to see someone climbing the track ahead of her. He looked around him as if uncertain of his direction, and she got the impression that she was overhauling a stranger. He walked slowly, and eventually she caught up with him – a small man with grizzled dark hair and skin burned brown by constant sunshine.

'*Buon giorno, signorina . . . scusami, ma Lei puo aiutarmi?*' He spoke with the accent of a native-born Italian, but the words came slowly, almost rustily. '*Cerco la signora Pizzone.*'

'I know the signora,' Georgina agreed cautiously. 'Is she expecting you?'

The man shook his head. 'No, signorina, but I am Pizzone too.'

Dear God – Maria's long-lost husband? Georgina tried desperately to think what was to be done. She never mentioned him. For all they knew, she hated the very name of a man who'd abandoned her and two children, and was now calmly proposing to look her up ten years later.

'I'm not sure . . . perhaps I should . . .'

'Don't be anxious, signorina . . . I am Tommaso, Luigi Pizzone's brother.'

It was something, at least, that he should only be Maria's brother-in-law. He was watching Georgina, aware of her doubt but not offended by it. 'My brother died two months ago,' he explained carefully. 'I promised him that I would find Maria and deliver some mementoes to her.'

She hesitated for a moment longer, then made up her mind. 'She lives with my grandparents in the house at the end of this track, but I think it would be kinder if I walked on ahead of you and warned her. Will you let me do that?'

'I should *prefer* it,' he said gravely. 'Thank you, signorina. I shall follow you in half an hour.'

He eased the rucksack off his back and settled himself without more ado by the roadside. She took with her the memory of a shy, charming smile that seemed to say there was nothing to worry about. Once during her breakneck rush up the hill to Poggio she looked back to find him still sitting there, gazing around – a man, apparently, who asked nothing better than to be allowed to sit and look at the Tuscan countryside.

Maria was in her usual place in the kitchen; Lucia was there too, and looked surprised at the sight of her granddaughter's flushed face.

'There was no need to run, *tesoro*, we weren't waiting for your shopping.'

Georgina mopped her face and helped herself to iced water from the fridge, trying to make up her mind how to begin.

'I followed a stranger up the hill. He said he was looking for Poggio and . . . Signora Pizzone.' The deliberate use of the name was enough to drive the colour from Maria's face.

'Mother of God! More trouble?' she whispered.

Georgina moved round the table and pushed her gently into a chair. 'He told me a little, *cara*, but not much. Luigi died two months ago. The man I met is his brother, Tommaso, fulfilling a promise in coming to see you.'

'Luigi dead after all these years . . . *povero* . . .' Maria was beginning to weep quietly, lost in memories and for the moment oblivious of the relative who'd come looking for her.

Lucia left the kitchen and returned a moment later with a small glass of brandy. 'Sip this slowly, *cara*, while we think what to do. If you prefer not to see Luigi's brother, Georgina will go out and tell him so. But I really believe that you should speak to him yourself.'

'Yes, yes. I think so too.' But it was a relief to be told what she must do. She stood up and took off her white apron. When it had been folded with extreme care she walked towards the door. 'I shall meet him at the bottom of the drive.'

'Then bring him here,' Lucia insisted. 'He may have travelled a long way and be in need of food.'

Overcome by the drama of the moment, Maria could only nod and go on her way.

Lucia smiled at her granddaughter. 'I think we'll take a little stroll, *tesoro*, to see how the *fagiolini* are coming on. If we don't do *something*, the strain will became unbearable!'

They were back on the terrace trying to wait patiently when Maria reappeared. Her face was reddened by weeping, but she was calm again.

'Tommaso's gone for the moment,' she explained. 'I offered him food, signora, but he refused – said he preferred to get something to eat in San Vicenzo.'

'Sit down, *cara*,' Lucia insisted gently. 'We should like to hear about it, you know.'

Maria lowered herself carefully on to the edge of a chair, then folded her hands in her lap like a child about to begin a recitation.

'He has things for us in his luggage at the *albergo*. He will bring them this evening. Luigi died of cancer, in a hospital in California. That's where he went when he left us – working his way across America until he came to the vineyards there. I didn't know that Tommaso had gone out to join him, but when their mother remarried he preferred not to stay at home. About six months ago Luigi fell ill. Most of their savings disappeared in hospital treatment, but Luigi made his brother keep enough for the journey back to Italy. Tommaso got off a cargo ship at Genoa two days ago.'

'What's he going to do now?' Georgina asked.

'Find work, what else?' Maria queried simply. 'His mother still lives near Greve, but he doesn't like his step-father.'

The tale was told as far as Maria was concerned, but she went over it again in her mind, feeling obliged to spend time in her thoughts with the memory of a man whose face she could hardly recall.

Georgina's voice, sharp with anxiety, interrupted her. 'You're sure he's coming back?'

'I told you . . . Luigi's dead . . .'

'*Tommaso*, Maria.' It was an effort not to scream the name at her. 'You said he had things to bring.'

'I told you: this evening,' she repeated patiently, unable to account for Georgina's burning desire to see her brother-in-law again. 'He'll walk up the hill after supper.' She got up and stood looking at them. 'I'm glad to know about Luigi. I can tell the children that their father did remember them. Funny, I always pretended to them that he went to America to find work, and it turned out to be true!'

Georgina waited for her to leave the room, then smiled tremulously at her grandmother. 'Are you thinking what I'm thinking? Yes, I can see you are! Will you put it to Gramps when he comes in?'

Lucia shook her head. 'I think you should do so. You're concerned in what happens at Poggio now, dearest. Enrico must get used to sharing decisions with you.'

She felt almost sick with impatience by the time he got back to the house, but Enrico had much to say himself, and he was determined to say it first.

'I went to see Moroni at the bank,' he began at once. 'He is a good friend. When I explained that money would be coming from England he made no fuss about a temporary loan – said he could trust my word. I should think so, after knowing me for fifty years, but it will be helpful all the same. Then I came back past Palmato's cottage and called in on the off-chance. He's busy with his own plot of ground, but he offered to help until he does his own harvesting, and he'll bring his son as well. Stop-gap, of course, but it's better than nothing.' Then his face darkened again at the memory of the rest of his conversation with the bank manager. 'Moroni said there *has* been talk in the town. Someone's been putting round the tale that Poggio is finished. If I knew who it was I'd . . . choke the lying villain.'

Lucia put her hand over his clenched fist and patted it consolingly. '*Amore*, there's more to think about than malicious gossip, and people will soon see that Poggio is *not* finished. It's the future we have to think about.'

'I think about nothing else,' he said simply.

'Our luck is turning,' she insisted. 'Listen while Georgina tells you *our* news.'

It was her cue, but by now she was hoarse with fear. It was one thing to want to hire an unknown man she'd done no more than speak to for five minutes in the lane; quite another to convince her grandfather that he might be the answer to their prayers.

'Gramps, you won't believe it, but Tommaso Pizzone has come back.'

'Pizzone?'

'Maria's brother-in-law. Her husband died recently in California, but Tommaso came to bring her some things from Luigi before he starts looking for a job. Now, and this is where the unbelievably good news comes in – he's been working in the vineyards there for the last ten years! Don't you think he sounds like a gift from Heaven?'

He smiled in spite of himself as the breathless torrent of words broke over him. His usually serene granddaughter was suddenly more Italian than English, reminding him vividly of Olivia.

'Whoa now, *cara*, we know nothing about this man. He may not know his job, may not *want* this job.'

'No, of course not; but you will *see* him, won't you, Gramps? He's coming back this evening to talk to Maria again. If he hasn't got anywhere to live, we could even offer him Giuseppe's old quarters in the farmhouse. Don't you think it seems *meant*?'

She *was* exactly like a young Olivia all over again, willing him to agree to something she'd set her heart on.

'You're just like your mother, after all! Reckless – a mad creature!'

'The higher they fly, the further they fall,' Lucia agreed calmly. 'It's the way they're made, *amore*; you can't change them.'

'I don't want to change them, but I don't want to see them hurt. I'll meet Pizzone when he comes back, but first I must talk to Maria. For all we know, she might hate the idea of having her brother-in-law at Poggio.'

'I hadn't thought of *that*,' Georgina had to confess, suddenly downcast. 'Vaulting ambition o'erleaping itself as usual!'

She went away to change back into working clothes and resume her struggle with the weeds round the olive trees; hard work was the only way to get through the suspense of the next few hours. Hidden at the far end of the orchard, she wasn't aware of the stranger coming back, or of her grandfather driving him down into San Vicenzo again two hours later. But when exhaustion finally sent her indoors Enrico was in the courtyard at the back of the house, putting the car away.

He walked towards her and she could see that he was smiling.

'You liked him,' she said at once. 'I can tell from your face. Oh, Gramps, what did he say? Is he going to stay?'

'He looked like a man who couldn't believe his luck, and when I offered him rooms in the farmhouse, I thought he was going to burst into tears. He's heard enough in the past few days to wonder whether he was mad to think of staying in Italy – people have regaled him with stories of unemployment, and of land no longer worked because of people flocking to the cities to find work. But he'd promised Luigi that he would come back and find Maria, and he was homesick for Tuscany.'

'Maria didn't mind him being asked to stay?'

'She *did* burst into tears again, but your grandmother assures me they were tears of joy! Pizzone met the children as well – Alessio for the first time, although he dimly remembered seeing Caterina as a small child. He seemed overcome at the prospect of belonging to a family again. The upshot of it is that he's going to start a three-month trial tomorrow, and at last we can begin working on the vines.'

Georgina's tired face broke into a smile. 'It's almost too good to be true, and if you hadn't had quite enough tears already, I'd follow Maria's example and weep! Shall we throw economy to the winds and ring Washington? It's time to tell Mama that Poggio's coming out of the shadows into the sunlight again.'

Chapter 9

A taxi bumped up the track next morning, bringing Tommaso, with a trunk and a couple of suitcases that contained the sum total of his worldly possessions. Lucia made him welcome, and then handed over to Maria the pleasure of showing her brother-in-law what would be his home. An hour later it was obvious that a change had come over their lives. The *padrone* and his new assistant were already setting out on a tour of inspection. Beside them walked Alessio, hands locked behind his back in unconscious imitation of the two men, while Nero dashed backwards and forwards, pretending to be a full-grown retriever looking for rabbits. Lucia sat on the terrace, stringing beans for freezing, and from somewhere in the courtyard the strange sounds could be heard that meant Maria was singing. Poggio had come properly alive again.

Rather to her surprise, when the men returned Georgina was invited to join them for a council of war. Her part in it was only to listen intelligently because she knew only the little her grandfather had taught her about viniculture, but Tommaso clearly knew a great deal. He confirmed Enrico's view that Cabernet Sauvignon grapes should be planted to improve the eventual quality of Poggio wine.

'I know that one or two outstanding producers of Chianti Classico no longer limit themselves to the traditional mixture of grapes,' Enrico admitted. 'It will mean a lot of hard work and a lot of investment in new vines, but there's no alternative if we want to get back into the ranks of vineyards producing first-class wine.'

Tommaso's eyes fixed themselves on the wilderness beyond the window. 'For the future it must be done,' he agreed. 'For now, *padrone*, we must get the best harvest we can from the grapes we've got. There's a mountain of work to be got through.'

He didn't ask why it had been neglected up till now, and Georgina waited to see how much her grandfather would feel obliged to explain.

'Estates like Poggio, worked in the "old-fashioned" way, suffer nowadays because young men, especially, have lost their taste for hard work. But at the moment we're dogged by another handicap – local gossip about the estate being finished frightened off the help we needed.' His beetling eyebrows frowned at the newcomer. 'If you don't feel like a struggle, you'd better say so now.'

'Let's get to work, signore,' said Tommaso, smiling at him.

A week later a routine of work had been established; Georgina and the children toiled among the olives and kept the gardens in order, while the two men, helped by Taddeo Palmato and his son, laboured from early morning to dusk among the vines. Row upon row now showed a rim of turquoise-blue round the edges of their leaves where the copper-sulphate spray had dried, and the ground in between was being systematically rotovated and cleared of undergrowth. Taddeo and his son worked with the slow methodical pace of countrymen, but Tommaso flung himself into each day's onslaught like a warrior going into battle. Then, breaking off from her own back-breaking labours one morning to consult her grandfather about the pruning of a tree, Georgina realised what she hadn't known before – that their work-force had been increased again, because walking slowly between the vines with a tank strapped to his back and spraying as to the manner born, was Professor Adam Fleming!

The long days grew steadily hotter, and they began to work earlier to take advantage of the coolness of the morning. Georgina took to sheltering under one of Lucia's old straw hats, and even Adam's pale skin began to change colour. The contrast between a darkening tan and hair bleached almost white by the sun gave him a strangely distinctive appearance, and she wondered whether any of his Oxford colleagues would recognise him as he looked now. It took an effort of the imagination to clothe him in the college don's black gown which she supposed he sometimes had to wear.

Alessio was chased reluctantly back to school, but rushed home each day to join the others and pretend that he was a man among vine-growing men. His most treasured possession, apart from his skates, had become a little pocket-knife with the haft beautifully damascened in silver, which his uncle had brought him from America.

'It belonged to my father,' he explained proudly to Georgina. 'Zio Tommaso told me.'

'Something to treasure,' she agreed, smiling at him. The word 'father' had been meaningless to him until Tommaso Pizzone's arrival. Now, the small object in his hand was enough to create for him the precious sense that he wasn't much different from his peers after all; in a way it was even more to boast about that *his* father hadn't been content with San Vicenzo.

Il suo padre had gone a long way away, but still remembered in the end that he had a son called Alessio.

'Will Zio Tommaso stay, Gina?'

'Would you like him to?'

His face broke into a sudden grin. '*Yes*. He makes us laugh, even Mamma! She's happy since he came, and Caterina's cheered up a bit, too.'

'Your uncle looks to me like a very contented man. I think he certainly wants to stay.'

She could say it confidently, knowing that he was thankful to be back where he belonged. He'd tried to explain to her one day how his heart had yearned for the colours of Tuscany – heavenly blue sky, silver-green of olives, dark green of cypresses, and terracotta warmth of old, tiled roofs. He hadn't minded California, and he'd learned a lot there, but it wasn't Tuscany.

Taddeo and his son chugged home each day at lunch-time on their ancient motor-scooter, but the rest of them shared the mid-day rest and meal, sitting on the terrace in the shade of a vine that now spread over the pergola. Georgina looked occasionally at her grandmother for the pleasure of knowing that she was serene again, or watched Enrico pouring wine, just to be able to smile at his bubbling cheerfulness. Her most recent letter from William had confirmed that the sale of the flat and the transfer of money to Italy was going through smoothly. Their future was still uncertain, and circumstances might defeat them in the end, but somehow confidence, not failure, was in the air.

There was a great deal to be happy about, and she forced herself to remember it whenever the tiredness that came from working too hard made her feel low. Her grandparents tactfully left the subject of Roberto alone, and she clung to the idea that he was involved in some new project that absorbed all his time. Even so, she hadn't expected to be left quite so severely alone since their restaurant meeting in Siena. She missed him, felt starved of his bright company, and badly needed his reassurance that the disagreement over Poggio hadn't really damaged them.

Signora Artom, encountered occasionally in San Vicenzo, at least confirmed one day that he was only just back from another trip abroad.

'Then I shall expect to hear from him,' Georgina said, smiling cheerfully, 'and I hope he's been missing me as much as I've been missing him!'

Looking at the beautiful tanned face in front of her, Erica Artom had the grace to admit that he probably had. A connoisseur of women, as her son undoubtedly was, couldn't overlook Georgina Hadley for long.

* * *

It seemed that her message *was* delivered by his mother, because Roberto telephoned that same afternoon. She must forgive his neglect of her to the extent of driving to Siena to see him, he insisted, because he couldn't manage without her any longer. In any case, it was time she inspected his home to see if she liked it enough to live there.

'And suppose I don't?' she asked teasingly. 'Will you instantly agree to move?'

'Not without trying to persuade you to change your mind!' he admitted with a smile in his,voice. 'It's a very nice home.'

She was content to know that they were friends again; whatever irritation he'd felt was over and they could go on from where they'd left off. The evening that followed confirmed it. By mutual consent they left the subject of Poggio alone, and Roberto was at his charming best – tender, amusing, and ready to admit that it had been very hard to stay away from her. His home in one of the beautiful old houses lining the Campo had only one fault – it lacked a garden of any sort; but now it was her turn to yield and she promised to make do with growing things at Poggio or Casagrande.

She was aware when he kissed her that he wanted very much to urge her to stay, but he seemed to understand without being told that while she remained at Poggio she would observe her grandparents' way of doing things.

'Never say that I'm not behaving like a perfect English gentleman, *amore*,' he murmured when it was time for her to leave. 'Your father should feel very proud of me!'

'I think he would,' she agreed, smiling at him, and my mother will be overjoyed to know I've balanced things for her – by choosing an Italian *galantuomo*!'

She drove home warmed by the memory of their goodnight kiss, and happily aware that there was no need to mark time much longer; they were both certain now of what they wanted: to be together as lovers, man and wife.

Observing her granddaughter the following morning, Lucia was able to report to Enrico that whatever difficulty with Roberto had been troubling her had gone now, leaving Georgina serenely attending to her own work outside. At the moment she was concentrating on the vegetable garden again, and she was there one morning transplanting lettuces when Tommaso came to find her.

'I've a question for the *padrone*, signorina. I thought he might be here with you.'

'He's doing paperwork indoors. I'm going in anyway – I'll call him for you.'

She walked into Enrico's office a minute or two later, and felt her heart miss a beat at the sight of him slumped over the desk.

'Gramps! You're ill. Shall I fetch Granny?'

The words tumbled out as she ran across the room, rousing him to lift his head and look at her. The brown skin of his face seemed to have turned grey, and in place of the cheerful bustling man of recent weeks was a defeated ghost.

'Not ill,' he muttered with difficulty. 'Just sick – at my own stupidity.'

'Tell me what's wrong.'

His hand crashed down on the sheet of paper lying in front of him. 'I should have known . . . guessed . . .'

'Gramps, *tell me!*' She shouted the words at him, trying to penetrate the fog of despair that wrapped around him. By way of answer he pushed the paper across the desk towards her. Her eyes flew to Roberto's signature at the bottom of the brief message, then went back to the words themselves; a polite demand for the immediate repayment of his original loan. The politeness didn't disguise a brutally clear request; if the repayment wasn't forthcoming, proceedings would have to be started to lay claim to Poggio, which was his security for the loan.

She collapsed into a chair by the desk, because her legs were trembling, read the letter again, and then stared at her grandfather.

'I can't believe it – he was concerned to help,' she muttered hoarsely. 'I thought he wanted to go on helping. How could he call the loan in *now*, when he knows we're struggling to save Poggio?'

She'd thanked him for his kindness, once had to reproach herself for being surprised that he should have behaved like the staunchest of friends. Only a night or two ago she had left him convinced that there would be no more misunderstandings.

'I've been a fool, *tesoro*,' her grandfather was painfully trying to explain. 'But there was no time-limit fixed when the loan was made. As long as I repaid the interest, which we've been careful to do, I thought the loan would stand for as long as we needed it. It even became irrelevant once it seemed that you were going to marry Roberto; then Poggio would have come to you both in the long run, anyway.'

She nodded, reluctant to believe even now that Roberto meant what he had written. He wasn't a man who enjoyed not getting his own way, but only a megalomaniac would insist on never being thwarted. She knew she hadn't been mistaken, Their long, chequered friendship *had* flowered at last into something that seemed full of promise. There had to be some reason why he'd suddenly withdrawn his help in this abrupt and brutal fashion.

'I think it's my fault, Gramps,' she decided slowly. 'He was a bit scornful about us managing without his help, and probably I was to blame for giving the wrong impression – he may think it won't hurt us to repay the original loan because we're swimming in wealth. Will you let me see him and explain? He's a businessman; he'll understand that we need the capital we've got until the estate is back to being a going concern.'

Her face was still ashen-white, but she was composed again. Roberto's letter had been a shock just when they seemed to be sailing sweetly along, but it was always a mistake to get into a panic too soon; the letter was a temporary problem they could solve together.

Enrico gave a little shrug. 'See him, *cara*, if you want to, but I think you'll be wasting your time. I didn't realise it before, but Roberto wants to own Poggio *now*! Combined with Casagrande, it would make him the biggest landowner in Tuscany – a powerful man. That's his addiction now, not more wealth than he already has, but more power.'

'You may be right, but I think we have to give him the chance to change his mind,' she said gently. 'Promise me we'll go on for the moment as if Poggio *wasn't* threatened.'

His smile was full of tenderness tinged with sadness. 'Do you realise what irritates the rest of the world about the English? They never know when they're beaten! Sometimes, of course, it turns out that they're not beaten at all, but this time . . .' He stopped speaking because his voice failed him, and she put her arms round him in a loving hug. After a moment she remembered why she'd come looking for him.

'I came to tell you that Tommaso needed some advice.'

'I'll be there soon.' She was almost at the door when he called her back. 'Gina, just in case you have it in mind, we are *not* going to ring Washington about this. In the end we might have to let Olivia know, but not until we have to.' Her face said that she was going to argue with him, and he banged sharply on the desk. 'I insist, *cara*.'

It was her turn to shrug. 'All right, if you insist. But I think it's wrong. It hurts them to be kept in the dark.'

'Everything hurts,' he said harshly.

She nodded and went away to telephone Roberto's office in Siena. A cool female voice conceded that Signor Artom was there, but so *occupato* that a last-minute appointment with him was out of the question. Nerves stretched, and temper not improved by a manner she found irritating, Georgina refused to be put off.

'I shall come anyway, and simply wait until you can fit me in. The matter is urgent.'

'All Signor Artom's affairs are urgent.'

'Then you must be able to understand *my* problem,' Georgina insisted shortly.

'Come at three, signorina,' the girl snapped. 'He may have a moment or two free between other appointments.'

There was time to shower and change, and eat a mouthful or two of food to conceal her lack of appetite. Enrico, sunk in a silence of his own, nodded when she asked if she might borrow the car. To Lucia she explained merely that she had an appointment.

'I may be late, so don't delay supper for me.'

Lucia refused to ask questions as usual, but her face looked drawn again. The respite from anxiety had been short-lived, and the threat of some new disaster seemed to hang in the air. Presently she would make Enrico tell her what it was, but only when Georgina had left them alone.

Chapter 10

Roberto's secretary, as cool and confident as her voice had sounded on the telephone, looked surprised when he appeared the moment his visitor arrived. She'd felt certain that he would want to keep someone from Poggio waiting.

'We'll go upstairs,' he said briefly, ushering his visitor out of the room with the elaborate courtesy that she thought women like Karen Kramer probably found irresistible. His secretary must be accustomed to it by now, but a glimpse at the expression on her face induced an unexpected twinge of pity. The girl was in all likelihood his slave, in and out of office hours, but deliberate attentions to other women helped to remind her that she mustn't forget her place in the scheme of things. Georgina offered her a smile in the hope of recognising her as a fellow human-being, not an automaton, but the girl's face didn't change; it was only Roberto she cared about.

He led Georgina up the curving staircase to the top floor of the old house, and opened the door for her into the large and beautiful room overlooking the Campo that she remembered from her previous visit. In July and August the square's herring-bone-patterned brick floor would be hidden by a seething mass of people there for the running of the Palio; now it was only pleasantly busy, with the first wave of tourists photographing the Palazzo Pubblico that glowed rose-red in the afternoon sunshine. The Mangia Tower thrust its head into the blue sky, and she could see at the top of it the bell that would be rung by hand throughout the processions and the running of the race. The view was breathtaking, and the room itself was comfortable and serene. It wouldn't be difficult to live in it, but she was beginning to doubt whether he cared if she lived in it or not.

'A glass of white wine, *cara*, or some English tea if you prefer?'

'Nothing, thanks. It's not a social visit. My grandfather got your letter this morning.'

Roberto smiled politely. 'I hope he finds himself able to do something about it.'

'I think you're aware of his difficulties. They're what gave rise to the loan in the first place.'

His little shrug suggested that, sorry as he was, he had no suggestions to make, and she was suddenly overcome by a feeling of disbelief; it was a nightmare she was in, not a conversation that was actually taking place. She couldn't really be pleading for her grandparents' home with the man she'd thought she was going to marry.

'Roberto, I have to make you understand,' she began calmly. 'The money we now have will only enable Poggio to carry on, no more than that, and I'm sorry if I gave you a different impression. But with experienced help again, hard work, and investment, we *can* make the estate profitable; Gramps got discouraged because he was left alone, but in time we shall be able to pay off the loan.'

Her eyes looked more vividly green against the present brownness of her skin and they pleaded with him to listen. He turned away so as not to acknowledge the fact, but he could still see her in his mind's eye. The bones of her face were revealed too clearly now, and the sun had put a patina of gold on her chestnut hair. He knew women more voluptuously beautiful, and women who would make him a more biddable wife, but none that he wanted so much as this one. Marriage, likely to be so dull otherwise, would have been a contest with her, always challenging. But she insisted on wasting her youth and beauty on a rundown estate in the middle of Tuscany while the most ambitious scheme of his business life was being frustrated. Ever since they were children, he'd been torn by the need to yield to and dominate her at the same time, and both emotions fought inside him still. There wasn't a single battle in the past that he'd been allowed to win if what he'd wanted her to do had gone against some stubbornly held conviction of her own. It was the same now, and her conviction was to fight for Poggio.

He poured himself a glass of wine, to show that the interview must go at whatever pace he dictated. 'I should *like* to be patient, Georgina, but you don't understand the problem. If I'm not to have Poggio, I must have the return of the loan. The matter is now becoming extremely urgent, and even if I were prepared to wait there are other people involved who can't be expected to care what happens to your grandfather. For them it's a straightforward business matter.'

She suspected him of inventing the 'other people', and decided that she had nothing to lose now by being blunt. 'Gramps thinks it has nothing to do with anyone else. He's convinced that you want Poggio in order to amalgamate it with Casagrande.'

Roberto's smile was convincing this time. 'He should know me better than that. I'm happy to inherit my father's estate when the time comes, but I have no personal interest in making wine or cutting a fine figure in the countryside.'

'Then I don't understand why you invested in Poggio at all,' she said flatly.

Roberto looked disappointed in her. 'Now you're being obtuse. I rather expected you to guess the night you met John Kramer; he talked a little too much, and you were such an attentive listener!'

Her face went white at the recollection. 'He went on about some new holiday village in Tuscany. Is *that* what the pair of you had in mind? To convert Poggio, or destroy it altogether?'

'A beautiful holiday village, *cara*; intended only for the most beautiful people,' he said lightly. 'Nothing cheap about it!'

She closed her eyes against a vision of concrete villas, complete with swimming pools and gaudy sun umbrellas, peppering the hills all the way down to San Vicenzo. Vines and olive trees and flowers would be uprooted, and ancient houses bulldozed into rubble – all in the cause of a little more wealth for men who were indecently rich already. When he finally broke the silence in the room she scarcely registered that his voice had changed. No longer mocking her, he sounded suddenly sincere.

'Listen, Gina, please. If I don't go ahead with this scheme someone else will, sooner or later. The sort of old-fashioned husbandry your grandfather clings to *can't* survive. We want to put the land to a more realistic use, that's all. You'd agree with me if it wasn't Poggio we were talking about.'

'I doubt it,' she said steadily, 'but it *is* my grandparents' home we're talking about. That's why I sold my flat in London to raise the money they needed.'

She saw his face flush with sudden rage, even before the explosion came. 'God in Heaven – it's *your* money that's keeping them going. That's why you kept so quiet about where the windfall was coming from. How *dared* you interfere, and nearly ruin months of patient work, and still pretend that you liked the idea of marrying me?'

'It wasn't a pretence,' she managed to say above the sickness in her throat. 'I thought we loved each other – another of my mistakes. But you won't get Poggio if I can help it, and I hope you don't get anywhere else. There's no need to start proceedings – we'll find the money; you'll be paid before the case gets anywhere near a court.'

'If you say so, of course I accept what you say.'

'Then accept one more thing before I go. You offend me, Roberto. Sympathy for Enrico, affection for me . . . They were simply steps to getting what you wanted – a despicable fraud. But your planned rape of our countryside is almost worse. You should be ashamed to call yourself a Tuscan.'

She imagined that the interview was over and turned towards the door. He was there before her, because it was suddenly intolerable that she should go without properly understanding him. His hands bit into her skin through the thin material of her dress; he could feel its softness and smell the faint flower perfume she used. Self-control slipped and his mouth fastened hard on her own. But she held herself rigid under his hands and finally he had to release her.

'You weren't entirely right,' he said unevenly. 'It wasn't all a fraud – I could have loved you, easily enough.'

She wiped trembling fingers across her lips as if to remove the impression of his own. Then, without answering him, she got to the door and let herself out of the room.

The staircase in front of her looked long enough to be winding down into Hell, but clinging to the banister like an old woman, she reached the bottom of it, and stepped out of the house. Siena looked normal, going about its affairs in the late-afternoon sunshine that fell warmly on her skin. After a moment or two she managed to dredge up the memory of where she'd left the car, but found that she couldn't drive straight back to Poggio and face Lucia. Without conscious thought she turned away from the road that led to Florence, and climbed instead the long snaking hill to the towered skyline ahead of her.

San Gimignano, crouched on its hilltop, was just as she remembered it, windblown and starling-haunted. She left the car outside the town's encircling wall and walked up towards the square. That was unchanged, too – with the usual gathering of birds round the ancient cistern in the centre, and with all the local youth and beauty clustered at pavement cafés enjoying the late sunshine. Reaction had set in and it was an effort to drag herself to an empty chair. Automatically she ordered a glass of the local Vernaccia white wine, tasting deliciously of nuts and honey, but it was still untouched in front of her when a quiet English voice spoke just behind her.

'Mind if I join you? I hate drinking alone.'

Before she could pull herself together sufficiently to answer him, he was drawing out a chair. A quick sip of wine helped, but the sting of it against her cut lip reminded her that she'd done nothing about her appearance since stumbling out of Roberto's apartment. It was the final humiliation that Adam Fleming should be there to see her in this moment of defeat. She was tempted to put her head down on the table and indulge in a full-blooded Italian bout of weeping that might embarrass him sufficiently to drive him away. But even that couldn't be depended on; he was a man who obeyed no rules but his own.

If her appearance was distraught, it didn't seem to bother him; when she glanced at him he was merely engrossed in watching the birds wheeling in and out of the arrow-slits of the tower across the square.

'Lucia thought you'd be here,' he remarked at last. 'She had the feeling your appointment might turn out badly. If it did, *this* was where she reckoned you'd come for comfort.'

She tried to smile in case he should look in her direction. 'Granny comes from a long line of witches and she's hardly ever wrong, but this time she is, Professor. I was merely enjoying the view.'

His eyes did skim over her face then, before returning to the starlings.

'Your upbringing must have been deplorable; there's no truth in you! Never mind . . . drink your wine and then I'll take you to look at the patron lady of this little town – St Catherine. She must have been watching over it during the war. There was a good deal of damage, unfortunately, but by a miracle Ghirlandaio's frescoes *weren't* blown to smithereens.'

Laughter, uncontrollable and hysterical, bubbled up inside her – a lesson in art-history was all she needed to round off the afternoon nicely! She fumbled for her glass with trembling hands and took another gulp of wine, praying that she wouldn't go to pieces in front of him.

'Georgina, I know you're wishing I'd just go away,' he said gently, 'but I'm not about to. You don't have to tell me what's wrong – we'll just pretend that we've met here by chance. Go and ring Lucia to stop her worrying, and then we'll enjoy a pleasant dinner together.'

His eyes met hers across the table, and the kindness in them steadied her.

'Excuse me a moment,' she said abruptly. She disappeared inside the café and returned ten minutes later outwardly restored again: hair brushed, and lipstick doing its best to disguise her sore mouth.

'Lead on, Professor, I've told Lucia I won't be back for supper and now I'm ready for St Catherine.'

They looked at the frescoes that told the saint's brief life story, wandered in and out of the shadows thrown by San Gimignano's medieval skyscrapers, and finally ended up at the restaurant Adam had marked out. At the far end of the room their table seemed to be suspended in space, and the windows overlooked a vast landscape over which dusk was softly falling. He lifted his glass with a smile she knew she would remember. 'Let's drink to Tuscany . . . "lovely beyond the singing of it", as someone once said of a very different view.'

She echoed the toast, but added soberly, 'Lovely but threatened by barbarians.'

'Recurring twin themes in its history – the miracle of achievement coupled with the miracle of survival. Barbarians are nothing new.'

'No, but there's a different threat now.' She had intended saying nothing about her visit to Siena, but suddenly the need to talk was overwhelming. 'You know so much about our affairs that you might as well hear the rest of it. My grandfather was lent money by Roberto's company when Poggio first began to run into difficulties. Neighbourly kindness, we thought, and I was even deeply grateful for it. By the time Roberto made another offer, I was here to throw my flat into the scales and avoid more borrowing, so Gramps was able to refuse his offer. I knew that Roberto was bitterly disappointed, but I didn't know why – until today. His letter calling in the original loan arrived this morning. Either we pay, or he takes Poggio anyway, and I now know that Poggio is what he always wanted.'

'I got the impression that *you* were what he'd always wanted.'

'A side-benefit,' she said in a voice that shook slightly, 'an extra thrown in, let's say.'

'Don't let's say anything so bloody stupid. It was perfectly obvious that Artom was in love with you.'

She shrugged aside the memory of Roberto's parting comment. 'Perhaps, but he wanted Poggio much more – though not in order to keep it going. The plan was to tear it to pieces so that he and his precious American backer could build a holiday village there.'

'Did Enrico realise what Artom had in mind?'

She shook her head. 'Gramps merely suspected Roberto of wanting to make sure he could combine it with Casagrande into one huge estate. But the matter was made clear to me this afternoon. If not Poggio, then he must have the loan back so that he can buy land elsewhere. A straightforward business matter, he assured me!'

'When I caught sight of you, it didn't seem to have been entirely a business matter,' Adam said gently.

'True! A tinge of good, old-fashioned lust coloured our final parting. Perhaps Roberto thought I was desperate enough to accept him on any terms.' She made a little gesture with her hand, pushing the words away. 'Unfair, I expect – I *had* tried him rather far.'

Adam wondered whether the wildly theatrical town they were sitting in explained his very undonnish desire to batter Roberto Artom into the ground. He'd never thought of himself as a violent man, but there was something to be said for the roaring days when men with a passion for vengeance built a tower higher than their neighbour's and simply let fly!

'What happens now?' he asked after a moment. 'Your contribution will be mopped up in repaying the debt instead of being used as working capital?'

'The problem in a nutshell, and for the moment, at least, Gramps refuses to let me tell my parents about it.' She stared at Adam, brow wrinkled in thought. 'I'm not sure why, when they're both the nicest of men, but my father and Gramps have never quite got on with one another. I think Daddy feels he's never been forgiven for taking Olivia away from Italy, and Gramps has always felt the need to impress my clever, successful father. Admitting to the mess we're in now wouldn't be easy for him.'

Adam stared at the plate that had been put in front of him. 'I realise that you're hell-bent on keeping Poggio going, but why? Enrico's reached the age when most men are thinking of putting their feet up, his land is hilly and difficult to work, and it's not as if he has a flock of sons and grandsons waiting to carry on the name of Casali. Is it worth all this terrible effort just to wipe Artom's eye?'

The question took her by surprise, but mounting anger was mixed with a sharp sense of disappointment in him. 'You don't understand any more than Roberto does. He thought all he had to do was offer the bribe of a price that would let my grandparents live in comfort. But Poggio *is* their life; they know no other, want no other. When Gramps is too old to work, he'll still be able to walk out over the hills, or just sit on the terrace and tell the rest of us what to do, and Lucia can enjoy the garden she's watched grow for fifty years. It isn't even just them, either. There's my mother, clinging to some inward vision of where she really belongs, and Maria with a shattered life remade here for her children, and Tommaso home again like Ulysses after his wanderings . . .'

'. . . and Caterina, yearning for the joys of city life,' Adam suggested, 'like a thousand other youngsters brought up in the country!'

'I know she can't wait to get away, or thinks she can't. But Alessio *will* stay, especially now that his uncle's here; every day I can see him a bit more aware of his heritage, and a bit more certain of the value of what he shares in.' Afraid that she hadn't convinced the man watching her, she added vehemently, 'I know Poggio's only a little bit of Tuscany, but every acre we can hang on to is something saved from people like the men behind Roberto, prepared to carve up an antique landscape for the sake of pulling in a few hundred more tourists and making a fortune out of them for themselves. As if tourists didn't infest Italy already!'

The argument had become general and he was obliged to take issue with her. 'Infest . . . To "visit with evil intent"? It's a strong word; did you mean it?'

'I don't care how strong it is. We are infested with them. They're like a horde of locusts, drifting on the breeze, and just about as mindlessly destructive. Have you seen Florence and Siena at the height of the summer? Even *this* enchanting place doesn't escape.'

'Of course I've seen them, I know the trail of tawdry rubbish the holiday industry spawns, and the mess it often leaves behind. But if a housewife from Doncaster wants a plastic model of the Leaning Tower of Pisa to take home with her, who are you to say she can't have it?'

There was a slight edge to her voice when she answered, but the assorted strains of the day had pushed her beyond the point of remembering caution. 'The lady from Doncaster probably wouldn't come here at all if it weren't for people like you telling her she must see the "Birth of Venus", or Michelangelo's "Pietà" before she dies. What's the point? Watch a herd of tourists being dragged from one "masterpiece" to another; by the end of a fortnight they can't even remember which town they're in, much less what they've seen.'

'It's the high-nosed attitude of someone who can afford to say, "Thank God *I'm* not a visitor,"' he said sharply. 'You forget something, Georgina. You've been made free of all this since you were a child; others haven't been so fortunate. Think of the people who lead desperately humdrum lives in ugly towns, where the dead hand of a materialistic society crushes out of them everything but the need to acquire one more useless gadget to fill the emptiness of their days. They *must* be allowed to see Michelangelo's masterpieces for themselves, and glimpse what the human spirit has been capable of producing.'

She was halted on the brink of another tirade by the need to think about what he'd said.

'You look struck,' he said, suddenly smiling at her. 'Did I shout at you?'

'No, but the effect was similar! I have to grant what you say, or be condemned as stupid, selfish, or arrogant. But tourists in large numbers *are* a threat. I *know* it doesn't matter about the plastic Tower of Pisa, or the rest of the tasteless rubbish they're offered. But there's a rich living to be made out of such customers, and it's more easily earned than money made working this land. There's a delicate balance between the land and the people who live by it; let too many of them be enticed away and it will become less beautiful and less fertile. I think *that* matters too, because in its own way it's just as much a reflection of the human spirit as the masterpieces you cherish.'

There was a little silence that lasted until she looked up to find him staring at her. 'I began this conversation by asking you why you wanted to keep Poggio going. You've just answered me,' he said simply.

She went back to the *bistecca a la fiorentina* now congealing on her plate, thinking that it must be the result of a thoroughly emotional day that she'd given away far too much about herself; but the strange thing was that she didn't seem to mind. They finished the rest of the meal and walked out of the restaurant into a street now theatrically lit by moonlight. The car park was empty except for their two cars eyeing one another across the tarmac. Adam walked with her to Enrico's Fiat, but stood with his hand holding the door.

'This is a rotten way to end an evening, driving home in separate cars, but perhaps it's just as well.'

She wasn't sure what he meant by it. With any other man the meaning would have been clear and she'd have known what he'd have liked to suggest instead. But his voice had been lightly amused, reminding her that if she knew anything about him at all it was that he was a solitary man who didn't see loneliness as a curse. The kindnesses that he was capable of were almost inhumanly disinterested, requiring nothing in return.

'Thank you for putting the pieces together for me,' she said, smiling at him. 'Miss Hadley is herself again!'

He opened the car door for her, and waited for her to drive away; but although he climbed into the MG afterwards he sat there for a long time making up his mind what must be done. Then, at last, he put the car into gear and went home.

Chapter 11

When she went down to breakfast next morning there was no sign of Enrico, and she didn't have to confess immediately that her trip to Siena had been a failure. Lucia *was* there, having already lost patience with the doctor's instruction that her days should begin quietly with breakfast in bed. A half-drunk cup of coffee was in front of her, but it was clear that she'd eaten nothing.

'If you'll struggle with a roll, I will too,' Georgina suggested.

She thought her grandmother was about to refuse, but Lucia finally reached out a hand to the basket being offered to her. The hand, thin but beautifully kept, shook slightly, and it was obvious that she knew about the calling in of the loan.

'A pleasant evening, I hope, *cara*?' she managed to suggest.

'Pleasanter than it might have been – thanks to you! But I hope the professor didn't mind being shunted off to San Gimignano to keep an eye on me.'

'I got the impression that he went very willingly,' Lucia said. She broke her roll into small pieces, then stared at them, wondering what she was going to do with them next.

'My journey was a waste of time, Gran,' Georgina said abruptly. 'I went to see Roberto, half convinced at least that I might be able to make him change his mind. He turned me down, and then I probably made matters worse by telling him about the sale of my flat. Our rather abortive little love-affair ended there and then. I feel numb about it at the moment, but that's only because there's so much more to worry about.' She stared at her grandmother's face for a moment. 'I asked Gramps a little while ago if he really wanted to go on with the struggle, but I think I should have asked you. You look so tired and worn.'

Lucia gave a little shrug. 'Tiredness is one thing. Giving in to *force majeure* is something else again. Your grandfather might have done that a few months ago; but not with you and Tommaso here. Besides, what else would he do? Sit and think about the days when he made good wine and

109

lived the life of a real man? No, *tesoro*; let us go on fighting. Tell him so when he comes in, please.'

Georgina got up from the table and dropped a kiss on her grandmother's hair. 'Decision unanimous, then! Somehow we carry on, even though I'm not sure how. Did Gramps say you weren't to tell Mama?'

'Yes, but I persuaded him to change his mind. We've upset her enough already by concealing the fact that I was ill. In any case, your father has a right to know. He may think your money shouldn't be risked after all; in which case perhaps the sale of your flat could still be cancelled.' Her eyes were fixed on her granddaughter's face, searching for signs of regret about what had been done.

'I do believe you're trying to get rid of me!' Georgina said, trying to make a joke of it.

'You don't believe anything of the sort. Look at me, *cara*.'

It was the voice of authority, known and recognised as such since a very small girl had insisted that she *would* ride one of the beautiful white oxen that had still been used twenty years ago to draw the carts bringing in the grape harvest. The small girl had lost that argument, and it didn't occur to her not to obey her grandmother now.

She looked up as instructed but said gently, 'You're worried that I don't know what I'm doing. I *do* know, and I'm not going to change my mind.'

A smile like sunlight in winter lit Lucia's thin face. 'What is it Richard likes to say? "It's dogged as does it!" I shall tell your mother so when I write to her.'

Georgina poured fresh coffee into her grandmother's cup and then got up to go. 'I'm late – Tommaso promised me and Alessio a lesson this morning in how to tie up the vines.'

Uncle and nephew were already there when she went outside – Alessio, as usual when the weekend freed him from school, never far from where Tommaso was working. The two of them were becoming fast friends, and the sight of them together, happy in each other's company, caused Maria to weep happily. The change that had come over their lives was nothing short of a miracle, and it didn't occur to her to be jealous of Alessio's affection for her brother-in-law. It was the natural order of things that a family should have a man at its head.

Like everything else done by an expert, Tommaso's demonstration of how to tie a vine looked easy, but they discovered that it wasn't easy at all.

'Like *this*,' he insisted. 'The tension must be correct, you understand. Too tight and the strings will do more harm than good; too loose and they won't give enough support later on when the swags of fruit get heavy. A sudden storm will snap them off if they're not held firmly.'

At the fifth attempt she'd just tied one that passed muster when Maria called to her from the slope above.

'The signore's back, *cara*. You are wanted in his office.'

Georgina went indoors to find Enrico at his desk as usual, but what she didn't expect to see was Adam Fleming propping up the wall. The colour rushed into her face at the memory of the previous evening.

'You forestalled me last night, I gather,' Enrico said. 'Not that it matters; I should have explained our situation to Adam in any case.'

'There hasn't been a chance to tell you, but my visit to Roberto did no good,' she reported steadily, ignoring the professor. 'He said he needed the money to buy land elsewhere if Poggio wasn't going to drop into his lap. His ambition, by the way, is not to become the biggest landowner in Tuscany, but simply to raze Poggio to the ground so that he can build over it.'

'I know; Adam told me. Needless to say, that *wasn't* made clear at the outset. My God, if it *had* been . . .' He struggled to contain his rage at the thought of it, and finally managed to go on. 'Don't let us waste time talking about it; it's the future we have to think of. Georgina, our dear friend here is offering to take over Roberto's loan, on terms that are, in effect, no terms at all ; he would have us borrow the money free of charge.'

She scarcely heard the last part of the sentence, being too stunned by its beginning to take in anything else. When she shot a glance at Adam he was absorbed in the pattern of the rug at his feet. She was overwhelmed by a medley of emotions she couldn't even identify, but the most prominent one felt like anger that he should have felt obliged to get involved in their chaotic affairs.

'You refused, of course,' she said fiercely to Enrico. 'It's a madly quixotic offer which we have to refuse.'

'*Why*?' the professor asked mildly.

She was almost goaded into shouting at him, took a deep breath instead, and forced herself to speak as one humouring an idiot. 'Because of the risk involved. Keep your money, please. What *we* risk is our own affair, but Poggio has no claim on you.'

'Gina, at least sound grateful! We're being threatened by Roberto Artom, not Adam.' Enrico was very uncertain himself that the Englishman's offer should be accepted, but his granddaughter's way of rejecting it scandalised him. Georgina, with a wary eye on his face, tried to explain herself.

'We've been given help in the past and it's done us more harm than

111

good. It's time to manage without any more interference that masquerades as help.' Before Enrico could find words to admonish her, she admitted herself that an apology was needed. 'Sorry,' she muttered to Adam, 'that must have sounded intolerably rude. I have no grounds at all for thinking that you're tarred with Roberto's delightful brush. But if I'd had the slightest idea that you'd feel obliged to come galloping to our rescue, I'd never have mentioned the calling-in of the loan last night.'

'I *don't* feel the slightest obligation,' Adam said calmly before Enrico could charge into the conversation. 'All I feel is a keen desire to be allowed a share in what goes on here.'

He was just like her father, she realised – opposing hostility with an unshakeable, gentle courtesy that left his adversary disarmed. She was forced to change tack slightly.

'I take it that you're not so rich that you can afford to lose this money?'

'I'm not rich at all. What I'm offering Enrico represents just about all the spare cash I have in the world.'

The quiet reminder that his offer was being made to Enrico, not her, almost passed her by.

'Then you *are* mad. Kind, but definitely insane,' she insisted flatly. 'Financially speaking, you need placing under restraint!'

'Georgina!' Her grandfather's outrage was expressed this time but lost in the professor's shout of laughter, and the more she glared at him, apparently the more comical the situation became.

'Be serious, damn you.' She was scarcely aware of Enrico now. The issue seemed to lie between herself and a quixotic fool who needed protecting from himself, but the distress breaking her voice sobered him into taking charge of the conversation.

'Please listen to me, both of you,' he said firmly. 'I can't force you to accept my offer, but you must understand the spirit in which it's made. I own a house, I have an income which is more than I need to live on, and no wife and children dependent on me. What money I have is *spare*, and it wouldn't be the end of the world if I lost it. I'm simply making an investment that might or might not turn out well. I happen to think it will be *well*, but that isn't the point at all; my ambition is to help preserve something precious which shouldn't be destroyed. God knows, I talk enough about that: now it's time to *do* something. Now will you, please, take the wretched money?'

She could find no hint in his face of anything but the most disinterested concern. Roberto's business need to acquire Poggio had been complicated by his desire to acquire Georgina Hadley as well. In the professor's case

112

only a matter of principle was at stake; she could be quite sure of that. She told herself that it was a relief, and trod heavily on a small shoot of regret that he should be quite so immune to the passions that drove normal people.

She finally answered him with a little shrug that said she withdrew from the battle. 'Poggio belongs to my grandfather; he must decide. I've got work to do outside.'

She left behind her a silence in which Enrico awkwardly examined his hands as if he hadn't seen them before.

'Not . . . quite herself at the moment, our dear girl,' he tried to explain. 'It's not to be wondered at, of course, but she's never difficult for long.' He stared hopefully at his guest to find the professor's eyes unexpectedly full of laughter.

'The "dear girl" is many things – beautiful and valiant to mention only two – but don't let's pretend that she isn't occasionally *very* difficult!'

Enrico gave a magnificent shrug that conceded the truth of it and asked at the same time what else men had ever expected of women. 'They think with their hearts,' he said forgivingly, 'it's the way God made them.'

'And sometimes we're very grateful for the fact!'

'True! Now, Adam, we must talk business. I agree to accept your offer provided we discuss the rate of interest and you let me first show you our plans for the future.' An hour later, the matter had been settled, with Enrico defeated on the matter of interest because Adam simply refused to charge any at all.

Over lunch he explained to Lucia and a rather silent granddaughter that the professor's money was available immediately, and would be used at once to pay off Roberto's loan. The money from the sale of the flat would be used, as they'd intended, as working capital.

'All we have to do now is pray to God for a reasonable harvest, and work, work, work ourselves to contribute what *we* can,' he finished up exuberantly.

'What *you* have to do is remember that you're seventy-one, not fifty years younger,' his wife reminded him.

Enrico's programme didn't seem to differ much from what they'd been doing for the past two months, but Georgina roused herself to smile at her grandmother.

'Don't fret, dearest. We'll hound him indoors from time to time, if only to stop *you* from worrying! Speaking of harvests, by the way, there *will* be an olive crop after all. They fool you because fruit and leaves are so similar in colour, but now that the dead wood has gone, they're beginning to look a good deal better than I expected. If the winter killed off a lot of trees elsewhere, oil of Poggio's quality will be in short supply and we shall get a high price for it. The sooner we can start paying back Adam's loan, the better.'

When she'd wandered into the kitchen with empty plates for Maria, Enrico looked ruefully at his wife. 'She's not happy about Adam's help. I'm not sure why; she was grateful enough to Roberto originally.'

'Roberto seemed to have given it for love, and she thought she loved him all the more because of it. Her confidence has been badly shaken.' Lucia hesitated, then put another anxiety into words. 'What will she do here when winter comes? Without friends at Casagrande she is going to be lonely.'

Enrico nodded, knowing that what his Lucia said was undoubtedly true. But the winter was months away. They had the summer to think about first, and the all-important *vendemmia*. God knew *that* was enough for a man to have to worry about, and for the moment all their effort must go towards that. There'd be time afterwards to remember loneliness or grief.

The days lengthened into a summer that Georgina knew she would remember for the rest of her life. There would be others as full of sunlight and shared work, and other seasons full of a different richness of their own, but they wouldn't be shot through with *this* summer's extraordinary mixture of emotions – urgency, joy, and grief. They worked in the knowledge that Poggio must succeed, and that if it didn't, it would fail completely. But as the long days passed they could see that what now remained to be done was less than what had been achieved. Row upon row of vines clothing the lee-sides of the hills had grown luxuriantly after a wetter spring than usual, but at last they were sprayed and neatly tied; in between, the weeds had been rotovated and turned in.

In a procession of brilliant days Enrico and Tommaso walked the hillsides, watching, judging, almost praying over the grape clusters forming on the vines. Sundays were officially days of rest, but even then the two of them, with Alessio and Nero at their heels, still patrolled the rows – like dignitaries inspecting a guard of honour, Lucia said – but Georgina saw them as physicians anxiously assessing the state of their patient's health. When she murmured that they were working too hard, her grandmother simply smiled.

'They're happy, *cara*, what else matters?' But her eyes examined the strained face in front of her. 'It's *you* I worry about!'

Georgina shook her head, deliberately misunderstanding what she knew her grandmother had meant. 'I enjoy work and I'm used to it, Gran. My dear William was a slave-driver at Kew!'

'Perhaps,' Lucia agreed, 'but you miss him all the same, miss your life there, I think. That was too much to give up for us.' It seemed safer than touching the wound left by Roberto. But she looked so tragic that Georgina gave her a little hug before she answered.

'It was a lot to give up William because he's special; you'll think that yourself when you meet him. But he's still my dear friend. Losing what I thought I had with Roberto has been harder to bear. All our ups and downs of childhood and adolescence seemed to have been meant to lead to wonderful fulfilment at last – we were going to love each other so richly, so passionately, for the rest of our lives. Instead of that, I was really nothing more than a pawn in the game he was playing; I was blinded by my own vanity and *his* powers of persuasion. I'm still very sore, Gran, and angry with myself as well as him; but I *won't* have you worry about me. I shall get over him, and learn in future to put my faith in goodness and solid virtue!'

'As found in William Bird perhaps?' Lucia asked with a faint smile.

'Perhaps,' agreed Georgina to please her.

Then a little silence fell between them until Lucia thought of something cheerful to say. 'I'm glad Paolo is back in Siena. His professional help could be useful to Enrico, and his family will be able to provide friends for you. Filippo, especially, has a knack of attracting people, or so his mother tells me. Put him on a desert island, she insists, and other human beings would crawl out of hiding to meet him!'

'It's not how I remember him,' Georgina pointed out. 'I met him here once or twice as a child and spent the whole time running away from him. He was always waiting with the largest spider he could find – a horrid small boy, I thought.'

'I don't suppose you'll have that trouble now, *tesoro*, he'll have outgrown an interest in spiders.' She hesitated for a moment. 'There's Adam, of course, but you seem determined *not* to make a friend of him; I can't think why.'

'It upsets Caterina, for one thing; she regards the professor as her property, only to be shared with Alessio when she can't avoid it. I just hope she remembers occasionally that he'll eventually go back to England. In fact, I hope you and Maria do, as well – you're all equally besotted about him!'

'Not besotted,' her grandmother protested mildly, 'but we shall certainly miss him. It seems all the more reason to enjoy his company while we can. But he's part of Poggio now; we shan't lose touch with him completely.'

'True! The professor will want to check up on his investment occasionally.'

Georgina saw her grandmother's face stiffen with disapproval and knew that a retraction was expected. 'Sorry, Gran. I'm growing into an acid-tongued old spinster! Our sense of obligation is as light as he can make it, I know that.'

Lucia leaned over to kiss her cheek. 'What has happened has made you unhappy, but don't let it make you bitter as well.'

Georgina smiled and promised to do her best. 'To prove it, I'll even smile at the professor!'

But she saw little of him even though his course of lectures had now come to an end for the summer. There were still days when he went off on occasional forays among the archives and libraries of Florence and Siena in search of the material he needed, but otherwise his time was split between morning work in the vineyard and afternoons and evenings at his desk. Their paths seldom crossed, but one morning he passed her trying to coax a bonfire into flame at the bottom of the vegetable garden.

'I'm afraid you were never a boy scout,' he said solemnly. 'No draught! You'll never get it to burn like that.'

He took the fork out of her hand, lifted up the smouldering mass, and after a moment or two a little flame obligingly sprang into life.

'There's no end to your accomplishments, Professor!'

'Nor to your talent for being snide. My accomplishments could even include up-ending you across my knee.'

Before she even had time to realise that his anger was real, he stuck the fork in the ground and stared at her. 'I'm not sure why it irritates you so much to see me out here, but if you're about to suggest that I want to make sure the rest of you don't slacken and endanger my investment, I shall probably beat the hide off you.'

Coming on top of her lecture from Lucia, his reaction induced in her an agonising need to laugh. So much for her brave new effort at cordiality! She could feel bubbles of laughter rising inside, tried to subdue them, but finally caved in, because the mixture of anger and frustration in his face was too much for her. Tears began to stream down her cheeks which he suddenly feared were the tears of hurt or hysteria, and at once his hands reached out to offer the comfort he would have given an overwrought child. She shook her head, struggling for self-control.

'I'm not distraught,' she finally managed to explain. 'Lucia gave me a lecture about being silent and sour, and I was doing my best to be chatty. All I achieved was to make you angry again.'

'Not angry; urbanity at all times is what we also pride ourselves on at Oxford!'

'Then Italy is destroying you,' she assured him gravely. 'There are times when a man-eating tiger could give you points on urbanity.' His still-unsmiling face seemed to suggest that she'd gone wrong yet again. 'I spoke in jest, Professor,' she insisted. 'I honestly wasn't trying to needle you.'

'I didn't suppose you were. I was merely struck by something – I haven't seen you laugh like you did just now since you came to Poggio.'

His gaze on her face was intently questioning; she needed to escape from it and from regret that she'd refused the touch of his hands – there would have been comfort in them, she felt sure. 'Lucia worries about you . . . thinks you're missing Artom. Are you?' He made a speciality of these quiet questions, she thought, thrust home when they were least expected.

'Yes, of course,' she said slowly. 'It's hard to explain about Roberto. You scarcely know him, and no doubt dislike what you've heard, but we grew up together here and all my memories of Poggio include him. I always half expected him to know that we belonged together. When it seemed he *did* know, I was very happy. Now, I'm a bit like a train that's unexpectedly been shunted on to another line, with nowhere else to go for the moment, and nothing to get up steam for!'

The odd analogy made him smile, but he thought it described very well the confusion that he sensed in her; she'd been damaged by Roberto Artom.

'The condition won't be permanent, I'm sure,' he said, with such gentleness in his voice that she was tempted into talking about another anxiety not shared with her grandparents.

'My own state of muddle is one thing, but there's something else bothering me that concerns other people. I now see that I didn't know Roberto as well as I thought I did, but there was one trait I was always sure about – he never liked being beaten. I suspect that he dislikes it even more now, and we *have* beaten him, thanks to you. I don't know what he can do about it, but I can't help feeling that he will want to do something.'

Adam saw no reason to confess that the same thought had occasionally occurred to him. He smiled at her instead. 'The trouble with you is that you're a born worrier. It's a condition I recognise because I shared it as a child! At the age of ten or so I could agonise over almost anything, as riven by the possibility of a wet day when I needed it to be fine, as by the fear that the world might fall into space during the night, leaving us all to

117

drop off it one by one! Shall we both agree *not* to worry about Roberto?'

'Very well, Professor,' she said obediently. 'I shall concentrate instead on giving – what was it, draught? – to my bonfire!'

He nodded at her and walked away. The scene hadn't lasted very long but to Caterina, watching it from her window, it had marked a kind of turning-point. She'd always liked the fact that her room overlooked the kitchen garden. When Giuseppe's sons had worked there she'd always brushed her hair at the window, knowing they were trying not to look at her. For a while after they went away she'd missed them, but that was before she became aware of Adam. She'd thought him old, to begin with, and so pale and thin as to be someone to laugh about with Alessio. But her brother had quickly changed his mind, and the day had come when, holding a door open for her, Adam had smiled. She'd gone to bed dreaming that she wasn't the housekeeper's daughter, and hadn't stopped thinking about him since. If only Georgina had stayed in England. Her visits had been looked forward to in the past, because there'd been more fun and laughter when she was there, but now the *padrone*'s granddaughter had become the enemy. With no *fidanzato* or *sposo* of her own at twenty-six, she was really to be pitied, if not despised; but she had the crucial advantage of belonging in the salon, not the kitchen, and it was obvious that Adam had noticed her at last.

Caterina hitched up her skirt by turning the waist-band over and over, then stared at herself in the mirror. The cruel truth was that her legs weren't as good as Georgina's. She lengthened her skirt again, but undid instead the all-important button on her shirt. When it came to bosoms, there was no doubt about it – even now she was better endowed than the enemy.

She found Adam in the courtyard, filling a tank with the copper-sulphate solution used to spray the vines. His smile welcomed her as usual, but he went on with what he was doing, and didn't notice that she'd arranged her hair in a new way.

'Why do you work out here like a labourer?' she asked sharply.

'Because I enjoy it, and because I've come to feel involved in what goes on.'

'I suppose that's because Poggio belongs to you, now.'

If she hadn't had his full attention before, she had it now. His eyes held hers over the tank he was still holding, and she had the feeling that she'd disappointed him in some way.

'Ill-informed gossip, Caterina. Don't ever bother to listen to it, and don't repeat it, please. Poggio belongs to the signore, as it always has.'

He sounded almost stern with her, but for once she felt minded to argue.

'Mamma said so. I heard her talking to Zio Tommaso.'

'Then you misunderstood what she said; I have a great interest in this lovely place, but who wouldn't if he was lucky enough to know it at all?'

Caterina fingered the button on her shirt, not even with the intention of making him look at it. 'Lovely maybe, but I don't want to stay here. Will you take me back to England with you when you go?'

She tried hard to sound provocative, but her eyes implored him to accept what she offered. They were balanced on the knife-edge of disaster, and he told himself he deserved it for being so foolishly self-confident when Georgina had tried to warn him of the danger. Even the instinct to take Caterina's hand by way of comfort had to be ignored in case it made matters worse. There seemed to be only lightness left to see him through.

'You'd hate England, you know. It's often cold and wet, and people would expect you to speak the dreadful language you find so difficult.'

She closed her eyes, overcome by the anguish of not being taken seriously because she wasn't yet quite sixteen. She offered herself to him, and he spoke of the weather! 'What do those things matter? I should be with you.'

He put down the tank, and led her to a bench against the wall. Comfort there had to be now, no matter where it left them. 'Listen to me, *cara*. I'm much more than twice your age; old enough to be your father, in fact. I live in an English village as quiet as Poggio, though not quite so beautiful. If you don't like it here, you'd like my home even less.'

'I wouldn't care . . . I just want you to love me. But you won't, and it's nothing to do with being too young. It's because I'm Caterina Pizzone, the housekeeper's daughter. That's not enough for you, is it?'

It was worse, more complicated than he'd ever imagined. His command of Italian had improved by leaps and bounds, but it was scarcely up to a conversation that held as many possibilities for misunderstandings as this one did.

'If you ever say that again, I shall be very angry with you. You're the daughter of a good and much-valued lady without whom Poggio couldn't function. Is there anything to be ashamed of in that? Your mother works here, and so do you, but so do we all, the signora included. There's no shame in it, believe me.'

'Then *why* won't you take me with you?' she whispered.

'Because you'd be homesick and unhappy; and because, fond though I am of you, my . . . heart was given long ago to a lady in England.'

He couldn't have brought himself to say it in English, but it sounded less mawkish in Italian, and if he didn't insist that his heart was involved, he knew he would never convince her.

The silence lasted a long time before she said, 'Why is this lady not here, taking care of you?'

'It isn't possible.' It sounded so terse that Caterina, scenting tragedy, accepted it. If he suffered as well, she could bear her own unhappiness somehow. She fetched a huge sigh, and smeared away her tears with the back of her hand, while he smiled at her with infinite kindness.

'I dare say life looks rather hopeless at the moment, but I promise you it won't stay that way. Have you thought what you're going to do when you leave school?'

She nodded unenthusiastically. 'Mamma has arranged it; I'm to go to Signora Minelli's salon in San Vicenzo to learn hairdressing.'

He didn't make the mistake of enthusing about a prospect she viewed so poorly, but dredged up out of the distant past memories of Amanda.

'My sister wanted to do that; she used to rearrange her hair half a dozen times a day, but I'm afraid she didn't have your skill; it always ended up looking like a bird's nest!'

The thought of the salon might still be dreadful, but he *had* noticed her hair after all, and she knew that she *did* have a skill that her friends at school lacked.

'It's a beginning,' she agreed after a while, 'but I want to see more than Poggio and San Vicenzo.'

'I'm sure you will, but don't lose sight of this lovely place altogether; it's your home.'

If she was about to deny it, the sound of her mother's voice calling from the house interrupted whatever she was going to say. She stood up, gave him a smile in which suffering and bravery were nicely mixed, and wandered off in the direction of the kitchen. Adam gave a sigh of relief and tried to comfort himself with the thought that adolescent hearts didn't stay broken for long. He hefted the spraying tank on his back again and went back to work, hoping that Caterina would at least remember to do up her blouse again before Maria caught sight of her.

Chapter 12

That evening, the first of two long-distance telephone calls came from William Bird, and confirmed to Georgina that the sale of the flat was being concluded. 'My cousin will be ready to move in by mid-September. Can you get over here before that to clear the flat out?'

'Of course I'll come before then. I've sent all the papers back to my solicitor, by the way, but I suppose he'll sit on them for ages.'

'No he won't. He's got my solicitor breathing down his neck, and I've put the fear of God into *him*. They know the money's needed in Italy, not sitting on their desks.'

'Oh, William, we'll never be able to thank you enough.' Her voice was hoarse with the gratitude that wanted to find relief in tears, but she knew that weeping would irritate him. She sniffed instead and wished he could see the effort she was making. 'You *are* coming for the grape-picking, I hope? We're counting on seeing you then.'

'I have that intention,' he said with dignity. 'Things I *don't* want to do have been known to slip my memory, but harvesting grapes is something I shall enjoy.'

'How's Kew looking?'

'Beautiful, despite the worst my new assistant can do.'

She was still smiling when she put down the telephone. Held over whatever distance, a conversation with William brought him vividly to mind, and for a moment she was engulfed in homesickness for him and for London. There was no going back on what had been done, and Poggio was now her only home. When the grapes were in there would be the olives to gather and press, and by the time that was done she would be able to start thinking about the spring again; there were changes she wanted to make in the gardens. She also had it in mind to ask Lucia if she could make a new home for herself in the farmhouse Adam Fleming would be vacating at the end of the summer. She thought it was a good thing she'd kept her head about *him* when all about her were losing theirs. Her first task of the winter would be to cheer up everyone who felt abandoned when he went back to England, the farmyard cats included!

When the telephone rang again, Lucia answered it, and a radiant smile spread across her face.

'Darling!' Olivia's voice sounded bell-clear across the wire. 'I can't make head nor tail of your letters, and my daughter's are even worse. One moment she's about to marry Roberto, then she's not; Poggio's ruined, then it's saved; and Pizzones seem to be popping up like mushrooms in a meadow. It's beyond me what is going on.'

'Dearest, only *one* Pizzone: our splendid Tommaso,' Lucia pointed out, struggling between tears and laughter. 'It's true that rather a lot has been happening, but I promise you there's no need to worry now. Apart from the fact that they work too hard, all your dear ones are well.'

'I don't trust you to be truthful any longer. I want to see for myself. Richard says we shall be ruined, but it's his idea anyway that we should come over for your birthday.'

'Never mind my birthday, that's nothing – but to see you again, *tesoro* . . .' Her voice failed at the thought of so much joy, and Georgina took over the telephone in time to hear her father's voice at the other end.

'Lucia mine, we can't afford the air fare *and* the cost of your daughter's telephone calls, so I shall be very brief!'

'It's me now, not Granny,' his daughter said quickly. 'Shall I meet you somewhere?'

'No need, love. We'll take the overnight flight to Milan, and hire a car there – be at Poggio in time for dinner on Friday, God willing. We must leave again on Monday morning, but a glimpse of you all will put your mother's mind at rest.'

When he'd rung off Lucia wiped away her tears and went in search of her husband. He was grinning broadly when he came into the room a few minutes later. 'Would you like to see two completely happy women, *cara*?' he asked Georgina. 'Your grandmother and Maria are now *both* weeping in the kitchen, in between telling each other all that has to be done before Friday!'

By the following morning it was clear that Lucia's plans included not only the spring-cleaning of the house from attics to cellar – for which reinforcements would be drafted in from among Maria's friends on the estate – but a full-scale party to mark Olivia's home-coming.

'This Saturday?' Georgina asked doubtfully. 'It's very short notice; don't be disappointed if people are already booked up.'

'They'll come, booked up or not,' Lucia said with confidence. 'Some will come because they're curious about Poggio, but most will come as friends, for the pleasure of seeing Olivia and Richard.'

'And for the pleasure of seeing *you*. We shall certainly mention that it's your seventieth birthday, and they'll all feel obliged to bring rich gifts!'

'*Tesoro* . . . what an idea!' Lucia sounded faintly scandalised, then a smile touched her mouth. 'I wonder if they will!'

On her way to the telephone Georgina stopped short at the sight of a name on the guest list in her hand. 'The Artoms? Surely we aren't going to ask them!'

'Why not? We have no quarrel with Dino and Erica, and they're still our nearest neighbours.'

'They won't come. I bet you anything you like dear Erica will be otherwise engaged.'

She returned from the telephone five minutes later to confirm that she'd been right. 'They're getting ready to leave for Paris next week – *desolated* that they can't come, but there isn't a moment free between now and then.'

'Well, I can't say I'm sorry, but we've behaved correctly. That's all that matters.'

'*Toujours la politesse*, dear Gran! Now, I shall cool down and then go and ask Cousin Paolo's wife if she can remember who I am.'

Over supper, when they were busy making lists and sharing out tasks still to be done, Enrico reported some news of his own.

'I heard from Moroni this morning. Adam's loan has been transferred, and will be sent on to Roberto immediately. Poggio has nothing to fear from *him* any longer, thank God.'

'And thanks also to Georgina and to Adam,' Lucia suggested gently. 'We must never forget that, *amore*.' She gave him a loving kiss, but anxiety quickly drew her brows together in a frown. 'There's no reason why Roberto should know how the loan has been settled?'

'Certainly not; let him think we dug the money up from under an olive tree.'

The knowledge that Adam's money had arrived put the final touch of grace on the prospect of their daughter's visit. Excitement rose in the house as steadily as the heat of summer outside, and only Caterina worked without sharing in the general feeling of joy. Georgina sympathised with Alessio's candid opinion that his sister was a pain, but she couldn't help remembering the agonies of being half child, half adult. At going on sixteen, life could often seem cruel; and was probably more so for a girl who preferred to live in a dream world where anything was possible rather than in one where floors still had to be washed and chickens fed.

Crossing the courtyard from the *cantina* the following morning, Georgina found her there, staring blindly into space.

'*Ciao, cara*, I never see you these days. What about coming into Florence with me? I have to find a birthday present for my grandmother, then we could drop in at a pizzeria.'

It was a temptation. An outing was an outing, even when offered by the enemy and Caterina nearly gave in. But she could still see in her mind's eye Georgina talking to Adam in the garden, keeping him there while she tried to make an impression an him. She wasn't going to marry Roberto Artom now – everybody knew that; she was probably desperate to find another man.

'Thanks, but I've got something more important to do. Adam relies on me to keep his rooms and his clothes tidy – he says he can't work in a muddle. I like being there alone with him.' The hint of all kinds of erotic possibilities hovered in the air, but Georgina was conscious of nothing but disappointment that an intelligent man should have been so stupid. Caterina was as far from seeing in him an 'elderly gent' as she was from flying to the moon, and if his way of dealing with the problem was to invite her into his rooms, then it could only be that her adoration pleased his vanity.

'I dare say you like helping the professor,' she said gently, 'but will you please try to remember that his real life is in England? He'll return to Oxford before long, and it isn't very likely that he'll even come back to Poggio.'

She'd expected anger, tears perhaps, but not that Caterina's face would suddenly reflect an almost-adult grief. 'He has a woman in England,' she admitted tragically. '*She* should be here, taking care of him. I wouldn't leave him alone if he belonged to me, no matter how many difficulties stood in the way.'

Georgina remembered what he'd said when the loan was being discussed. He had no wife, no children who needed his care, so perhaps the woman was someone else's wife. It would explain the detachment she'd sensed in him. Kindness was second-nature to him, but it was kindness of a very impersonal brand.

'He didn't tell me about his life in England,' she said at last.

There was comfort for Caterina in having known something the *padrona*'s granddaughter didn't know. She was almost able to smile, confident of another pleasant certainty – for once she was about to have the last word.

'I must go: Adam will be waiting for me.'

* * *

A thunderstorm that evening caused some anxiety, but by morning the sky had cleared and Poggio was looking as it was required to look for Olivia's return – a shifting kaleidoscope of green upon green, under a sky as blue as a Sienese painting. The terrace urns spilled the pink and crimson of summer flowers, and indoors the house smelled of roses and beeswax polish.

Enrico was halfway down the lane looking for the car a good two hours before there was any hope of it arriving, and Alessio had walked all the way to San Vicenzo twice before Richard Hadley's hired *macchina* finally turned on to the track towards home and picked him up for a ride up the hill. The world was complete and perfect again, and even the knowledge that he must face his son-in-law couldn't spoil Enrico's joy. He'd steeled himself for signs that Richard despised him for the mess he'd made of things – a man must be allowed to resent the fact that an inheritance given to his daughter was being used to prop up his father-in-law. It made things no better in Enrico's view that at the moment of reunion Richard's smile and hand-clasp seemed as affectionate as ever – here was simply more proof that he was a professional diplomat, trained to hide his feelings. Lucia and Olivia stood hugging each other while Enrico waited for his son-in-law to say something that would give his feelings away.

'Poggio's looking beautiful,' Richard said instead. 'With Giuseppe not here you must have been working like ten men.'

The words fell like balm after all and, moved by sudden affection for a man he'd never quite understood, Enrico hugged *him* in case his first welcome hadn't been sufficiently warm.

'Tomorrow I'll tell you what's been happening, *caro*; but not tonight. Tonight is only for the happiness of being together again.'

Supper had to wait while everyone was greeted and even Tommaso, now reckoned to be part of the family, was brought over and introduced. Then, without any feeling of surprise, Georgina saw her grandmother whisper to the man beside her. A moment later Richard Hadley wandered across the lawn, obviously sent to bring to the supper table a guest he didn't know. With Lucia's usual good sense, the two Englishmen were to be allowed to meet each other in peace, without fighting to make themselves heard over half a dozen excited Italian voices.

Enrico's best wine was poured, and one of Maria's turkeys, sacrificed for the occasion and roasted to perfection, brought to the table. A thanksgiving dinner, said Lucia, in every sense of the word.

The next day, her birthday, they did no outside work at all. Enrico supervised the preparation of the terrace, which meant that Richard listened patiently to a hail of conflicting instructions while Tommaso, assisted by his nephew, got on with the actual work of arranging tables and hanging fairylights. Georgina tactfully suggested that two women in the kitchen – three, counting Caterina – were enough, which left Olivia free to talk to her mother.

'We ought to be helping,' Lucia said remorsefully when her granddaughter took them coffee halfway through the morning.

'We *are* helping, by keeping out of the way. Isn't that so, *tesoro*?'

Georgina grinned at her mother's question. 'Something like that.'

She went away still smiling, but Olivia had noticed with a sense of shock the thinness of her daughter's face. At first glance its attractive tan was all she'd seen, but hollowed cheekbones and the tautness around Georgina's mouth spoke of much more strain than had been communicated to her parents in Washington.

By mid-afternoon it seemed impossible that they could ever be ready in time; by five o'clock the frenzy was subsiding; and by half-past five there was suddenly nothing left to do but tell each other how beautiful it all looked, and go upstairs to change. Far from being finished, Poggio was *en fête* again.

Colours deepened outside as evening crept across the sky, and Nature, entering into the spirit of the thing, produced the delicate silver crescent of a new moon to fly above the chimneys like a house pennant. Lucia appeared in her ancient black dinner dress, adorned with the new collar of white lace that had been Georgina's exquisite birthday present to her and framed her brown face and silver hair like an antique ruff. Bowing ceremoniously over her hand, Adam told her that he was now very confused as to time and place, because she seemed to have stepped out of a seventeenth-century Dutch portrait – a compliment of which she was secretly rather proud. Olivia fluttered down the stairs gorgeous as a butterfly in iridescent chiffon, but Georgina opted for the simplicity of a white silk shift in which she planned to retire unnoticed into the background. It was to be Lucia's and her mother's night; her own part in it would be only to keep an eye on things and make sure her father didn't get left too far behind in the roar of Italian conversation.

In the middle of this unselfish programme she was suddenly wrapped in the embrace of a smiling young man who reminded her slightly of Enrico.

'Filippo,' she gasped when breath allowed. 'My little second cousin,

126

as I live! You've grown very handsome; it's to be hoped you've also grown nicer than you were as a small boy.'

'The spiders still rankle, I see! I'm a reformed character, *cara*, loved by everybody,' he said modestly. 'You've changed too, but the changes are all for the better! Kind of Fate to bring you back to Poggio just as we come home to roost in Siena.'

'For good, or is it a fleeting visit?'

'Definitely permanent. Rome's so damned international these days that you hardly know you're in Italy at all. Anyway, it's time to settle down. *Eccomi* . . . wild oats sown, a responsible citizen from now on!'

She smiled at his laughing face, trying hard to fit him into the constraining sobriety of his father's law firm. 'I can't for the life of me picture you knee-deep in wills and red tape, but perhaps you'll grow more dignified in time, as lawyers seem to do in England.'

'It's the climate there, I expect. The poor things are permanently sodden with rain!' Then, to her surprise, he did become serious. 'My father heard from Enrico about your problems here – too late, I'm afraid, for us to help. Remember us in future, please, if you have any more trouble with Roberto Artom.'

She thanked him, but felt reluctant to discuss Roberto, and it was Filippo who went on.

'He's making a huge success of things, but getting himself disliked in the process. I know that because we represent some of the people he's steam-rollered out of his way.'

Her mind went back to the past; a younger Roberto she *could* talk about. 'When we were children he always wanted to win. I suppose we all did, but the rest of us learned in the end to accept a failure here and there. Roberto never did – still doesn't, I think.'

Filippo's eyes scanned her face, noting its sadness when she wasn't smiling. 'I remember that the two of you were very close – that was why I was always trying to get your attention! I hated him because, however fast I grew, he was three years ahead of me, and the terms we competed on were never equal. Now when they are it's going to be interesting!'

'Why? Are you thinking of competing?'

'Hoping to. I think I've done enough lobbying to get myself elected.'

The look of puzzlement in her face cleared as understanding dawned. 'The Palio! Gramps said something about that. Have you been chosen?'

His dark eyes sparkled with pleasure. 'The usual lad has had to drop out, and since the Ostrich *contrada* has traditionally been Casali territory and I'm not a bad amateur jockey, I think I've persuaded them to let me ride.'

'Roberto's riding for the Centipedes. Does he know about you?'

'He certainly soon will – taking stock of the opposition is a vital part of the fun.'

She wouldn't have described the race as fun at the best of times, but if the traditional rivalry between *contrada* and *contrada* was going to be complicated by the paying-off of old scores, this year's Palio looked like providing even more opportunities for mayhem and general skulduggery than usual. The thought depressed her enough to hope that she could avoid going to Siena when the day came, but more immediately there was a warning to pass on.

'Filippo, it's up to my grandfather to talk to you about Poggio's affairs if he wants to, but I can at least admit that Roberto and I finally came to grief after thinking we had a future together. It's been painful for me, and it's only fair to assume that he hasn't found it easy either. On top of that, I interfered in the big project he had planned for Poggio; and you must take my word for it that he doesn't feel kindly disposed towards us at the moment. He certainly won't want to be beaten by one of our family, so please promise me that you'll try to stay out of his way during the race.'

Her face was so grave that it wasn't the moment to remind her that nothing went according to prior arrangement during the running of the Palio. Filippo had as much chance of planning to avoid Roberto as Roberto had of planning to get alongside *him*. It was usually chaos from start to finish.

'No one wants to be beaten,' he said finally. 'But thank you for the kind advice. If Roberto's horse tries to bite mine, I shall remember that he's a disappointed man, and that all's fair in love and war and the Palio!'

It was the end of the conversation because Olivia's signal from across the room summoned Georgina to be introduced to Filippo's parents. She went, smiled, and talked her way through the rest of the evening, surprised to realise that she would be glad when it was over. The more elderly of the guests congregated in the drawing-room, whose long windows opened out on to the lamplit terrace. Outside, someone had begun to play a guitar and another amateur musician with a mouth-organ joined in. The combination made a sound that was peculiarly haunting, and Georgina blamed it for the fact that she felt sad. She was alone in her sadness because the party was clearly a success, and the rest of her family looked entirely happy. Enrico was at his best when offering hospitality to his friends, Lucia looked serenely content, and Olivia beautiful – for a little while she was among her own people again and homesickness could be forgotten.

Georgina stared at the starlit sky and the lamplit faces on the terrace absorbed in listening to the music, knowing that she couldn't even identify the desolate longing that filled her. It was impossible after what had happened to go on longing for Roberto, but it was at a party like this that she seemed to miss him most, and be most aware of her heart's loneliness. A slight breeze moved one of Tommaso's fairy lights, and showed Adam a wraith of a girl in a simple white dress, who moved away when he turned towards her, to hide the shine of tears in her eyes.

Back in the salon afterwards, she caught glimpses of the professor and found that what she might have expected was exactly the case. He remained unshakeably himself in the midst of the press of mostly unknown people around him. Most men or women changed, consciously or not, in the middle of a social group, but not Adam Fleming. He looked as unnoticeable as usual and talked just as quietly; but the people he was with not only listened, but seemed to enjoy what they heard. A lecture on Ghirlandaio's frescoes perhaps, or Uccello's use of perspective? She couldn't guess, but whatever it was, the face of the woman beside him was very animated and – unlike him – she was really exerting herself to please. Lucky woman to have the professor's company! Georgina examined that thought suddenly clear in her mind, and told herself very firmly that it was born of nothing except her present lowness. He happened to be there, that was all, and on the whole she would prefer it when he went away and left them to organise their lives without him.

With that settled once and for all, she could pin a smile back on her face and enjoy the rest of Lucia's birthday party or die in the attempt.

Chapter 13

She rose early next morning, anxious to help in the mammoth task of clearing up, but discovered that the Pizzone family had been up since dawn. Tommaso and Alessio were outside, hosing down the terrace; indoors, the house was already ordered again. She found Maria in the kitchen, now ready to begin making the ravioli needed for Olivia's favourite lunch. The housekeeper smiled at the sight of her, and brushed aside Georgina's apology for not arriving earlier.

'No need for you to come at all, *cara* signorina. It's *our* job, and Tommaso's like me, only happy when he's working.'

'It's hard to remember now how we managed without him,' Georgina said gratefully. 'Heaven was looking after Poggio the day he came to visit you.'

Maria's nod confirmed that this was her view too; the Blessed Virgin Mary had seen they needed help. 'Tommaso's a good man – kinder than his brother was, and much more reliable.'

'Alessio still worries that he won't stay – in fact, that none of you can stay – but I've tried to convince him that Poggio looks safe now, though we might need a little *more* help from Heaven in the way of good weather later on!'

'Tommaso *will* stay,' Maria said firmly, 'this is his home now. But I think we must find him a good wife.' She wasn't even considering the possibility of Poggio failing, Georgina could see; only running through her mind the unmarried candidates for her brother-in-law's hand that the neighbourhood might supply. It was too serious a matter to be left to chance, or even to Tommaso. The bride who came to live in the farmhouse must fit happily into the close-knit circle at Poggio.

Georgina stared at the serene woman in front of her, remembering her own sense of disgruntlement the previous evening with a feeling of shame. Maria lived entirely in the service of other people, and not only managed to see nothing demeaning in it, but found in the regular pattern of her days the contentment that others looked for feverishly and never discovered at all.

131

'It was cruel of Luigi to leave you for so long without a word,' she remarked suddenly out of the silence in the room. 'You might have married again . . . still might, now that you know you're free.'

'No, once was enough,' Maria said simply. 'There's no reason to blame Luigi; he never wanted to marry me. Nowadays I suppose that kind of marriage doesn't happen, just because a child is coming. The only thing I grieved over was the children growing up without a father when he went away, but it mattered less here at Poggio, thanks to the signora and the *padrone*.'

'Alessio's ambition is simple – to stay here and learn to be a vine-grower – and perhaps that won't change. But I have the feeling that Caterina wants to see the world.' Georgina chose the words carefully in case Maria hadn't so far wanted to acknowledge the truth about her daughter.

'She's like her father: restless. The old ways won't do for her. Imagine it! She'd rather buy ready-made pasta!'

As she spoke, Maria dropped eggs, broken one against another, into a well in her large heap of flour, then salt, and a small amount of olive oil. The ritual had been repeated countless times, day in and day out, but in her view that only made the task more, not less, satisfying. She worked the flour into a soft, pliable ball, then began to roll it out on the cool slab of marble kept only for this purpose. The ball was rolled until it was paper-thin, and almost translucent when she stretched it over her rolling-pin and held it up to the light. Pasta, in one form or another, they ate every day; *ecco*, pasta in one form or another must be made every day. It was as simple as that, and life itself was simple provided you simply accepted the pattern marked out for you.

'Caterina wants everything,' her mother said slowly. 'At the moment, as soon as she's free of school, she's prepared to work in Antonia Minelli's salon in San Vicenzo. But she'll leave in the end, like Luigi, and I'll be able to do nothing about it except pray that no harm comes to her.'

Her eyes suddenly lifted from her work to stare at the girl in front of her. 'Is it enough for *you*, *cara*, to stay at Poggio?'

The question took Georgina by surprise, making her wonder whether the previous night's depression still clung to her in some way that was visible.

'The old ways *will* do for me,' she answered after a moment. 'I love Poggio just as it is and only ask for it to stay as it is. But the world around it is altering, and it must adapt in order to survive. Helping my grandfather change it to the extent that it must be changed without destroying anything precious in the process – that's going to be more than enough for me.'

Explaining it to someone else helped to clear her own mind, she decided. Last night's lowness was simply the result of weeks of hard work compounded with a new apprehension – she deeply disliked the idea of Filippo and Roberto riding against each other in the Palio. With all that finally settled, she was able to smile serenely at her father's suggestion of a walk after breakfast.

As soon as Olivia and Lucia had driven down to San Vicenzo to attend Mass, the two of them set off together, untroubled by the fact that the English passion for tramping over the countryside still gave their Italian relatives incredulous amusement. Olivia even liked to insist that her husband's first ambition as soon as he reached Heaven would be to identify some like-minded old friend with whom he could begin strolling the fields of Paradise.

Nothing was said until they'd climbed the neighbouring hill and stood looking down at the land spread out below them.

'You're looking a trifle worn down, my dear,' Richard Hadley said out of a companionable silence. 'In fact, your mother insists that you've lost too much weight. Artom's behaviour must have been a cruel blow, in more ways than one.'

'Yes, but I've come to realise that it wasn't all his fault. I simply didn't understand the man he'd become. He didn't conceal the fact that he was intensely ambitious; I just didn't see that success is the thing that matters most in his life, and that interfering in his affairs as I did held out no hope of a future together. The truth is that I was flattered – too much so to think clearly. He seemed to have been waiting for *me* when he could have taken his pick of any number of women over here.'

'Vanity, vanity, sayeth the preacher!' Richard agreed, smiling at her. 'Enrico insisted on filling me in this morning. If we'd known the size of the problem here we wouldn't have left it on your shoulders.'

'You didn't, strictly speaking. It was Adam Fleming who rang the very day you left London and told me in no uncertain terms to get myself out to Poggio.'

'Did he do that? Odd . . . He gives the impression of a self-effacing man who'd never dream of dictating to anyone else.'

'The impression's false,' she said tartly. 'He can dictate with the best of them when he feels inclined.'

Even before her father's face told her so, she knew she'd been betrayed into intemperateness again; it was the effect the professor always seemed to have on her. 'Sorry – I should be ashamed of that remark,' she admitted with some reluctance. 'We'd have been lost without his help.'

'Is that what irks you – the fact that he or anyone else was needed? Did you want to save Poggio single-handedly?'

The quiet question was typical of her father, shrewdly hitting the nail on the head, but so courteously that the hammer didn't hurt too much. She was obliged to think about what he'd said, but finally shook her head.

'I honestly don't think I mind who helps, as long as it *is* saved. My quarrel with Adam Fleming is that he misleads people. What did you call him – self-effacing? I know that it *seems* true, but everyone else here now depends on him to a quite ridiculous extent. That wouldn't matter if he was always going to be here, but the day will come when he'll walk away, leaving them to manage without him.'

She'd been careful to disclaim dependence on him herself, Richard noticed, and feared it meant that she still hadn't got Roberto Artom out of her system.

'What about you, love?' he asked. 'I know it would be late in the day for you to change your mind, but are you still content to stay here? You're scarcely approaching the sere and yellow yet, but the future has to be thought about.'

'There's no hurry.' Her gaze lingered on the landscape round them, as softly brilliant in the sunlight as the pages of some ancient illuminated manuscript. 'England seems a long way away. I shall be homesick for it now and then, I expect, just as Mama is for Italy, but I don't regret anything.'

Richard Hadley accepted what she said and reverted to the subject of his father-in-law. 'I was glad Enrico insisted on talking business this morning; it gave me the chance to ask why the hell he didn't come to me when he needed help.'

'I can guess what he said. You'd done what you could for me, and couldn't be expected to beggar yourself on *his* account.'

'Something like that, but I told him I took it amiss that he was prepared to accept help from a stranger and not from me. Of course, I now realise that Fleming is anything but a stranger.'

'Gramps particularly didn't want you to know. For one thing it would have worried Mama, of course, but the main reason is that he can't bear not to seem a success in front of you.'

'Dear, daft man! Well, with the help of someone as good as Tommaso and with capital to reinvest in the estate, the chances of avoiding failure begin to look quite good. But you have to promise me something. If Poggio *should* fail in the end I insist on knowing about it beforehand, not afterwards. Promise?'

134

She nodded her head. 'Word of a Hadley!'

'Good – then we've got that out of the way. Now I think I've got enough breath back to race you to the top of the next hill. Last one up is a sissy!'

Lunch was being laid on the terrace by the time they got back, and the meal spread in its usual Sunday fashion right across the afternoon. Georgina half listened to her father's humorous account of diplomatic life in Washington, enjoying the incongruous mixture of America described in his ultra-English voice, in a setting which could only be somewhere in the heart of Italy. Beyond the vine-shaded terrace the garden shimmered in the heat of mid-afternoon. Nothing moved except for a small summer breeze that ruffled the leaves of the olive trees. Even Maria's hens had fallen into a post-luncheon slumber, and it was left to the cicadas to provide background music to the sound of her father's quiet voice.

Across the table she watched Olivia withdraw her attention from what was being said to concentrate on the scene around her. It had to be drawn into her heart again to enable her to survive another exile. Enrico occasionally sipped the glass of wine in front of him, or smiled at something Richard had just said, while Lucia tried to conceal her astonishment that anyone could live in Washington and remain sane. Beyond the terrace the garden lay wrapped in Sunday peace; the greenness of Tuscany was all around them, and further off the hills were a lavender blue, deeper than the sky.

The end of the school term released Alessio into the glorious freedom of the summer holiday – long hot days spent out of doors with his uncle, almost from dawn until dusk unless hunger sent him and Nero indoors for refuelling. The race against time of Tommaso's first few weeks at Poggio had settled now into a less feverish cycle of work. There was always something to be done, but they could relax enough to enjoy the doing of it, and begin to think of the future. Old vines that must be grubbed out in the autumn needed to be marked, and the sites for new plantings prepared. There was no question of Tommaso not wanting to stay – this year's harvest was looked forward to, but already he and Enrico were thinking about next year's, and planning the changes to be made the year after that. Alessio listened to them talking, nodding sagely to show that he agreed, and confided to Georgina that he was happy again; the fear of leaving Poggio had shrivelled and died in the conviction that the ground was firm beneath his feet once more. Caterina had frightened him for nothing; he should have remembered that she was only a girl, unable to understand things that came naturally to men.

135

Georgina accepted the solemn pronouncement without surprise. Tuscan male chauvinism was alive and well, and Alessio would grow up as convinced as her grandfather that women were delightful and necessary in their way, but better excluded from the running of serious things.

'I don't see much of Caterina these days,' she remarked next, watching Alessio obligingly scratch the spot on Nero's back that he couldn't quite reach himself. 'Does she like working for Signora Minelli?'

'She likes not having to go to school any more. Two weeks working there and she talks as if she runs the place. She wishes she did; it's old-fashioned, apparently. Everything should be coloured black and white instead of pink, according to Caterina's magazines. I can't see that it matters what colour towel she ties round a lady's neck. Still, it gives her something to think about instead of mooning over Adam. We don't see much of *him* now, because he has to work on his book. But come and look at Florence, anyway.'

She knew what she was being invited to inspect – the model of fifteenth-century Florence that he was constructing with the professor's help. Buildings that he could still see virtually unchanged in his own visits to the city were being lovingly fashioned out of cardboard, painted, and then assembled on the large sheet of hardboard that Adam had got for him. Caterina had been inveigled into the project as well, her job being to dress the figures who peopled the streets, in the scraps of silk and satin that Lucia unearthed from her sewing bag.

It was an imaginative way to teach them the history of their own inheritance, and one day when Adam had been persuaded to lunch with them Georgina told him so.

'It's a Pizzone heirloom in the making. One day Alessio will let *his* children play with it as a special treat, and he'll tell them all over again about the summer when a famous English professor came to stay at Poggio!'

Adam smilingly waved that aside. 'I think he'll forget about the English professor sooner than I shall be able to forget Poggio.'

She found herself believing what he said, and suddenly there was no difficulty in acknowledging the extent to which they were in his debt; it was hard, now, to know why she hadn't been able to do it before.

'Even apart from repaying Roberto's loan, you've done a great deal for us,' she said abruptly. 'I'm afraid I may not always have seemed appreciative enough.'

His mouth twitched at the understatement, but he resisted the temptation to say that she'd never seemed appreciative at all. Careful not to look at him, she went on with the job of making amends.

'Poggio seems to have rather taken you over – I hope the book hasn't suffered too much as a result.' She didn't mention that she knew what late hours he kept, because when she went to bed at night the lamp was always burning in his window across the garden. It would be something else to miss, glowing in the darkness, when he went away.

'The book's a bit behind schedule, but nothing I can't make up by keeping my nose to the grindstone from now on. The *vendemmia*'s going to be a fearful temptation, though!'

'You must forget about us and concentrate on what's important for you. I doubt if your publishers would think Alessio's history lessons very important in the scheme of things.'

'I don't much care *what* they think. Provided I deliver the manuscript on time, I'm free to cling to my own priorities. Poggio's important, and so is Alessio.'

A flicker of something like pain disturbed her brown face, and he was almost certain that she was still remembering Roberto Artom – a man whose view of what was important hadn't coincided with her own.

'It's a good yardstick,' she agreed slowly, 'what people regard as important. Perhaps another one is what strikes them as funny.'

Adam nodded. 'Find a man and a woman who share both and you have the basis for a perfect marriage.'

She wondered if he'd once had one himself that was less than perfect. Did it explain why the woman Caterina had told her about was in England instead of taking care of him here? If she was free to come, she *ought* to be here, for his sake and everybody else's.

'Your parents struck me as having got the combination right, even though it must be especially hard to make a mixed marriage work,' he said thoughtfully.

'They've certainly needed to laugh at the same things. Imagine being cooped up together in Brazzaville or Bogotá without a shared sense of humour!'

'What will happen to your parents in the end? Will they retire to "England, home, and beauty"? I couldn't help noticing how your mother blossomed in the short time she was here. She's very striking anyway, of course, but on the night of Lucia's party happiness made her wonderfully beautiful.'

Georgina smiled over a shaft of pain that took her by surprise. New twist to an old story, surely, if a daughter were stupid enough to discover that she was jealous of her own mother! It wasn't the case, of course – she was just surprised that even Olivia had made such an impression on the professor.

'I think my parents will come back here eventually,' she answered at last. 'My father looks and sounds like everybody's idea of the perfect Englishman, but he's very adaptable. Mama's trailed around the world with him for years; when he retires he thinks it will be her turn to choose, and there's no doubt she'll choose Poggio.'

'Where would that leave you? Free to resume your own life somewhere else? Will the pull on your mother's heart-strings work in reverse for you?' He added a quiet afterthought after a glance at her face. 'Sorry – it's a silly question when you've committed yourself here so thoroughly.'

She took her time about answering. 'The question isn't silly, but I can't answer it. The odd thing is that, much as I love Poggio, I still feel English, not Italian, and I doubt if that will change however long I stay. So perhaps I'll go back one day, and hope that my dear William will be able to find me a job again.' She spoke her friend's name with so much nostalgic affection that Adam wondered whether he'd misread her recent sadness. Perhaps she wasn't even sure herself which of them she missed most – Roberto or William.

He wouldn't have asked, but Enrico came up then to interrupt the conversation.

'Adam, I know you're making up for lost time, but leave your work just for tomorrow morning. I promised Alessio I wouldn't start the tasting without him, but now that he's finished school I can make a beginning.'

It wasn't an invitation to be refused. Next morning, with Nero lassoed to a tree and protesting loudly, outside work was abandoned while they moved into the cool gloom of the *cantina*. Tall oak casks ranged along the walls contained the wine maturing from previous vintages; once bottled, it would be ready to sell, but the timing was critical. Bottled too soon, the wine wouldn't have reached its maximum quality; left longer in the cask than its quality merited, it would lose colour and richness, and finally emerge hardly worth drinking at all. Enrico had to be the judge of each year's quality and of the length of time it could be left to mature in the casks. The time-honoured ritual of testing was well known but never lost its fascination. A bamboo spigot was inserted into each cask in turn, and the sample withdrawn was smelled for bouquet, examined for colour, held up to the light for clearness, and finally tasted for its quality.

The whole performance was enthralling, but Adam found himself watching the actors more than the play. Enrico revelled in his role at the centre of the drama and added an extra flourish or two for the benefit of the audience. Tommaso was quietly absorbed in what was going on, and Alessio's gaze was riveted on the *padrone*. Just so would *he* be judging the wine one day, with the same air of a magician performing some trick of which he alone knew the secret. Poggio's eventual fate might still be uncertain, but looking at them wrapped up in what was going on, Adam had no doubt that he'd been right to get involved in its survival. Let Artom build his shiny villas if he must, but not here at Poggio.

Having settled the details of the loan to Enrico, he wasted no more time thinking about it, and hoped that no one else did either. He knew that both Maria and Tommaso had been entrusted with some knowledge of Poggio's affairs and it was inevitable that what they talked about the children would overhear; but for the sake of Enrico's self-esteem, he hoped that the existence of the loan wasn't common knowledge in San Vicenzo.

Caterina was surprised to discover that Signora Artom visited the small town occasionally; she wasn't a regular client of the Minelli salon, of course, but now and then she called in when she hadn't time to drive into Florence. She noticed the new apprentice and took the trouble to speak kindly to her about beginning a career. Caterina was flattered, and hoped her colleagues had noticed.

A few evenings later she hoped even more that they noticed a long white Alfa Romeo come to a stop outside as she left the salon.

'A lift, Caterina? I'm going your way.' She'd never been at ease with Signor Roberto but it was a triumph all the same.

'Out in the big world at last, I see.' His eyes flicked over her as she climbed in, noting the first small attempts at sophistication.

Signora Minelli wasn't within hearing and she could be honest. 'Not very big yet, but I have to start somewhere.'

'True! I don't suppose you can wait to get away from Poggio. It's a dead-end place for a girl like you. Sad, all the same, to see it going downhill.'

His calm certainty suggested that he knew what was going on; she didn't know whether to agree or argue with him, but he changed the subject before she could make up her mind.

'Is the peculiar Englishman still there, or has he gone back to his own dismal island now?'

Roberto's contempt for Poggio was bearable; his scorn of the professor was not. Caterina swelled with the pride of being able to correct him. 'He's still there, Mamma calls him our saviour.'

'Because he pays a little rent for his apartment? It will take more than that, *cara*, to save Poggio.'

'Not because of that.' She couldn't be precise but she could be emphatic. 'Adam has done something marvellous. I don't know quite what, but Mamma says he's given the *padrone* an enormous sum of money.' Her hands sketched a towering heap that imagination could hardly encompass, and only in the act of saying the words did she remember that Adam had been angry when she'd talked about him owning Poggio; but it was too late now, and in any case something told her that for once she'd made an impression on a man who'd never bothered to take much notice of her before.

'My apologies. I didn't know the professor had it in him to do such heroic deeds!'

She couldn't identify what lay behind the compliment, but it had sounded not like a compliment at all, and she suddenly wished that she hadn't been tempted into saying the little she knew. It was a relief when he stopped the car at the bottom of the drive and let her get out. Then he turned and drove back the way they'd come, and she wondered why he'd changed his mind about where he was going.

Adam was at his window, and waved as she walked past. She saw very little of him now that she was in San Vicenzo all day, and even at weekends he was either writing at his desk or in some library or other, deciphering archives written in Latin or fifteenth-century Italian. She thought in her heart of hearts that it was a strange way for a man to spend his time, locked in the past; surely it was the present that mattered. But he always smiled and shook his head when she told him so.

Adam was in Siena one evening, as he often was, when he had the unnerving impression that he was being watched. It must be the strain of weeks of concentrated work, he told himself, on top of which something had to be allowed for the melodramatic effect of a town whose alley-ways were still medieval. A plate of spaghetti at his favourite restaurant in the Campo would make up for a missed lunch and restore his overactive imagination to its proper place again. He was waiting for the food to arrive, and looking at the silhouette of the Palazzo Pubblico against an evening sky when someone pulled out a chair and sat down opposite him.

'*Buona sera, Signor Professore*. The research goes well, I trust?'

'Kind of you to ask – extremely well.' It was said courteously, but the tone was not encouraging.

Roberto persevered. 'Better than Poggio's affairs in that case.'

'About those I'm not qualified to comment,' Adam said gently. 'All I can tell you is that the estate seems to be a hive of happy industry.'

'You must hope that it's not only happy but profitable.'

'Don't we all hope so? Such effort certainly deserves the reward of success.'

Georgina could have explained that it was a typical example of the well-known Oxford style. Not knowing it, Roberto was conscious of trying to find a foothold on a surface of polished steel.

'Shall we not beat about the bush, Professor? Siena's a small place and I happen to have a lot of influence in it. I know the exact extent of your interest in a bankrupt estate.'

Adam's face showed nothing but a mild curiosity, 'How? By bribing some wretchedly underpaid bank clerk to give away information he should keep to himself?'

Roberto smiled. 'The clerk kindly confirmed some details, but your little admirer, Caterina Pizzone, gave the game away. I should never have thought it of *you*, but she couldn't resist telling me that you were Poggio's . . . er, "saviour", I think was the word she used! I hope you don't end up losing your money.'

He was rewarded with a sweet smile over the rim of his opponent's glass. 'What I suspect you mean is that you hope I *do*!'

'To be strictly truthful, I shouldn't shed any tears on your behalf. Your interference has been irritating. But I'll give you a friendly tip all the same. Don't waste any more of your money betting on Filippo Casali's chances of winning the Palio. I can tell you now that I shall beat him.'

'More bribery?' Adam enquired. This time their eyes met with the inimical kiss of sword-blades clashing. Roberto disengaged first, stood up, and then pushed back his chair.

'*Buon appetito, Professore!*'

Left alone, Adam discovered that he now felt slightly sick instead of hungry, but he forced himself to eat the food the waiter put in front of him and drink the small carafe of wine. The effect of a day spent absorbing the power struggles of Renaissance nobles could be discounted, but the fact remained that he was in a country where modernity was still only skin-deep. Vendettas were alive and well, and the philosophy of 'vengeance is mine, sayeth the Lord' had never greatly appealed to Italians, who still preferred the satisfaction of settling their own scores. He walked back through the dark, narrow streets, irritated to find that his breathing was faster than usual. Imagination was all very well in a writer of fiction, but it wasn't supposed to get out of hand in a staid historian. He found the MG where he'd left it that morning, climbed in unmolested, and drove away feeling rather foolish.

Chapter 14

He drove home more slowly than usual because a sudden shower of rain had made the road surface greasy, but an empty stretch tempted him to speed up. Then, immediately, there was a heart-stopping explosion. The car swerved for no apparent reason like a frightened colt, and he could do nothing to stop it slewing across the road, nine-tenths out of control. He tensed himself for the inevitable somersault that it was bound to take into the deep ditch bordering the road. The somersault didn't come, but he ricocheted instead off a gate-post and hurtled unevenly into a field of sunflowers. They were already growing tall, and in the sudden quietness his disordered imagination suggested that their faces peered at him through the windows of the car, enquiring what he was doing there. After a moment when it seemed impossible to do anything at all, he climbed out and saw how he'd been saved. God's mercy had provided a grassy track bridging the ditch between the road and the field, and the MG's drunken swerve had carried her neatly across it. The side of his face was beginning to throb, reminding him that his head had connected with the windowframe when the car hit the post. One of its wings was very dented, but otherwise he could see nothing wrong except the blown tyre that had sent it plunging off the road. He told the MG that she'd behaved like a perfect lady, then set off to walk to the village he'd passed a mile or so back. With the Fates continuing to watch over him, it boasted not only a garage but a young proprietor eager to be helpful, who clucked sympathetically over the grazed bruise beginning to show itself on his face. Within half an hour they and the car were back in the garage, and the mechanic was staring at the off-side front wheel.

'That tyre didn't burst on its own, signore. It's been slashed. Look! You can see the clean stroke of the knife. Holy Mother of God, what a world we live in when you can't even park a car in the middle of Siena without it being vandalised.'

Confronted by the tyre, Adam wondered what else was likely to have given way at some crucial moment when he was driving along. 'If I leave it here can you give it a thorough check, as well as do something about the dent?'

'But, of course! It would be a pleasure. She's a *carina* little piece of motor car.' Her wounded flank received a tender pat, and it was obvious that she was being left in appreciative hands.

Adam handed over the keys and hitched a lift to San Vicenzo from the next car that stopped for petrol. It wasn't until he was set down and starting on the long climb up the hill to Poggio that he was free to think again about his conversation with Roberto in the restaurant. There wasn't a shred of proof that the slashing of the tyre had been organised, but it was surely in character that Artom would have wanted it known that a man who thwarted him didn't go unpunished. It might have been intended only as an inconvenience or a scare, but it would have been easy enough to have killed someone else in an oncoming car if the tyre hadn't blown on an empty road. Relief outweighed anger for the moment and made him light-headed. He had the night and the hillside to himself, and he might have been dead by now; instead he had the pleasure of a peaceful, starlit walk. He quite felt like bursting into song.

Georgina was letting herself out of one of the estate cottages when she heard a light tenor voice carolling Gilbert and Sullivan on the track further down the hill.

> There's a fascination frantic in a ruin that's romantic.
> Do you think you are sufficiently decayed?

The voice could belong to only one man, but even when the starlight showed her the shadowy figure of the professor rounding a bend in the lane, she could scarcely believe that she wasn't dreaming. Then he caught sight of her standing there and hastily abandoned his second verse.

'I used to be able to remember reams of it, but now it only comes back in snatches,' he said apologetically. 'I'd have chosen something more appropriate if I'd known you were going to be there.'

She'd never seen him anything but completely sober, even in the face of Enrico's formidable hospitality, but a note of reckless gaiety in his voice hinted that tonight discretion had been thrown to the winds. She was sure of it a moment later when he reached her and took hold of her hand.

'Leave it where it is,' he said sternly when she tried to pull herself free. 'Poggio looks its beautifully peaceful self, but there are villains lurking everywhere.'

It was said with such ponderous gravity that she grinned in spite of herself. 'I'm ashamed of you, Professor. You've been led astray! Thank goodness you had enough sense to leave your car somewhere and walk home.'

It had the effect of making him laugh, but she was aware that what she heard was a chuckle of real amusement, not the senseless giggle of a man less than entirely sober.

'Georgina mine, you're a treasure! I'm light-headed with relief, as a matter of fact, not drunk on alcohol. That's why I was singing so blithely. A slight contretemps on the way home from Siena landed me in a sunflower field, right side up, but with a burst tyre. The car's with a helpful young man at a garage somewhere between here and Castellina.'

She wasn't his Georgina and might have told him so except that her mouth had gone dry with fear, making it difficult to say anything at all.

'You might have been killed,' she managed to mutter at last.

'I might have killed someone else,' he said with a sudden change of tone, 'but it didn't happen, so we won't lose any sleep over it.'

At the point where the drive divided he released her hand, but found her still walking beside him in the direction of the farmhouse.

'You live over there,' he pointed out.

'I know I do, but I've been listening to old Signora Galleani all evening and it's thirsty work. If by any chance you were going to make yourself some coffee, I thought you might offer me a cup.'

'Shameless wench! Very well, one cup of coffee; then I shall resist temptation and escort you home.'

The professor was definitely not himself this evening, but it wasn't until they were inside and the lamps were lit that she saw why. Blood had dried darkly on his hair and temple, and a livid bruise ran from it down to his jawbone. Grey eyes overbright in the pallor of his face spoke of some tension that didn't match his light-hearted behaviour.

'I think it's time you told me what really happened this evening,' she suggested quietly.

He was tempted to lie, but Roberto's conversation had seemed to include a warning that needed passing on.

'The burst tyre was true,' he said slowly. 'What I didn't mention was that, according to the garage mechanic, it didn't happen accidentally . . . the tyre was deliberately slashed.'

She said nothing for a moment, staring at him with huge, troubled eyes. Then she turned and walked out of the room, and returned a moment later with a cloth and a bowl of warm water. Only when she'd gestured him to a seat at the table, and her hands were gently swabbing his face, did she manage to find something to say.

'It could have been anyone,' she insisted almost desperately. 'There are mad, wicked people about . . . sick people . . . even here.' Adam hesitated over how to answer and she read the expression on his battered face. 'You think Roberto is responsible – why should he be? He knows nothing about your loan.'

'He knows everything about it, I'm afraid – he was kind enough to explain that to me this evening. Caterina unwittingly put him on the right track, and he bribed some unfortunate bank clerk to confirm it for him. He told me so when I was at the *ristorante*, eating my supper.'

'And what happens next, when he discovers that he didn't succeed in getting you killed this evening?' Her voice barely trembled, but Adam's hand covered her own for a moment.

'Nothing happens next. Roberto's not stupid enough to repeat himself. I've been made to feel his displeasure, that's all. Now he regards the honours as even. There's one other thing, though. He warned me not to bet on your cousin at the Palio because he intends to win himself. I don't know what the rules technically allow in the way of tactics, or what the riders can get away with unofficially; but your cousin must be told to keep as far away from him as possible.'

'I've tried to warn Filippo already, because the idea of them competing in the same race has bothered me all along. He thought I was being merely female and hysterical, but now I shall talk to him again.'

She emptied the bowl of water and then occupied herself with making coffee. Sitting down again, she put her hands round the hot mug for comfort, and went slowly on. 'I suppose I'm not surprised about what happened this evening. I always had the feeling that Roberto wouldn't take defeat lying down; it's not how he's made. You may prefer to think that he'll behave like a gent from now on, but I don't have your confidence in him. Will you please go home and forget about my family? We shan't work any the less hard without you here; in fact, we'll work all the harder to ensure that you *don't* lose your investment. Just go back to England and finish your book there.'

She suddenly found that she'd managed to upset the man in front of her more seriously than he'd been disturbed by the other events of the evening.

'I warned you once before of the danger of suggesting that my only concern is to collect a profit from my investment. If you ever hint at such a thing again I shall forget myself enough to give you a sound beating.

Does that make things sufficiently clear?'

She was torn, unable to decide whether to burst into tears or hysterical laughter. Unable to decide, she finally nodded instead and heard Adam speak again.

'The only other thing to settle before we forget this little episode is the fact that Caterina mustn't know the reason for it. As far as she's concerned, the tyre simply burst and I banged my head. The same story must also stand for Enrico and Lucia.'

She nodded, without looking at him, aware of something gathering strength inside her, like a wave glimpsed far out to sea that was readying itself for an engulfing rush upon the shore. The upheaval beginning inside her had the same inevitability, and when the moment of engulfment came she would be equally powerless to resist it. The silence in the quiet room seemed beyond breaking because there was nothing she could safely find to say. Adam stared at her hanging head, only wishing with all his heart that they hadn't always been at such cross-purposes with each other. The lamplight made a nimbus round her hair and he wanted to stretch out his hand and touch the silkiness of it.

'I'm sorry,' he said abruptly. 'What you said just now was meant for my own good and I took it amiss as usual. But even if I wanted to go home, which I don't, it isn't as easy as you might suppose. My house is let to a visiting American academic until the end of the summer, and we're not supposed to hang around during sabbaticals in any case, getting under the feet of the people left behind. But if you're going to let the thought of Roberto keep you awake from now until I leave, I'll find somewhere else to hang my hat.'

'Do whatever you like,' Georgina managed to murmur. 'It's nothing that really concerns me.'

Her eyes met his across the table, denying what she'd just said, and something hung in the balance, quivered in the air between them. But before he could decide what to do about it, she'd turned towards the door. 'It's time I went home.'

'Yes,' he agreed flatly. 'Are you ready for the long trek across the lawn?'

He found it easier to explain his accident than he'd feared; Enrico didn't question the version given to him, and Lucia, knowing nothing about tyres, calmly accepted the idea that they could disintegrate. She was still reliving the pleasure of Olivia's visit, and happy to think that the birthday party would have informed the entire district of her granddaughter's presence at Poggio. Even without Filippo's intention of involving Georgina in whatever went on in Siena, there was less likelihood, now, that she would be lonely. Paolo and his family had become, with years of living in Rome, a little too sophisticated for Lucia's taste, but they were kin when all was said, and though friends were good, family was better. At weekends, now, she could count on one or other of them dropping in, knowing that the more relatives Enrico could cluster round his dinner-table, the happier he became. Georgina seemed glad to be absorbed into her cousins' circle of friends, although she explained with inward amusement to Lucia that part of her attractiveness for them lay in being half English and consequently '*un po' diverso*'; her novelty would wear off, but for the moment she was greatly in demand.

One day, with her grandfather's permission, she gave Filippo a fuller account of what had been happening at Poggio, in order to be sure that he would take her next warning about the Palio seriously. She even mentioned Adam's mishap with the car, but added the severe rider that her grandparents weren't to know about it, and nor was he to repeat what she'd said to half Siena, Filippo sounded indignant.

'Georgina, darling, how can you suggest such a thing? I'm a walking safe-deposit of other people's secrets. They don't call me close-lipped Casali for nothing!'

Beneath the surface fun she saw that she'd offended him and hastily begged pardon. 'Of course, professional pride; I should have remembered. Now tell me about the race – is it certain that you're going to ride, and, if so, have you got a chance?'

'Yes to the first question: the Ostrich have agreed that I'm to be their jockey. The answer to the second question largely depends on the draw for the horses. With a halfway reasonable one we have a hope of winning, but no hope at all if what we get is a spavined beast gone in the wind!'

He was all set to get her lost in a welter of equine technicalities, but she refused to be diverted from the matter in hand. 'You'll think I'm obsessed about Roberto, willing to see Artom manipulations everywhere, but do you suppose his supporters could find some means of rigging the draw for the horses?'

Filippo took the question seriously for once, being aware that his charming cousin had not only been hurt by Roberto Artom, but also deeply shocked by what she was discovering about him.

'You're not obsessed,' he told her gently, 'but you're letting anxiety get the better of you, *cara*. I doubt if anyone *could* rig the draw, and although the Palio isn't what you'd call a gentlemanly race, there are certain rules that everyone has to abide by – so stop worrying!'

'Then I won't say another word,' she promised him with a rueful smile.

It was one thing to promise, another to reason away the sense of dread that grew in her as the beginning of July approached, and the first running of the race in honour of Maria Santissima in Provenzano. But the complicated preliminaries came and went without disaster, the horses were drawn, and Filippo reported jubilantly that the Ostrich *contrada* had got a good one. The eliminating heats were run, and then the usual Masses were said, with the horses themselves persuaded with the usual difficulty to go inside their *contrada* churches to receive divine blessing.

Then on the morning of the Palio itself, after a day or two of feeling unwell, Lucia awoke with a throat infection uncomfortable enough to keep her at home. Georgina ignored her plea that no one else should miss the race on her account, and confessed that she was ready to seize any excuse not to go to Siena. Enrico was to go with Tommaso who, having watched his last race ten years ago, was determined not to miss this one. The children tossed a coin for which of them should occupy the passenger seat in Adam's MG, now repaired and restored to him. Alessio lost, and Georgina watched his sister being installed there instead. She was wearing her sunflower skirt, there were yellow flowers in her hair, and joy illumined her. Present happiness might never again seem quite enough to wipe away any past or future woe, but just for this once it was. If she gave a thought to the woman in England, that country was far away; *she*, Caterina, was going to the Palio with Adam.

After they'd driven away Georgina found that her own mind was full of the woman who, for one reason or another, hadn't come to Italy with him. Either she was kept at home by commitments she couldn't avoid, or she was very confident that, because of her, he would never be anything more than impersonally kind to other women. There was even a third possibility of course. Maybe she'd simply been defeated by some self-sufficiency that protected him from needing other people in the way that they seemed to need him. Lost in this last thought, Georgina wasn't even aware that she was being anxiously stared at by her grandmother.

'*Tesoro*, your mouth smiles, but sometimes your eyes are sad, and that worries me. I'm afraid you're missing London. Your work at Kew meant a lot to you and you've had to give up friends there like William Bird.'

Georgina knew that there would be no comfort for her grandmother in a lie, even if she could have offered one. 'Dear Gran, you're being very tactful,' she said instead, 'not to mention that I came a bit of a cropper over Roberto as well. I think I've got that sorted out now, and I shall feel better still when I've been back to London and cleared out the flat. As a matter of fact I was going to ask if I could move into the farmhouse when Adam leaves. I'd bring my books and suchlike things back from London and feel settled again.'

'Of course,' Lucia agreed immediately. 'Somewhere of your own where you can be independent of us and entertain your friends. I should have thought of it myself.' She looked distressed at the oversight, and Georgina had to comfort her with a kiss, and a little teasing.

'The truth is, of course, that you can't bear to think of saying goodbye to the professor! You'll manage it when the time comes, but we shall have a very distraught teenager on our hands. Caterina went off to Siena with him looking as if her cup of happiness had overflowed. She'd even managed to forget that he's not heartwhole and fancy-free after all – there's someone in England, apparently, who matters a great deal. She'd have done us all a kindness by not letting him come here alone.'

Lucia nodded, wishing as well that she knew her granddaughter's state of heart and mind better than she did. When unobserved the girl looked sad. When she was being watched, she clothed herself in a bright, brittle gaiety that was enjoyed by Filippo and his friends but didn't, for Lucia, hide the loneliness underneath. Asking more than she already had was out of the question, though, and she turned the conversation away to local matters until the rest of the household returned from Siena. It was obvious at a glance that Filippo's horse certainly hadn't won. The children looked disappointed and Enrico was red-faced and angry.

'It was a bad race,' he said heavily. 'A thoroughly badly run race – arranged beforehand, of course, that Filippo should be boxed in. He did very well to get himself out of it, but he couldn't make up the lost ground.'

'Yes, but is he all right?' Georgina demanded anxiously.

'A bit bruised, I should imagine, but he would expect that; nothing broken.'

'Well, I hope that's the end of Casali participation in the Palio.'

Enrico stared at her. 'How can it be? There's the second running of the race in August. If the Ostrich horse is lucky enough to be drawn next time Filippo will ride again. I'm telling you, child, that he did very well!'

Lucia intervened. 'You still haven't told us who did win.'

'Artom, of course.'

No one felt inclined to pursue the subject after that, and Georgina had to wait to hear the details from Filippo himself. She found that he had an ungrudging admiration for the man who had beaten him.

'Gramps said you were boxed in deliberately.'

'One looks for excuses,' Filippo said honestly. 'The truth is that Roberto's a brilliant rider; professional standard, and absolutely fearless. Still, I've got the hang of it better now, so tell Maria to pray her hardest for the next draw! We've got to have another chance at it, and next time, dearest cousin, I shall expect *you* to be there, cheering the Ostrich on!'

'I hate the thought of it, but if you can bear to ride I suppose that I can bear to watch. Next time I've no doubt that we shall *all* be there.'

She had no chance to ask the professor what he'd thought of the race because he nowadays seemed to make a point of avoiding her. It was true that he was hard at work on his book, but she suspected him of wanting to forget the strange episode of his night walk because he was aware of having been shaken out of his usual behaviour, and still regretted it; Lucia's invitations to join in their meals on the terrace were even refused on the grounds that he could eat while he was working. But one morning Georgina caught him cleaning the car, and short of crawling underneath it he had to stay and speak to her.

'No more problems with this?' she asked, pointing to the MG.

'As good as new, thanks to my garage friend.'

'And you now park somewhere in Siena where an easily recognised English car doesn't leap to the eye?'

'I hide it under a toadstool,' he confirmed gravely.

She smiled but the smile didn't dispel the anxiety in her eyes, and he was conscious again of the extent to which she'd changed since coming to Poggio. Surface indifference had gone, along with surface sophistication. He could do nothing about whatever else disturbed her peace of mind, but he *could* refuse to add himself to the list of things she worried about.

'You agonise altogether too much. I had occasion to mention it once before.' It sounded ungratefully stiff, and he wasn't surprised when she retreated behind a practised smile.

'We can't help feeling responsible. It gives us a bad name when our tenants get roughed up by the local brand of Mafia!' That made clear enough, she thought, what he was to understand – her concern had nothing personal in it; she was concerned only with Poggio's good name.

'Don't worry; I shall speak only good of this place, which I find delightful in every way.' He was polishing the bonnet of the car and it seemed safe to look at him. 'Quite delightful,' he insisted gently, and now she found that he wasn't looking at the car at all but at her, and the grey eyes she'd once thought cold and colourless were warm with amusement. It was hard – harder than she'd have believed possible – to nod and walk carelessly away; but she managed it by concentrating on another thought.

151

Roberto's opinion of the professor had been made plain – he didn't even propose to take the man seriously. But if the rest of his judgements were as wide of the mark as that, his business success was something to marvel at.

Chapter 15

The days got steadily hotter, provoking thunderstorms which brought needed rain but also the risk of damage to the grapes that were now becoming well formed. Enrico and Tommaso prowled up and down, almost talking the vines into flourishing, but Georgina's own dearest concern was for the olive trees. She found them more interesting and much more beautiful, contorted by generations of succeeding winters into strange and lovely shapes. A hundred years each to grow, to flourish, and finally to die, the old adage went, and she was fascinated by this slowly changing cycle of life and death. Alessio's children, and their children in turn, would nurture these trees and learn how to pick the olives – always in the direction in which the fruit grew so that the brittle twigs wouldn't be damaged. They would gather them by hand, and process them by hand – laboriously, it was true, but it was the time-honoured way to make Poggio's famous extra-virgin oil from the first cold pressing. She knew that the year's crop wouldn't be heavy because so much frost-killed wood had had to be pruned away, but still there would be some beautiful green oil. And there was always next year to look forward to. It was the age-old incantation offered up by everyone concerned with growing things: this year might be bad, but there was no harm in expecting that next year would be different!

August was upon them too quickly for her liking, and either Maria's prayers or the luck of the draw saw to it that Filippo was to ride the Ostrich *contrada*'s horse again. His father reserved an entire row of seats, and there wasn't the slightest excuse for them not to go as a family to watch this second and last running of the race. Even Maria, seized by the importance of the occasion, agreed to forsake her kitchen for once and appeared in the Sunday clothes she normally reserved for going to Mass.

They took their seats in the stand, grateful for a slight breeze that tempered the fierce late-afternoon heat. Siena was letting itself go with flags flying, Il Santo's bell being tolled in the Mangia Tower, and drums and trumpets keeping up an almost continuous fanfare. The entire population of the town, as well as thousands of dazzled visitors, seemed

153

to be jammed around the rim of the Campo or packed into the middle of the square. The processions went their leisurely way – they'd been seen a hundred times before, but were still as colourful as the first time. The *alfieri* – young men representing each *contrada* – wore their medieval costumes as if slashed crimson velvet, hooped black and white silk, or sky-blue satin were what they dressed in every day. They twirled their heavy, long-handled flags in the traditional displays of *sbandierata* and, in a final flurry of bravado, tossed them high in the air for each other to catch. The drums' insistent tattoo grew in intensity, and garlanded pages who could have stepped out of some illuminated missal finally appeared, walking gravely in front of the *carroccio*, drawn by four of the great white oxen of Tuscany. From its mast fluttered the Palio itself – the silken banner of the Virgin for which the race was run.

By the time the processions had brought in all the competing teams, and they and countless dignitaries were settled on the dais against the walls of the Palazzo Pubblico like rows of brightly coloured flowers, the huge crowd had settled down to anticipate the real excitement of the evening. The spectacle so far had been delightful, all part of a twice-yearly event that made Siena different from anywhere else on earth, but the race was what they'd really come to see. They were accustomed to waiting, and there were friends to wave to and forecasts of victory to be argued over; the usual last-minute delays only sharpened anticipation to fever-pitch. Georgina didn't identify the moment when anticipation began to be coloured by impatience, but at last a flicker of dissatisfaction caught and ran like a strengthening flame along the rows. Hitches were permissible, but not this too-prolonged wait for the race to begin.

Something finally did happen, but it only affected the Casali row. A man made his way to where Paolo sat and whispered in his ear. Paolo muttered something to Adam Fleming, sitting beside him, and the two of them got up and walked away. Now rumour was ready to ignite: one of the jockeys had failed to appear. The fragment of news was spreading like a forest fire – checked momentarily here, leaping over a gap to reappear somewhere else, but always gathering momentum through the crowd.

Paolo and Adam didn't return, the race still didn't start, and consternation began to seep through the ranks of the family. It was the unpardonable sin, to be chosen to represent a *contrada* and then fail to appear. Filippo's absence would leave family pride in the dust, and it seemed clear that public humiliation was just around the corner. Georgina thought of her laughing, light-hearted cousin – not the sort of man to be overcome by an attack of nerves, but she couldn't blame him if a repetition of July's ordeal had suddenly seemed more than he could bear.

The crowds were beginning to show signs of real disgruntlement, and the sky was beginning to darken. A race that was dangerous enough in full daylight would be murderous in the dusk, and the officials must soon decide whether the race should be run or cancelled. Then, at last, as signs of action appeared, the mood of the audience immediately changed from restiveness to excitement again, and cheers and clapping began to echo round the square. The horses were being brought in, jostling and rearing even more than usual, as if the delay had unsettled them as well. Georgina counted nine and felt like fainting with relief; Filippo must have arrived after all. The tenth horse, known as the *rincorsa*, would be galloped in at the beginning of the race, simply to galvanise the others behind the rope into wanting to run.

The starting-point was just below the Casali row of seats, and a little to the right. The jockeys had arrived there now, and were struggling to get their steeds into something that might be called a starting-line. She could easily make out the gold and white silk of the Ostrich jockey's colours. Behind it, kicking and rearing, was a horse whose rider was wearing the old rose and green of the Centipede – Roberto's black mount, doing its best to get alongside the Ostrich grey.

'Look out, Filippo . . . behind you.' The words were torn out of her uselessly; in the roar beginning to echo round the Campo there wasn't the faintest chance that they could be heard. But the jockey in gold and white glanced up at the Casali stand all the same and his whip touched his hat in a brief salute; but it wasn't the face of Filippo that just for a moment was looking at them.

The world swung upside down, went dark, and Georgina ducked her head on her knees in a desperate determination not to faint.

'*Tesoro*, are you ill?' Lucia's anxious whisper penetrated the fog and made her lift her head.

She wiped away the perspiration that she could feel wet on her forehead and tried to smile at her grandmother. 'It's too hot. I felt a bit faint – that's all.'

Lucia's hand tucked itself inside her own cold one. 'Am I going mad or is it Adam down there?'

Georgina stared at Roberto's horse, now making a spirited attempt to kick the Ostrich horse to death before the race had even started.

'That's the professor,' she agreed too brightly. 'He probably thinks he's about to take part in some gentlemanly point-to-point at home—' She had to stop abruptly, free hand clamped against her mouth, swallowing the nausea she could feel rising in her throat.

A moment later the stewards abandoned hope of persuading two horses that preferred to stay and bite each other to join the race; the *rincorsa* was set free; the rope jerked up. The Palio had begun.

At the end of the first circuit of the Campo one horse had fallen and another was riderless; the two that had been left behind were now enthusiastically storming into the back of an untidy bunch fighting its way up the slope on the northern side of the square. Georgina watched in a state of frozen calm, unaware of Maria beside her, head now buried in her hands, of Caterina praying out loud, and Enrico standing on his chair, lost to everything but the need to shout encouragement to the Ostrich. Only pure rage prevented her from imitating any one of them. No one should be so madly insane as Adam Fleming. Foolhardiness of *this* immensity simply wasn't forgivable, and God must protect him at least long enough for her to tell him so. Her hand clutched Lucia's when his horse stumbled, but recovered itself as if the man on its back had lifted it bodily, and then hurtled past them at the start of the second lap.

Mindful of Filippo's experience in the first running of the race, Adam had been at pains to keep on the outside. But the Centipede horse had now been edged alongside him, deliberately pushing him near the barriers that blocked off the most dangerous of the alley-ways leading out of the square. The two horses were much too close together. Georgina heard Enrico's roar in her ear: 'That *mascalzone*'s trying to unseat him!' She closed her eyes but found it more unbearable that way; whatever was to happen there was nothing she could do but watch. When she looked again, Adam was still there. He'd lost his whip, but by some miracle man and horse were still together.

By the time they were into the third and last lap Siena had gone wild with excitement. The Hare *contrada*'s horse cannoned into the padded barrier meant to discourage it from bolting down the Via San Martino, and unseated the rider next to it as well. The riderless horse almost immediately proved the undoing of a jockey in buttercup and pale blue, and now there were effectively only two contestants left in the race. Forgetting to breathe, she watched Roberto edge his horse close to Adam's again. His whip arm came up, slightly mistimed the blow, and caught not only his opponent's shoulder as intended – which was nearly allowed – but the flank of his horse as well, which was not. The effect was to send it forward in a demented leap that all but unseated its rider. Completely deaf now to the uproar all around her, Georgina waited for Roberto's next blow to immobilise the only man who could prevent him from winning the Palio outright. But Adam's horse wasn't to be caught again. Still smarting from the cut of the whip, it went up the hill at a finishing speed that would have done credit to a Derby winner.

The race was over, and the gold and white banners in the crowd waved triumphantly to Heaven. Nothing they said to each other could be heard, but they were beyond words anyway. Enrico and Lucia simply hugged each other, Maria and her daughter burst into tears, and Tommaso came back to earth to discover Alessio locked in mortal combat with a small Centipede supporter.

Georgina sat through the tumult, torn between the weakness of relief that unbearable suspense was over, and rage that they should have been made to feel such terror. Beneath those contradicting emotions was something else as well, that in a calmer moment would need dealing with. The truth would have to be faced that throughout the running of the race she'd felt more alien, more English, than ever before. She needn't ever watch another Palio, but she *was* committed to a future in Italy, with all that that entailed. Living there wasn't the same thing as visiting Poggio for long, carefree summer holidays, and just at the moment she wasn't at all sure that what she loved about the place would be enough to see her through things she intensely disliked – like mismanaged running of today's race, with its unchecked cheating and violence.

Lucia's voice reached her from a long way away. 'It's all over, *cara*. Adam seems to be all right, and I rather think he's won.'

'Yes, it's over,' she agreed faintly. 'Or is it? We still don't know what happened to Filippo.'

'Yes – Paolo's been telling your grandfather. He didn't come back because he had to speak to Filippo, calling on the telephone from Rome.'

'From *Rome*? What in the world was he doing there?'

'The poor boy doesn't know! There was the usual *contrada* dinner last night after the horse had been taken to the church to be blessed. Filippo remembers drinking a last glass of wine, nothing more than that. When he woke up, feeling dreadful, he was in the back of a lorry going south. He was put out without a lira in his pockets, walked into Rome, and looked up some old friends who provided him with the use of a telephone.'

'He once assured me there were accepted limits of behaviour,' Georgina said with difficulty. 'The limits seem remarkably elastic here, especially when you're dealing with men like Roberto Artom.'

'Dearest, think what you like; but neither you nor Filippo must be foolish enough to say it publicly. You'll get nothing for your pains but a writ for slander. Paolo is very insistent about that. You can be sure there'll be no shred of proof, and in any case Roberto himself *may* be innocent. Perhaps his friends arranged it all.'

Georgina shook her head. 'It's too neat, Gran. Roberto wasn't just removing an opponent who nearly beat him last time and might have managed it today. He's been waiting to get his revenge on the family. I hope he never forgets the moment when he discovered that the Ostrich horse *was* being ridden against him after all.' She heard herself say the words, then went deathly white. About to add that Roberto would have discovered by now the identity of the winner, she just managed to remember in time that her grandmother didn't know the true reason for the damage to Adam's car.

Lucia looked from her pale face to Maria, now slumped in her seat and overcome by too much emotion.

'I think perhaps we'll go home, *tesoro*. Let Tommaso bring the children back when they've seen enough of the celebrations. Your grandfather must go with Paolo to find Adam and stay for the dinner, but you, Maria, and I will go back home and recover.'

The road out of Siena was empty, since no one else would dream of leaving for hours yet. After the heat and noise and overcharged atmosphere of the town, Poggio had never seemed more peaceful or more beautiful. Lucia prescribed calming English tea, which they all drank, even Maria, before she left them to go back to her own room. Alone with Lucia, Georgina broached the idea in her mind that now gleamed with the same desirability as a green oasis in the middle of a desert.

'Gran, you know I must go back to London to clear out my flat? I'd planned to go at the beginning of September, but it's hanging over me rather and I'd be happier to get it done. I think I might just as well go straightaway.'

She spoke calmly, but her face was still very pale and her fingers were gripped too tightly round the fragile china cup.

'Why not?' Lucia agreed after a moment's pause. 'There's no need to wait at all; leave tomorrow if you want to.'

Georgina blew her a little kiss that thanked her for not asking questions difficult to answer, and then paid her a compliment that came from an overcharged heart. 'You're above price! I hope you know that.'

'Because I don't ask to be told too much?' Lucia suggested, smiling at her.

'Because you don't ask anything at all. I'll go tomorrow – need to be away a week, probably. That should give me time enough to get the flat ready to turn over to William's cousin. I was planning to sell my car, but it seems a much better idea to drive it over here; then I can load it with everything I want to bring back.'

When Tommaso brought the children home later in the evening and heard of her departure the following day he refused her request that he should drive her into Florence so that she could catch the train to Pisa.

'I know what the *padrone* would say: "the *aeroporto*",' he insisted stubbornly. 'So that is where I shall take you, signorina.'

She was outside putting a small suitcase in the back of the car after an early breakfast when the farmhouse door opened and Adam walked down the steps. His left arm was in a sling and there was another weal down the side of his face. As usual, the sight of him excited Maria's hens and turkeys to a flurry across the lawn, in case they missed his next move, and the procession they made threatened to catapult her into hysterical laughter. It seemed safer to leave it to him to find something to say.

'Going somewhere?'

'London.' It was said curtly, and he raised an eyebrow, then winced because he'd chosen the wrong eyebrow.

'You make it sound rather final, but I take it that you're not going for good?' The question was asked so casually that she wondered why he'd bothered to ask it at all. The mad desire to laugh of a moment ago was suddenly swamped by a return of yesterday's rage. She fought with herself not to shout at him.

'I'm going to clear out my flat. Perhaps you'll have gone yourself by the time I get back.'

He didn't answer that, and she was goaded into shouting because his face looked drawn and tired.

'You could go and lie down, instead of walking about with those damned stupid birds. You could lead the quiet life you presumably came here for, instead of joining in yesterday's mayhem at the Palio and making a mortal enemy of Roberto Artom. Do you ever behave like a sensible man?'

'All too often,' he answered with a faint smile. 'I'm not complaining about a dislocated collar bone and a few bruises in unmentionable places!'

'You might have got yourself killed,' she raged at him. 'How do you suppose my grandparents would have felt about that? Thankful that they wouldn't have to repay your loan? Wrong, Professor – they'd have been heartbroken; but you do what pleases you, regardless of people's feelings.'

Dimly she was aware of the unfairness of what she'd just said; now it would be his turn to shout. But he spoke quietly, as if she were an overwrought child who needed humouring.

'It wasn't as rash as it seemed, as a matter of fact. I was riding horses bareback on the Berkshire downs at the tender age of nine – the summit of my ambition at the time being to become a circus performer!'

'And what happens when Roberto decides to make sure this time of punishing a man who's thwarted him once too often?'

'Nothing happens,' Adam said gently. 'Artom has shot his bolt. He may have landed himself in real trouble over Filippo. No doubt his henchmen are well paid, and they're unlikely to give him away unless they're leaned on heavily by the authorities; all the same, he's well aware that he mustn't step out of line in future.' His good hand reached out as if to touch her but he thought better of the idea and let it drop again. 'Filippo's all right and so am I; you can stop worrying about us, if that's what you *are* doing.'

She was, in fact, fighting a terrible temptation to burst into tears, but she managed to find something else to say.

'Leaving aside the people here who've grown ridiculously attached to you, you might give a thought to . . . to relatives in England who expect to see you returned to them in one piece.'

It was as near as she could get to mentioning the woman he'd had, for some reason, to leave behind. He didn't know that Caterina had spoken of her, and probably would have resented the fact that his private affairs had been bandied about Poggio.

'You're being so tactful,' he surmised gently, 'that I suppose Caterina's been talking again. Well, I have every intention of going home in one piece, so you needn't worry about anyone else kind enough to be attached to me.'

She was being told, she thought, not to pry into his real life in England; it had nothing to do with them. It was the moment to nod and leave, but she suddenly heard herself say one last thing.

'For a man who didn't become a circus performer after all it was a very creditable performance yesterday.'

'All-round versatility,' he explained gravely. 'We pride ourselves on that at Oxford!' Then he smiled and walked away, followed by his little retinue, and she found she still wanted to burst into tears.

Chapter 16

Tommaso said goodbye to her at the airport and, freed from the necessity to talk to him, she drifted into a strange kind of limbo. Fragments of other people's conversations overheard suggested that she was still part of the human race, but it seemed to have little to do with her. She hadn't experienced this kind of numb detachment before, and couldn't even decide whether she wanted it to last or not. It seemed to promise protection from pain, but excluded any hope of joy as well; on the whole she hoped that something would soon matter enough to jolt her back to reality again.

By the time the plane touched down at Heathrow the weather was predictably the gloomy dampness of a wet August in England, but for that she was certainly aware of gratitude. She wanted what she'd arrived at to be as different as possible from what she'd just flown away from. Italy never went in for understatement, and in her present state of mind and heart she needed the soft, grey English sky and the grey English river not far from her front door.

After being shut up for five months the flat was full of dust and the sour smell of disuse. It seemed cramped after the spaciousness of Poggio, and she stared round the rooms, having to recognise again treasured ornaments and small pieces of furniture happily acquired by patient ferreting about in junk shops. It was hard to believe in the fact that she was there only to dismantle it all. The rooms had been changed by the identity she had given them; now, a new owner would put *his* imprint there, wiping away the image of Georgina Hadley. The reality of what she had done must be accepted fully at last; she no longer belonged in England. If she came at all in future, she would come as a visitor. Homesickness had her by the throat, intensified by the exhaustion that had settled on her like a fog.

She went thankfully to bed, and awoke ten hours later to a watery gleam of sunshine slanting through the window that inspired fresh hope. Life wasn't over after all, and some of her misery last night had probably been the result of hunger. The local corner shop provided her with bread and milk and coffee, and after breakfast she felt calm enough to ring William. He was never a talkative man, face to face or on the telephone, but this morning it seemed that more time than usual was needed for him to find something to say.

'I've obviously taken you by surprise,' she said into the silence at the other end. 'It's sooner than I intended, but it was suddenly a sensible moment to come back to London.'

'First bit of good news so far today,' he muttered finally. 'It's been a lousy morning – an unidentified disease romping through my best begonias, and a whole border knocked flat by some bloody depression coming in from the Atlantic. Can you tell me why that ocean never breeds anything but wind and rain?'

'No, I can't, dear William. I'd offer to come and help, but there's a lot to do here, and I probably ought to apply myself to getting on with it.'

'Stay where you are . . . I just wanted to have my usual little grouse! We've got things to talk about, though, and seeing as how it's you I'll throw caution to the winds for once and chance a restaurant meal. Pick you up at half past seven?'

She was sufficiently cheered to grin into the telephone, remembering his deep distrust of eating out. 'Noble of you, Mr Bird! I'll look forward to it.'

What she'd said, she realised, when the conversation ended, scarcely described the spring of pleasure that had come from just talking to him again; seeing him would be even better. The company of Filippo and his friends was enjoyable enough, and she was grateful for it, but none of them would make any lasting impression on her or leave a gap if they went away. Poggio's most serious drawback was that it could never offer her the richness of her friendship with William, even if she outgrew her longing for everything else that was English and dear. She buried the knowledge in her mind and set to work, heaping on one side everything she intended to take with her, and on the other what would have to be disposed of if William's cousin had no need of it. By the time she stopped to strip off working clothes and change for dinner, quite a lot had been achieved. Cupboards had been emptied, and a start made on sorting clothes and books for taking back to Poggio or donating to Oxfam.

She was browsing through a volume she hadn't looked at for years when William's ring sounded at the door. He stood there so spruced up for the occasion that he looked unfamiliar for a moment, but there was something else different as well – William had grown a beard, and it not only suited him but seemed to transform his whole appearance. She wanted to say so, and most of all wanted to confess how much she'd missed him, but in place of the necessary words came hot, stupid tears instead, to trickle down her face; because of them, all she could do was stare at him.

Embarrassed or appalled as she supposed he probably was, he nevertheless rose nobly to the occasion. 'I'm no oil-painting, God knows, but women don't usually take one gander at me and burst into a fit of weeping – I suppose you don't like the beard?'

It was a long and rather wistful speech for him, and by the end of it she'd more or less recovered herself. 'I like it very well,' she managed to insist tearfully. 'I was only crying because I'm so happy to see you again!'

'Typically daft and feminine, if you ask me,' he said quickly, but he planted a kiss awkwardly on her wet cheek all the same, and didn't explain whether he was happy too, or simply acknowledging an odd sort of compliment. Then he stood back to inspect her with the considering stare she recognised – he normally offered it to a plant he was especially interested in. 'Brown and gorgeous, but too thin,' he decided. 'I expect you've been working too hard.'

She was able to smile now over the bottle of sherry she'd thought to buy that morning. 'Partly too much work, partly anxiety. The past few months have been rather stressful.'

He could see that for himself; though he reckoned her even more beautiful than before. With her tanned skin and the gilding of sunlight on her hair, she looked changed – more experienced, he finally explained to himself. He needed to find out why, but began by asking about Poggio instead of about her.

'Things going better out there now?' he suggested.

'Much better than they were,' she answered slowly. 'You know already what I found when I arrived. Granny was still in hospital, and my grandfather had all but given up. The men who worked for him had left, and the loan that had kept Poggio going was running out.'

'That was when you decided to sell the flat, I take it?'

'Yes – we could have borrowed again, but it would have meant still more debt for Poggio.' Her face was shadowed by the memory of what had happened next, and William had to prompt her.

'Still not plain sailing after that?'

'Not quite! Our original lender was so displeased with us for refusing another loan that he called in the first one. Then we discovered why – he'd only wanted Poggio in order to destroy it. The land was to be built over with a holiday village!'

'You might have battled your way through to solvency – then he wouldn't have got it at all. Didn't he think of that?'

'He was sure my grandfather would fail, but in any case he had a second string to his bow. We'd been friends since childhood, Roberto Artom and I; then teenage sweethearts. When I went back this time it was as if he'd been waiting for me, and I felt sure he was the man I was going to marry!'

William digested this in silence for a moment, no longer wondering at the change he found in her. 'You made a mistake there, girl – the man sounds a thorough-going sod,' he finally allowed himself to say.

She nodded but felt obliged to explain a little more. 'You'd have to meet him to understand that he's also clever, persuasive, and extremely handsome! It's easy enough now to see how mistaken I was – and, I'm afraid, how mistaken *he* was – but to begin with I was deeply grateful for the help he'd apparently given my grandfather. I was also blinded by vanity – I knew that Roberto could take his pick of women, and he'd chosen me!'

'I hate him sight unseen; I'd rather hear what's happening to Poggio now.'

A happier smile touched her mouth. 'Something harder to believe! We found a *true* saviour this time – an English academic renting Poggio's empty farmhouse for the summer. Out of affection for my grandparents, I think, he insisted on investing in the estate to the extent of taking over Roberto's loan himself, which meant that we could still use the money from the sale of the flat to haul Poggio into the black again.'

'*Can* it be hauled back?'

'We believe so. Gramps came unstuck because he hadn't been prudent in good years and there have recently been several bad ones. The whole wine-making scene has changed, but the making of Chianti has changed more than most. Poggio hadn't kept up with the changes because my grandfather couldn't see any of us being there to carry it on in the future and lost heart. Now everything looks different.'

'You said he had no help; the two of you can't work an estate that size by yourselves.'

'That was almost the worst problem to begin with, because once Giuseppe and his sons had gone the word went round that Poggio was finished. But Heaven still hadn't done with us. I haven't told you that there arrived out of the blue a man related by marriage to Granny's housekeeper, who'd spent ten years working in the vineyards of California! He was homesick for Tuscany, in need of a job, and asked nothing better than to be given the chance to settle down at Poggio. Tommaso is an expert as well as an enthusiast, and just having him there has fired my grandfather with fresh energy. So I think the estate *will* survive, after all.'

William nodded, but her pale face caused him to announce that he'd reserve the rest of his questions until she'd been given something to eat and drink.

Over the boeuf bourgignon, apple tart, ripe Camembert, and good red Burgundy, he was made to talk himself because she wanted to know about Kew. The spring had been dry and cold, the summer wet and windy – just what a gardener didn't want, in other words; but William explained it philosophically. Every season, bloody and cantankerous though it might be, had enough perfect days to keep hope alive.

'Forget your packing-up for an hour or two – come and see for yourself,' he suggested. 'Just for old times' sake.'

Georgina hesitated for a moment, then shook her head. 'I could spare the time, but I have a dreadful feeling that it wouldn't be wise; I'll just remember the gardens as I saw them last.'

'Homesick?' William enquired gently after another small pause.

She nodded, trying to swallow a sip of wine over the sudden lump in her throat. 'It's hard to explain, especially when I *know* how beautiful and precious Poggio is. I don't regret what I've done, but just now and again, something about life in Italy grates so badly that I can't help asking myself why I'm there. I shall get over it and settle down when I've sorted everything out; you don't have to feel sorry for me.'

He was inclined to feel sorry for anyone who didn't live in England, within striking distance of Kew; and he had, besides, a deeply held conviction that, as a race, the Italians usually proved charming but unreliable, if not worse – like the specimen she'd nearly married. But he remembered just in time where her own mother hailed from and clutched at the recollection of someone else. 'You mentioned a saviour: what happened to him?'

'He's still there, on a year's sabbatical from Oxford. Apart from giving lectures in Florence, he's writing a history of his special subject – Italian Renaissance art.'

'Peculiar,' William commented. 'I'm not personally acquainted with many academics, mind you, but the ones I do know wouldn't spend money on salvaging a rundown estate.'

She thought of Adam stripped to the waist, with a heavy tank of copper-sulphate on his back, spraying vines row for row with Tommaso. She wished she *hadn't* thought of him, because the image of his battered face was suddenly vivid in her mind, and in what other way might he not be crossing swords with Roberto when her back was turned?

'Professor Fleming's not one of your usual dons,' she said slowly. 'His services to our family don't even stop at lending it a large sum of money. There was some skulduggery that prevented my cousin from riding in the Palio that's just been run in Siena. You've probably heard of it – a bareback race round the square there, ancient and time-honoured, but terribly dangerous. Adam Fleming not only rode for us in Filippo's place against Roberto but won! I expect Siena is still talking about it.'

William couldn't decide whether she sounded pleased, proud, or strangely cross. 'Seems to me the professor's a nut, and you've been involved in some very peculiar goings-on,' he said severely.

She smiled and shook her head. 'You might not know much about High Renaissance art, and I doubt if he can tell a cotoneaster from a camellia, but I'm fairly sure the two of you would like each other.'

With the meal finally over, she promised to see William again before she left London, but spent the rest of the week working hard on her own, only interrupted when Lucia telephoned one evening to confirm that all was well at Poggio.

'And the professor?' Georgina found herself asking.

'He allows Alessio to clean the car for him, and remembers to put his arm in a sling whenever Maria's anywhere around, but he looks remarkably well.'

'What about Filippo – have you seen *him*?'

'He got back the day you left, determined to have a fight to the death with Roberto, whatever his father said. But by the greatest good fortune Roberto was already on his way to New York. Now Filippo's temper has had time to cool, and he's been persuaded that a public brawl would do neither of them any good.'

'Persuaded by you, I dare say.'

'No, by Dino Artom, I think. Rather bravely, he went to see Filippo – didn't admit in so many words that Roberto had been involved, of course, but the fact that he felt obliged to go at all meant that he was apologising for something. He said that they mustn't allow an old friendship between neighbours to be destroyed, and I agree with him. Even Filippo had to admit that Dino was unusually dignified, and afterwards they both came here and saw Adam. So I feel hopeful that this year's Palio can now be forgotten.'

'You can hope so, Gran, but I doubt if it ever will be. Alessio will probably see dozens more, but this is the one he'll be telling his grandchildren about.'

'Perhaps, and it's certainly the one Adam will be telling *his* grandchildren about. He's got visitors coming, by the way. He seems very pleased at the prospect; excited, in fact.'

Georgina's imagination leapt to the likeliest visitor of all – the woman in his life, who must have finally changed her mind about not being with him at Poggio. No doubt she'd been told about his Tuscan adventures and come to the conclusion that he wasn't safe to be left alone. The poor woman didn't know the ordeal in front of her, Georgina reckoned – not only Caterina but Lucia and Maria as well needing to be satisfied that she in any way deserved their *caro professore*. Then Lucia's next question interrupted this train of thought.

'When are you coming home, *tesoro*?'

'I'll catch the ferry on Saturday night; that way I can get well down through France while the *camions* are off the roads. With nothing to hold me up, I should be back at Poggio on Monday evening.'

'I shall fib a little and tell your grandfather Tuesday, then you'll be here before he's started to worry. Take great care, my dear child.'

Her last meeting with William began with an argument; there were things she wanted to leave behind for his cousin without charging for them, which William insisted he must buy. With this hammered out to his satisfaction, she pointed to something else – a Georgian wine-cooler, found battered in a junk shop and now restored to its original shining beauty.

'Not for your cousin,' she said. 'It's for you. I don't know how else to thank you for all your kindness.'

His mournful face stared at the small object for so long that she was afraid she might have offended him. Then he finally spoke at last, apparently to himself.

'The fool of a girl ought to know she doesn't need to thank me,' he muttered, but his hand stroked the smoothness of the wood as lovingly as he touched his plants. 'I dare say I shall treasure it, though.' He seemed to hesitate again and she was aware of him looking at some hurdle he could see ahead and wondering how to tackle it.

'It won't be long before we see you at Poggio,' she reminded him cheerfully, to fill the continuing pause. 'You haven't forgotten you promised to come?'

'I shall be there, at the beginning of October. A grape harvest's something I haven't experienced before.' But he spoke absently, as if his mind was on something else, and at last he managed to put it into words. 'I've been thinking about what you said the other day about not quite settling down at Poggio. You might reckon you'd *got* to stay there now, but that isn't so; there's always Kew to come back to. I'd fire my know-all assistant for excessive zeal and then it would be the old firm back again.'

His steady gaze was on her face, making no demands beyond the simple one that she should understand what he was saying.

There was no limit to his kindness and she smiled tremulously as she shook her head. 'Poor zealous young man! I should have him on *my* conscience even if you didn't have him on yours. In any case, it wouldn't be very easy to come back. I should have no home here.'

'There's always mine,' said William slowly.

For a moment she was unsure, afraid to say anything at all, in case what she read into an ambiguous remark was not what he'd intended. Then, when she glanced at him and saw his eyes fixed on her, she knew that she hadn't been mistaken. It couldn't have been called a flowery proposal, but that would be quite beyond him; even so, she was being offered all that William Bird had to offer, and she knew that it had never been offered to anyone else before.

'You're a peerless friend, William, but you carry chivalry much too far,' she said unsteadily. 'I have to go back, at least until the olive harvest at Christmas; after that if I'm desperate to come home, I promise I'll let you know – word of a Hadley, as my darling father would say!'

'That's all right then,' said William. 'Just as long as you know.'

He smiled at her with the joyous relief of an inarticulate man who'd managed to say his piece. She'd been very taken with the handsome Italian – there wasn't any doubt about that – and would need time to get over him. It might be *him* who'd put her off the place, but William tried not to feel grateful for that – the man deserved hating, after all. But at least she could go back for as long as she needed to, certain that she wasn't trapped, because a chap called William Bird – *not* handsome and, God knew, not clever with words even now – given the chance, would love her for ever and guard her with his life.

Chapter 17

By eight o'clock the next morning she was on the road out of Cherbourg, heading for the south-east. At the end of a long day's drive she stopped for the night on the French side of the Mont Blanc tunnel, made an even earlier start the next day, and finally bumped up the track from San Vicenzo at nine o'clock that night, tired and red-eyed, to be gathered into Enrico's arms.

'*Tesoro*, tomorrow, your grandmother said . . . You've come like the wind, driven all night, surely?'

Lucia appeared, weeping a little for the joy of seeing her. Maria stopped long enough to thank the Holy Virgin for watching over her journey, then gave her another hug. Nero, grown even bigger in the space of a week, almost knocked her over . . . She was safely home and they could all be happy again.

Still stiff from the long drive, she got up the next day in time for what was always her chief pleasure – walking through the gardens at the moment when the sun rose high enough to clear the opposite hill. The mist all round her thinned and floated away in tiny wisps of silver vapour as sunlight flooded in instead. Like Nero, the olives had grown in her absence, and the grapes were changing colour: it would soon be harvest-time.

Since leaving England she'd forced her conversation with William to the back of her mind while she concentrated on the car and the long road ahead of her. Now she was free to consider it again – must do so, in fact, because the unholy muddle she was in must be settled sooner rather than later. William's touchingly awkward offer had been more disturbing than he knew. She had a choice now, and must make up her mind which it was to be: Kew with him, or Poggio perhaps always in some fundamentally private way by herself.

Her dear William was as different from Roberto Artom as a man could possibly be, and what he offered was different, too. She might lack excitement with him, and the physical pleasures that her Italian lover would have known how to provide; although even in that he might surprise her.

169

What wasn't in doubt was the offer of contentment, security, and deep affection. They were things that should always have weighed heavily, but they looked all the more attractive when she was still humiliated by the nearness of her brush with disaster. Poggio's late-summer beauty was all around her, and after yesterday's welcome she knew how deeply she was loved there. But Tommaso would remain, to keep her grandfather out of future trouble, and she could come often to visit them. With the *vendemmia* and the olive harvest safely accomplished, it would be no treachery to return to what still felt like home.

She wandered slowly back across the lawn, unaware that she was being watched from the top of the stone staircase leading to Adam's sitting room.

'*Buon giorno*, Georgina. All ties with England finally severed?'

The question came so neatly to challenge what her mind had just been wrestling with that she half feared she'd been conducting her debate with herself out loud. 'Severed for the moment,' she finally agreed.

The professor registered the qualification, but asked an easier question. 'A trouble-free journey, I trust?'

'Apart from a tremendous thunderstorm coming across France, no problems at all.'

'You must thank Maria for that. She went down to church and lit so many candles that we knew the whole company of Heaven must be watching over you.'

He was smiling now and she could see no evidence of his ride in the Palio; in fact, he looked relaxed and well, more obviously happy than she'd known him ever before. The visitors Lucia had mentioned on the telephone, of course – *they* were the reason for the contentment that shone in his face.

'My grandmother said something about your guests,' she suggested coolly. 'Are they still here?'

'Yes, and I want you to meet them. In fact, here comes the one I want you to meet most of all.' He turned to a girl walking down the stairs behind him. 'Madame Blanchard . . . Georgina Hadley.'

Madame Blanchard had the rare combination of blue eyes and beautiful red-gold hair, and her smile was friendly. There was also something else about her not to be missed – she was very close to Adam Fleming. The ease of long intimacy was in the way they looked at each other.

'I'm not sure what's required – good morning or *bonjour*?' Georgina finally remembered to say, making a slight question of it.

'Adam's teasing; I'm as English as you are – no, rather more so, I think! How nice that you're back; we got the impression that your grandparents were missing you.'

She *was* nice; but how could she not be if she was the professor's choice? Georgina struggled to find something pleasant to say in return, but was interrupted by the sight of what seemed to be a herd of small boys tumbling out of the door behind Madame Blanchard. There were, in fact, only three of them, scaled down in size and age from ten to five. At the sight of a stranger, they came to an abrupt halt, bumping into one another.

'My sons,' she said unnecessarily, because they were too like her to be anything else. 'We call them François, Philippe, and Alain, but they're really the Three Musketeers. Alessio plays the part of d'Artagnan, but of course you know him already.'

Georgina stared at the children. She would have been amused at any other time by the sight of them bowing over her hand in turn with the grave politeness of a trio of elderly mandarins. Just now it seemed important to work out whose sons they were – surely not the professor's? He'd denied a wife and family when he offered his loan to her grandfather. A smiling nod from their mother released them, and they tore off in search of their confederate.

Then with the recollection of something Adam had once said, she thought she understood. 'Are they by any chance Mrs Fleming's French grandsons?' she suggested doubtfully. 'If so, it surely makes you—'

'Adam's sister – quite right!' Amanda confirmed, unaware that she could have been supposed to be anyone else. 'We thought it time to see what he was up to in Tuscany! Now, if you'll excuse me, I must return to getting breakfast for the tribe. I only came down to say hello.'

She gave the smile that was familiar because it could now be seen to resemble her brother's and climbed the stairs again. Georgina stared at her own feet, thinking about the woman in England. She was destined to remain a mystery, it seemed; they would probably never know any more about her than they now knew, because the professor preferred it that way.

'Jean-Paul's away at a medical congress,' she heard him explain instead. 'It seemed a good moment to let the children escape from Paris. I didn't doubt that they'd love it here, but the problem of persuading them to go home again and leave Alessio behind is beginning to assume horrendous proportions.'

'Your sister will think of something: she looks a very experienced mother to me.' Georgina nodded and walked away, leaving him with the impression that she'd scarcely heard what he'd just said. It was reasonable for her to feel tired after her journey, but he'd found in her no pleasure at meeting Amanda and the boys, and he could have sworn to something else – when he'd caught sight of her in the garden she'd been troubled; there was no joy for her in being back at Poggio.

The Blanchards stayed for a week that they and Alessio never forgot. The four children were inseparable, talking to each other in a mixture of French and Italian that baffled everyone else but seemed to work perfectly well for them. When Adam drove his sister to look at Florence, Siena, or San Gimignano, they pleaded to be left behind; sightseeing couldn't hope to compete with the delights of Poggio, where Georgina had been cast in the role of the princess who always needed rescuing. She enjoyed the game and only baulked when Alain, alias Aramis, suggested that in the interest of verisimilitude she really needed to be tied up with ropes. In the uncomplicated pleasure of the children's company she found it easy to relax; but she found herself stupidly anxious to avoid Amanda Blanchard, whose presence usually meant that her brother also wasn't far way.

Aware of the exclusion, Amanda was tactful enough to accept it without question. But, hanging out a line of small shirts and shorts one morning, she caught Georgina in the vegetable garden, gathering beans.

Her eyes went from the brown hands steadily stripping pods to the face bent over them, apparently concentrating on the job. It was a beautiful face, meant to express whatever its owner was feeling; but Amanda agreed with her brother – there was some unnatural reticence about Georgina Hadley at the moment that kept the rest of them at arm's length.

'You'll have to explain to me what you're doing,' Amanda began cheerfully. 'I live in a flat in the middle of Paris, and when I want flowers or vegetables I have to go out and buy them. It's a stupid way to live, and I'm nearly as besotted about Poggio as my sons are.'

'I'm picking French beans,' Georgina said, smiling at her. 'Most are picked young and green, and eaten like that, but these have been left on the plants to dry off. When they're shelled we shall have a store of delicious haricot beans for soups and stews in the winter.'

Amanda investigated the inside of a pod while she offered her next query. 'Adam says you're going to stay here now. Beautiful as it is, won't it be lonely for you?'

The question was so gently asked that only friendliness could have prompted it. 'I shan't know for certain till I've tried, but I don't think so,' Georgina answered, unable to hint at a probable different future when she hadn't mentioned it to her grandparents.

'I understand now why Adam's been so happy here. We shall have to tear the boys away when the time comes, but I think my brother's going to have a far harder job to leave. The strange thing is that he isn't normally very dependent on his surroundings – in fact I sometimes think he doesn't even notice them. That isn't the case here, though.'

Her companion went on stripping beans. 'Poggio is very near Florence – an art-historian's Heaven! If your brother enjoys being here, that's probably the reason. I expect it will be forgotten easily enough once he gets back to Oxford.'

Amanda watched her for a moment, wondering why her own comment had been deliberately misunderstood. The girl in front of her was a mystery altogether – so clearly attractive, but so solitary, and when she forgot to smile there was sadness in her eyes.

'I've a horror of loneliness myself,' Amanda suddenly confessed, reverting to the question she'd asked earlier. 'If something happened to Jean-Paul I should feel that my own life had come to an end, but at least I'd still have the boys. Adam didn't even have the help of children when Elizabeth died.'

'Elizabeth?' The query was a murmur only just heard.

'His wife. We'd all grown up together, known each other for always. Even now it seems unthinkable that she should have been struck down so young – a heart attack is supposed to be what kills elderly people. Adam changed after her death – not surprisingly, of course. We hoped he'd find someone else to love, but I'm afraid he has a constant heart; it's more unusual in a man, I think.'

Georgina stared at the bean pod in her hands, then dropped it on the ground. 'He seems happy enough as he is,' she said briefly. 'Everyone here seems to have fallen under the Fleming spell, and probably his Oxford friends have, too. It's impersonal kindness he offers, though, which I didn't quite understand before. Knowing about his wife, of course, I do.'

Amanda's eyes skimmed her face again but she didn't answer until she'd retrieved her laundry-basket and was about to walk away. 'We're not far from you in Paris. Come and visit us in the winter, when the theatres and the opera wake up again. It's no boast to claim that you'll enjoy meeting my husband – he's a lovely man – and I can promise that he'll like the look of you!'

'Perhaps I'll come when we've got the olives safely in,' Georgina agreed, rather unsteadily. She was disliking more and more the need to prevaricate, knowing that it would be a huge relief to be certain of what she must do.

* * *

173

When the Blanchards left for Paris Adam went with them. Amanda was of the opinion that it was time he saw his brother-in-law again, but he explained to Lucia that he was really going to deliver his family safely home. Amanda and Enrico had much in common, apparently, when it came to being in too-spirited charge of a *macchina*.

The farmhouse seemed empty when they'd gone, and Alessio loudly mourned his friends, but when Lucia also confessed to missing the professor, Georgina told her sharply that it was no more than she'd been warned about. They'd all got too dependent on him, and the sooner they learned to manage on their own again, the better.

He came back by train a week later, but only to immerse himself immediately in a book whose deadline was now approaching rapidly. Sleeping badly herself, Georgina often got out of bed to find his light still burning into the early hours of the morning. She couldn't help thinking about his dead wife, and about his constancy. How ready she'd been to accuse him of a self-sufficiency that had seemed arrogantly complete. It didn't seem quite enough of an excuse to say that she hadn't known about his past life – she must hope, with new-found humility, to be less opinionated in future.

The burning heat of high summer gradually softened into the perfect days of late September, and there was now a different sweetness in the early-morning air. The vines were meshed in a filigree of dew, and Enrico came in to breakfast looking content with the signs of a harvest better than the ones of recent years. It was exactly what Poggio needed most – a vintage that would help them on the road to recovery rather than drag them down into further decline. As he walked the hillsides with Tommaso, it was easy to see confidence returning to the set of his shoulders and the tilt of his head. God was good, and escape from disaster was beginning to look very possible. But he told himself and Lucia that success wouldn't be taken for granted again; he'd be on his guard against extravagance and easy optimism in future. Lucia smiled and merely added in her prayers a plea for this safe and unextravagant future he promised her.

Georgina rarely went to Florence while a river of tourists still flowed through the city more freely than the Arno in late summer, but sometimes a visit couldn't be avoided. One morning she went there early, despatched by Maria on an errand to the Mercato Centrale, close by the ancient church of San Lorenzo. Her favourite stall in the market offered *verdura* and herbs of varieties that didn't yet grow at Poggio. She was selecting choice leaves of pungent green *radicchio* and *salvastrella* when a voice spoke diffidently behind her.

'*Buon giorno, signorina.*'

She turned and recognised Franco, Giuseppe's younger son. He was smiling sheepishly, as if uncertain of her attitude towards him, but she gave him a friendly nod and gestured to the green bunches in her hand. 'Specially requested by Maria! I shall have to learn to grow them at Poggio. How are you, Franco – enjoying city life?'

He gave a little shrug, and she imagined that the brief conversation was over. Then suddenly he burst forth again with questions. 'The *padroni* are well? And little Caterina?'

'They're all well. Caterina, no longer very little, has left school – she's learning to be a hairdresser in San Vicenzo.'

'You're here for a holiday, signorina?'

'No, I live at Poggio, at least for the time being. We're just about to start the *vendemmia* and you'll remember *that* as being no holiday at all!'

'It was fun, though, the *vendemmia* . . . hard work but fun.' He spoke with a mixture of sadness and regret, like someone remembering a joy he'd known and thrown away.

She stared more closely at a young face that could have been pleasant without its incipient beard. It didn't suit him but was probably required among the urban youths he now lived alongside. 'Don't you like it here?' she asked suddenly. 'We thought it was what you wanted – higher pay, and an easier job than working at Poggio.'

'I hate it! Pietro's happy enough. He likes cafés and discos, thinks it's cool to be awake all night when he ought to be asleep, and yawn all day when he ought to be awake, but it isn't my idea of life.'

'Would you come back, if you could?'

He hunched his shoulders again, in a gesture that politely said the question wasn't worth answering. 'I have no home there. I share a room with Pietro, but whenever he wants it for himself and some girl or other, I'm told to disappear.'

'Why not go back to Giuseppe and Emma? Aren't they still at Greve?'

'I'm not needed there either; in any case, we had a big row – they said Poggio was finished and I didn't believe them. But I reckoned the *padrone* would be sick of my family . . . wouldn't keep me on alone.'

She hesitated for a moment, afraid that what he said was probably true. 'Franco, I can't speak for my grandfather, but I'll tell him you're unhappy here. If he decided that there *was* still a place for you, we could probably find you a room in the farmhouse. But you mustn't bank on it happening.'

The sullen unhappiness in his face was giving way to a gleam of hope.

'I'd work hard, signorina.' His hands cradled an imaginary plant, touchingly. 'I like growing things; selling them isn't what I want to do.'

She smiled, recognising a kindred spirit when she saw one. 'I'll speak to my grandfather,' she promised. 'One of us will come and see you again here.'

She went home and reported the conversation, but Enrico was unimpressed.

'He walked out once before, *cara*; he could do it again just when we needed help most.'

'Only because he was talked into it by his family. At least see him yourself, and let Tommaso meet him as well. He's working in the Mercato Centrale, and hating every minute of it.'

'Well, it serves him right!' Enrico looked severe but finally relented to the extent of promising to consider the idea.

Tommaso was sent to inspect the boy, and his favourable report brought Franco back to be interrogated by the *padrone*, who was stern but fair.

'You were persuaded to leave, I realise. But if you can't make up your own mind now and hold to it, I don't want you here. You must learn that loyalty is important; if you can't understand that you'd better stay where you are.'

'I'd stay, signore, I promise.' He didn't seem able to state his case more fully than that, but Enrico, never at a loss for words himself, wasn't blind to a longing that couldn't be articulated.

'Well, help us through the *vendemmia*,' he said finally. 'Then we'll see.'

Chastened but content, Franco was installed in Tommaso's part of the farmhouse and calmly accepted by Maria as another member of the family to be fed and cared for. The beard disappeared because Caterina at once insisted that it didn't suit him, and he was rewarded for this docility by being allowed to take her on the back of his moped for coffee with the rest of café society in San Vicenzo. She had no intention of becoming his girl, but he could be useful sometimes, and there was a certain pleasure in showing Adam a young man completely under her thumb. Maria was happy to mother him, and Alessio felt sorry for a fellow-male stupid enough to allow himself to be told what to do by a mere girl. Georgina had insisted, though, that stupid or not Franco must be made to feel welcome, and it was *something* to be said in his favour that he'd had sense enough to want to come back to Poggio.

Georgina herself watched him carefully, aware that Franco's arrival seemed to ease her own return to England. They would be able to manage without her now, except at harvest-times when extra labour was always needed. She could enjoy William's coming to Poggio, knowing that she'd be free to ask him to make good his offer to take her home to Kew.

Chapter 18

The day before grape-picking began Georgina drove to Florence to collect her guest from the station.

'Can't abide aeroplanes,' William explained briefly when she found him on the platform. 'I like to take my time about getting adjusted along the way, not be flung down in a different country before I properly know where I am.'

He sounded as if the rail-journey hadn't agreed with him either, but she understood him well enough to know that he also needed to take his time about the matter of their reunion. She thought she probably struck him here as a girl he'd have to get to know all over again – one who not only looked perfectly at home in a country he found strange and exotic but could even speak the lingo as well as any Italian. William's reluctant smile agreed with her; he felt out of his depth, and a bit of a fool for having come at all. But then she put out her hand to take hold of his and suddenly there was nothing to worry about.

'You're looking tired,' she said gently, 'but Poggio will fix you!'

From the moment of introducing him to the household it was clear that Poggio would. His gaunt frame at once put fresh heart into Maria, who'd had to relinquish all hope of fattening up the professor. And, on the receiving end of Lucia's slow, welcoming smile, William at once boldly announced that he would end up falling in love with her. His ignorance of Italian and Enrico's limited English only temporarily stalled their understanding of one another, and a friendship with Tommaso was struck up immediately. As Lucia said, when heart talked to heart a lack of words rarely got in the way.

Georgina suggested in vain that William needed to begin by having a rest. 'Daft idea,' he said discouragingly. 'I've come to pick grapes, not loll about while the rest of you work.'

She begged pardon, and smiled as he loped off to join his new friend.

The tempo of work would change again now and all the hours of daylight would have to be spent out of doors until the grapes were safely gathered. Every pair of hands they could find was pressed into service and even Filippo, come to pay an ill-timed social visit, was begged to stay. About to accept the invitation, he rushed off to Siena first to round up as many friends as possible, shepherding them back with the firm instruction that a few days' exercise in the fresh air would do them a great deal of good. From then on it was inevitable that the *vendemmia* should become an uproarious as well as a back-breaking affair.

Picking began early the next morning, to make the most use, Enrico said, of his augmented labour-force. Following Poggio's assortment of guests outside, Georgina was of the opinion that not even the most city-loving of them could wish for the moment to be anywhere else. The hillsides around them, bathed in mellow sunlight, almost seemed to be saying, she thought, that this year they'd given of their best, brought forth all the fruit they could. Her grandfather was at least content with the quantity of heavy green or purple swags along the cordoned vines; the quality of the grapes couldn't be foretold yet, and would only be revealed when the process of converting them into wine was under way.

She worked alongside William, both of them too intent on their task to do much talking, but content to exchange smiles when one or other of them tipped the next basketful of fruit on to the glistening heap waiting to be trundled to the *cantina*. Working together again couldn't be anything but a pleasure; more surprising was the discovery that her usually silent William was getting on like a house on fire with chatterbox Filippo. Altogether, her dear friend – ancient panama clapped on his head at a rakish angle – was having the time of his life and the sight of him was enough to make her smile whenever she looked at him.

The work was strenuous, and they were allowed occasionally to stop for a breather. William commented during one of them that if Poggio's 'saviour' was among the people scattered about the slopes, he hadn't spotted him.

Georgina shook her head. 'I haven't seen him, either, this morning. He's running out of time to complete his book, having helped us too much earlier on when we needed help most. It's sad that he's missing the best part of all, but the professor always operates only by his own rules, not by those we'd like him to keep to.'

William considered her flushed face beneath a wide-brimmed straw hat borrowed from Lucia. 'You speak of him always with a funny mixture of pride and exasperation – I don't know whether it means you like more than you dislike him, or the other way round!'

She thought before she spoke, knowing that if William asked a question he expected it to be answered with proper care. 'The truth is,' she said finally, 'that I don't know myself. I rather wish I did.'

They were interrupted by the arrival beside them of an enormous, overflowing basket apparently propelling itself unaided towards the wicker *bigoncia* waiting on the tractor. Then Filippo was revealed behind it.

'Enough of these sweet nothings, you two,' he panted, as soon as his basket had been emptied on the heap. 'You're supposed to be picking grapes like the rest of us, not holding hands in the shade!' He grinned kindly all the same and went away to report as he passed his fellow labourer toiling at the end of the row that his cousin and her very *simpatico* English friend seemed to be on the most affectionate of terms.

'I'm glad about that,' he added simply. 'Georgina deserved much better than our local Flash Harry! But I'm not altogether sure that she was right in thinking she could spend the rest of her life here without Roberto Artom. William will do nicely instead, except that he'll take my sweet cousin back to England.'

Adam Fleming, who *had* been working out there with them all along, nodded but went on picking. 'I agree with you about William Bird – I met him last night and liked him. Perhaps Georgina will manage to get it right this time.'

Filippo heard the cool, almost careless statement, wondering why the professor sounded unlike himself; it was odd for him to be so off-hand about a girl he must by now know fairly well.

'Collarbone still troubling you?' he asked sympathetically.

'Knitting nicely, thank you – in fact more or less knut!' Aware of being examined too closely, Adam offered a convincing smile. 'I *am* feeling a trifle let down, though. Where are the white oxen of Tuscany? I expected to see beautiful, garlanded beasts dragging the baskets to the *cantina*, not an all-purpose tractor!'

'Past history, thank God,' said Filippo. 'I prefer something more manageable myself.' He grinned and walked away, too kind to point out that the oxen had been a diversion; the professor had been feeling low about something else, and before the day was out, by observing him closely, Filippo was pleased to be able to tell himself that he knew what it was.

Adam's next pause, necessary because his damaged shoulder was still more troublesome than he was prepared to admit, was shared with Caterina, who arrived with a flagon of her mother's chilled homemade lemonade. She settled herself beside him, pulled the top of her muslin blouse a little lower when he wasn't looking, and then poured out Maria's delicious drink.

'Nectar,' he said smiling at her after a long cool swallow. 'But you mustn't stay and keep me company – everyone will be needing this by now.'

'Mamma and Alessio are delivering it as well, and I've already taken some to Georgina and Signor Bird.' Caterina then considered what she would say next. 'They looked very happy together. Mamma thinks so too, and she hasn't seen them as I have, behaving like . . . well, like *innamorati*!'

It was a slight exaggeration, she knew; what she'd seen the evening before was William carefully helping Georgina down a steep slope in the orchard. But after the disappointment with Roberto Artom, it was surely a kindness to suggest that another love-affair might be flourishing for someone of her age?

The professor continued to sip his lemonade, then handed her back the empty glass – not interested, it seemed, in commenting on what she'd just said. Instead, he chose to speak of someone else. 'The *padrone* is glad to have Giuseppe's son back; his only worry is that Franco seems determined to work himself to death to make sure of being kept on at Poggio. But I think the besotted young man is also hoping to earn *your* good opinion!'

Caterina gave a little shrug. 'He's *stupido*, that one. Why come back here when there's the whole world to choose from?'

'Because what he can do is here,' Adam pointed out, 'and what he loves is also here. That doesn't make him stupid; quite the reverse in fact.'

Her mouth quivered because the professor's voice, though gentle, held a note of faint reproof; but *he* was *stupido* too, not to forget a careless Englishwoman who left him lonely and accept what *she* offered instead. He didn't even look at her now and she knew, because Franco's eyes clearly said so, that she was worth looking at.

'*I* shan't stay,' she insisted. 'Perhaps a year or two more, and then I'll be old enough to escape from Poggio.' She blinked away the threat of tears and tried to smile at him. 'I'll come and visit you in cold, wet England!'

'Then I shall ask my mother to make you welcome,' Adam promised gravely. 'She's very good at welcoming my friends. But now I must get back to work, or Filippo over there will accuse me of slacking.'

Caterina had to take the hint and walk away, and Adam picked up his basket again. Who would be next, he wondered, to find it necessary to explain to him how happy Georgina was in the company of William Bird!

As it happened, the girl herself only crossed his path late in the day when they coincided for once at the *bigoncia*, Georgina emptying her basket, Adam – promoted to the tractor – getting ready to drive it to the *cantina*. She looked tired but content – he couldn't help noticing that for himself. Everyone was quite right who'd said she was happy; he must remember that and be glad, and in an effort to be glad he smiled cheerfully at her.

'I forgot to ask – do we go on picking by torchlight?'

'Certainly not,' she answered. 'Any moment now Alessio will be allowed to ring the bell that announces work is over for the day. We shall clean ourselves up, and then be expected to tuck into one of Maria's enormous suppers.'

Adam shook his head. 'You'll have to make my excuses, I'm afraid. I have some different work I've been neglecting all day.' He gave her no chance to protest, and pointed to where Enrico stood talking to William in the doorway of the *cantina*.

'Your friend from Kew looks very much at home here – but you obviously knew he would be.'

Georgina's face shone with sudden pleasure. 'I wasn't quite sure – William's a man who likes familiar ground under his feet. But he seems to be really happy here. I'm glad it shows so clearly.'

'Poggio and you – of course it shows!' Adam smiled as he said it, then seemed to think he'd done his best to take an interest in Georgina Hadley and William Bird. 'Your grandfather's fairly revelling in the proceedings too; the very picture of a contented *padrone*.'

'Thanks to you,' she said quietly. 'He doesn't forget that, and nor do the rest of us.'

'Then I wish to God you *would*.' The answer came with a sudden force that took her aback. 'You're not meant to go through life from now on bowed down with gratitude; I won't have it, Georgina.'

Even if she could have found anything to say, he wasn't inclined to wait for it. With a grinding of gears the tractor moved off, and the professor roared his way up to the *cantina*. She watched him go, and forgot to deliver his apology to Maria. It seemed more necessary to remember that he'd be glad to leave altogether; he'd had enough of Poggio now.

The rest of the weekend and the two days of public holiday that followed it became in Georgina's mind a kaleidoscope of shifting scenes and colours; the soft, bloomed purple and green of grapes, the gold of sunlight, and the heavenly blue of a sky now tempered to gentleness. She stored up pictures to remember – William's bearded face smiling at Alessio's brown one as they discussed some knotty problem concerning Nero's parentage, Franco tenderly lifting Caterina down off the tractor though she could easily have jumped, and Filippo crowned with a wreath of grapes – a laughing Bacchus, exuberantly enjoying himself. On the last evening, when the ringing of the bell signalled not only supper-time but the completion of the *vendemmia*, they all inevitably lingered at the door of the *cantina* where Tommaso was already roughly crushing the grapes to speed the process of fermentation. Another vintage lay within the glistening heaps and, although it would have been tempting Fate to say it out loud, Enrico's optimism was catching. It was beginning to look like a good vintage, perhaps even a very good one.

Maria bustled to and from the kitchen with enormous bowls of spaghetti; then the pasta was followed by salads and escalopes of veal crisply golden and faintly aromatic with herbs. Enrico poured wine with the gusto of a man who loved giving hospitality to true friends, and indulged himself with the pleasure of something else he greatly enjoyed – the making of an extempore speech. There was his wife, precious above the rest, to be toasted, and the future of Poggio to be drunk to – saved for them by his granddaughter and his dear *amico*, Adam. Tommaso had to be thanked, and William, Filippo and his friends invited to look on Poggio from now on as their second home. The delivery might have been superbly theatrical but the sentiments were sincere, and watching him wind up with the request that they should all drink Maria's health for producing so many huge and delicious meals for them, Georgina felt again the certainty of a train of events that had somehow been irresistibly set in motion. The scene around her had been pre-ordained – Lucia at the foot of the table, with Alessio proudly holding her hand because he sat next to her; among the rest of them, Caterina pretending not to know that Franco's eyes were fixed on her, and Adam – because for the final supper he *was* there – listening with his usual air of courteous but detached attention.

At that point in her circuit of the table, Georgina suddenly closed her eyes, aware of something more insistent than the contented certainty she'd just been feeling. Still unidentified, and still more unwelcome than before was the strange, unsettling sensation of a moment she must continue to wait for. It would come whether she wanted it to or not, but it cast a shadow on the future, not the light of some happiness that she might expect.

She opened her eyes and found William watching her across the table. He was smiling at her – for comfort, she thought, knowing that comfort was needed.

The following morning, while William made a final visit to the *cantina* with Tommaso, Georgina busied herself outside – it was a blessed thing about a garden; there was always something in it one could find to do. She was staking up great, gaudy dahlias when Adam's voice spoke behind her.

'Do I detect a little irritation in the gardener's tying of knots? Surely not – she loves all growing things, except bindweed, I seem to remember.'

Georgina turned round to glower at him. 'They're not my favourite things, dahlias; they haven't the sense to know they should stop growing while they can still support themselves.'

'You could say the same of us,' he pointed out. 'We often don't know our limitations, either.'

Irritation – she thought his own word would have to do for the malaise that still assailed her – was suddenly sharpened to knife-point; he had no right to sound so damnably reasonable and serene and self-sufficient. Just once she needed to get behind the professor's cool, unruffled façade.

'Amanda told me about your wife,' she said suddenly. 'You didn't mention her yourself – it's as if she never existed.'

There was silence for a moment; she regretted the words and would have cancelled them if she could, but it wasn't possible.

'You only didn't hear from me about Elizabeth's brief life because it had nothing to do with Poggio. Why should you have been interested?' he asked finally.

Georgina stared at him, thinking that the small distance between them might have been an ocean waste for all the hope she had of reaching him across it.

'We could have understood you a little better,' she said slowly, 'but that wasn't what you wanted, of course.'

He considered this for a moment, then shook his head. 'I'm afraid you still don't understand anything at all, even knowing about Elizabeth.'

The rejection sounded as final as she supposed he meant it to. It ended the conversation certainly enough, but also their chequered relationship as well. She saw him nod and walk away, and could only think how symmetrical it all was – they'd begun and ended by misunderstanding one another.

* * *

185

That afternoon William left for England and she drove him back to Florence to catch the train. They arrived at the station with less time in hand than she'd hoped in which to talk to him away from Poggio. But when the moment came she couldn't think how to begin, and he misread her hesitation. His hands suddenly cupped her face – gently, as he always touched everything.

'Don't fret, love, and don't be in a hurry to make up your mind. Come back if you want to, otherwise stay and be happy here. That's what matters, not what I want you to do.'

'Italy's making me emotional,' she muttered, blinking away tears. 'I keep finding myself wanting to cry – now, I expect, because I've got to say goodbye to you, and I hate doing that.'

'There's always next year's *vendemmia*,' he pointed out, hoping to cheer them both up. 'Lucia made me promise to come for that.'

'We'll both come – together!' It was out now, and suddenly she could smile at him. 'Dearest William, I have to stay and see the olives in – they've been *my* concern all along. But if you can't come back for Christmas, can I come to you? I mean, to stay.'

She was only just in time, because suddenly whistles began to blow as the great train got ready to haul itself across Italy and France. But William had heard and understood; she was pulled hard against him and his face was buried in her hair.

'Stay for ever, love,' he murmured unsteadily.

Released a little, she reached up to kiss him: a promise that it was what she would do.

'I'm not sure I believe it yet,' said William, 'but I shall spend the time from here to Calais grinning at my fellow-passengers, and telling them about the girl I'm going to marry!'

'Unless you miss the train instead,' she pointed out with an anxious smile as the commotion all about them rose to fever-pitch. He quickly kissed her mouth, then leapt on board the train, and stood leaning out of the window.

'Until Christmas,' he shouted above the racket, 'here or at home.'

The whistles gave a final hysterical shriek, the last door slammed, and slowly the great serpent of coaches was beginning to move. She stood there until she could no longer see William's wave, then turned away and walked along the now-empty platform. It was stupid to feel so forlorn; in three months, at the most, they would be back at Kew together. She told herself that she'd be perfectly all right as soon as she'd broken her news to Lucia and Enrico. Then, that ominous sense of something about to happen would finally dwindle and die in the certainty of having made her choice. There was nothing to fear, and everything to look forward to; and she must remember that she was the age she was, not a nervous adolescent, wishing with all her heart that it hadn't been necessary for William to set off for England alone, leaving her behind.

Chapter 19

Filippo wasn't sorry to be back in Siena. He'd thoroughly enjoyed himself at Poggio, and liked helping Enrico, but he wasn't a countryman at heart. It made him less critical than he might have been of Roberto Artom's ambition to buy up half of Tuscany, but the man's business methods were only just on the hither side of legal, and overconfidence might sooner or later put him squarely on the wrong side of the law. Filippo waited hopefully for that day, having felt obliged to promise his father that the matter of the Palio had ended with Dino Artom's apology.

Being so often away, Roberto wasn't difficult to avoid even though they worked in the same city, but one morning not long after the *vendemmia* holiday he was drinking coffee in the *ristorante* that Filippo favoured for his own early snack. To turn tail would have looked like a retreat, and the two of them smiled at each other – boxers weighing up the opposition before the bout began.

'You look well, Filippo,' Roberto said affably.

'A virtuous life; fresh air, early nights – not your sort of thing at all! Business is good, I hope?'

'Excellent, thank you. My purchase of Frescobaldi's place near Greve is just going through – another failed estate, but at least he had the sense to sell, unlike Enrico.'

'Poggio isn't a failed estate,' Filippo pointed out gently. 'I was allowed to help with the *vendemmia* there – a good one, everybody reckoned; the whole place was humming. It quite did my heart good!'

'Delaying collapse by a season or two, until Enrico's money runs out again.' Roberto shrugged the subject aside. 'Was Georgina still there? Well, I suppose she has to be, having rather rashly sold her home in London. Poor girl, she must be regretting that, and feeling very lonely.'

Filippo shook his head. 'Not lonely! All my friends find excuses to drop in at Poggio but I'm afraid she really prefers her own countrymen – not surprisingly!' Pleased with that little jab, Filippo sailed happily on. 'A very nice friend came over from London, obviously in the hope of enticing her back. Then, of course, there's the professor . . .'

'What about him?' Roberto snapped, forgetting to sound unconcerned.

Filippo smiled again. 'He's still there for the moment, with that irritating English habit of coming from behind and winning. I expect you remember that!' It had been beautifully true in the Palio, but Filippo had mentioned Adam Fleming now only in the hope of causing Roberto irritation. Watching Adam at the *vendemmia*, he'd seen no chance of him taking part in a different race against his own countryman; that wouldn't be his way. Filippo accepted the fact philosophically – after all, God had made the professor not an Italian. He stood up to leave. 'Now I must go or I'll be late for work, and that would never do. *Ciao*, Roberto, nice seeing you again.'

He sauntered away, feeling extremely pleased with himself; there was nothing like paying off a score for setting a man up for the day. Roberto remained where he was for a moment, then went to a telephone, because it was suddenly extremely important to know when the man they'd been talking about would be returning to England.

Georgina's turn to bump into Roberto came only a day later when she was walking home from San Vicenzo in the dusk of an October late-afternoon. The trip into town hadn't been necessary, but the morning's heavy rain had prevented work out of doors, and she'd seized on an errand for Maria when the clouds finally lifted. As usual, when she was alone, her tired mind insisted on seeing problems that didn't really exist. It was only what she'd expected – that Lucia and Enrico should have been disappointed by her decision not to stay at Poggio. They'd both taken a strong liking to William, there wasn't any doubt about that; but they couldn't help hoping that she might have found a man to love in Tuscany. Enrico, perhaps, even more than Lucia, had shared his daughter's view that life would be complete if they could all be reunited at Poggio. Georgina refused to be dismayed, but she couldn't help knowing that the future would depend on Tommaso; Poggio would only be safe if *he* remained with her grandfather.

Deep in thought, she was startled when the outline of a man materialised out of the dimness ahead of her: not anyone she might have expected. She recognised him with astonishment – Roberto Artom, for once on foot, walking down the track that higher up forked either to Poggio or over the hill to Casagrande. He came level with her and she made no effort to greet him pleasantly.

'Not your usual habit to go walking about the countryside,' she pointed out. 'Have you driven your car into a ditch?'

'Not at all, *cara*. You passed it half a mile back. I was doing a rare good deed, as it happens – directing someone who'd lost his way.'

The explanation came readily, but it occurred to her that he sounded less smooth than usual, slightly breathless perhaps from the unaccustomed exercise he'd had to take. It was an odd time of the day for anyone to be climbing hill tracks, but not even Roberto would have refused to help a stranger. She wanted to get away, but needed even more to stay and puncture his overweening confidence in himself if she could.

'Your parents are keeping you informed, I expect, about affairs at Poggio. Our *vendemmia* was earlier than Casagrande's and it went extremely well.'

'I know – Filippo told me yesterday. He sounded full of virtue for having been there, toiling for Enrico.'

'I'm surprised he brought himself to talk to you at all – you don't deserve that any of us should. But still, Adam Fleming did worst you in the end. You despised *him*, I seem to remember – wrongly as it turned out.'

The contempt in her voice stung like ice against his skin but Roberto was struggling with too many emotions for rage to get the upper hand. More than anything else, he was still aware of aching regret – this could, *should*, have been his girl, the lover and wife he'd wanted all along, and only lost because she hadn't been able to see the future they might have had together.

'I wrongly despised him, but I rightly loved you,' he insisted. 'You should have known that, Georgina. I'd have taken care of your grandparents – you should have known that as well.'

She was disconcerted for a moment by the ring of sincerity in his voice, then remembered that much of his success had come from his ability to sound convincing. 'You'd have "helped" by destroying Poggio. It wasn't much of an offer, and I'm thankful in my prayers every night that we were able to turn it down.'

Roberto's mouth twisted in a sneer. 'We're back to the *caro professore*, I see! Well, I hope he doesn't lose his investment as well as everything else – even a trusting fool like Adam Fleming doesn't deserve that. Now, I must regretfully *not* offer to escort you home, *cara* – I've work to do before I leave for Geneva in the morning. It's a more exciting life than watching the seasons change at Poggio!'

He smiled and walked past her, trying to block out the thought that he'd probably seen her for the last time. She'd go back to England and settle down with some cool and inarticulate islander who hadn't the first idea of how to love her. He *hated* waste, and the waste of Georgina Hadley might always haunt him, even when he was being offered the charms of some other woman. He hadn't yet found anyone else to laugh with as well as love.

But left to herself again, Georgina let out a sigh of relief; the encounter had been disturbing, not least for the venom in Roberto's voice when he spoke of Adam. Still, it was understandable; he'd been beaten twice by a man he pretended not to take seriously. She reached the courtyard at Poggio and heard the usual noises from Maria's sitting room – she'd be watching television until it was time to start preparing supper; the other rooms were unlit, because Enrico and Lucia were out calling on friends.

Tommaso would be busy in the *cantina*, of course, absorbed in hovering over the huge vats. The crust of skins and stalks that kept forming over the fermenting mass had to be regularly broken up; this allowed carbon dioxide that would otherwise make the wine diseased to escape.

There was no light in the farmhouse, which she glanced at out of habit, but Lucia had said the professor was making farewell visits, now, to friends in Florence and Siena. He had, though, gone out without properly shutting his door – she could see it standing ajar, and must go and close it for him in case the evening turned wet again.

She climbed the staircase and fumbled for the light switch just inside the door. Even as she did so, she was aware of something wrong. The door hadn't blown open – a visitor had left in too much of a hurry to shut it. There was, she could now see, only chaos all around her – papers torn up and scattered, the folders normally stacked on Adam's desk thrown down, to empty themselves on the floor; the deliberate ruin of months of work. There had been no stranger needing to be shown his way; there'd been only Roberto Artom directing his paid creature to the farmhouse, to destroy a man he hadn't been able to beat fairly. If he'd reappeared then she thought she would have tried to kill him with whatever instrument came to hand. But beneath anger lay something worse – with the destruction of Adam's work, the room felt abandoned as if he'd already gone out of their lives; this, she realised with a shock as physical as a blow over the head, was how it would always feel from now on during the years to be faced without him.

The moment she'd believed she could avoid had finally arrived after all – the moment of truth, the Spaniards called it. The wave of self-knowledge that she had been ducking ever since coming to Poggio was upon her now, as irresistible as an incoming tide.

The choice had seemed easy enough: Poggio or William. But even loving him, as she certainly did, the choice wasn't going to be easy now. Was she to welsh on the promise she'd made him, and destroy *his* happiness? Could she love him enough for the truth to be lived with that she dwelt with a different man in her heart's core? The man in question had no need of her at all, but William needed her.

She was still slumped in a chair, oblivious of the disorder around her, when Adam Fleming walked in. It was just possible to remember that she must find something to say.

'Lucia said you were going to Siena.' She muttered it, aware in some still-functioning corner of her mind that to sound angry with him was her only defence against breaking down.

'I went to Siena, now I'm back,' he explained calmly. 'I seem to have missed a visitor.'

Now, at least, she needn't pretend to be angry. Before he could point out, as he probably would, that calmness in the face of disaster was the Oxford way, she found herself shouting at him.

'Be *angry*, for God's sake – *feel* something, Adam; don't stand there pretending that this kind of vindictiveness doesn't matter. Be like the rest of us for once, instead of inhumanly detached – be vulnerable, hurt, enraged . . . *anything* but coolly amused.'

Her voice broke on the words and tears began to trickle down her cheeks, blinding her to the strange expression that touched his mouth for a moment. Then he closed the gap between them and knelt down beside her.

'Don't cry, please. I'll try to rant and rave if it will make you feel better, though it doesn't come naturally; but there's no need. My visitor went to a great deal of trouble here to destroy all my notes and research material – a nuisance, certainly, but not a tragedy. My completed typescript is locked in Enrico's safe.'

'You expected something like this to happen?' she asked, in a voice she still couldn't hold steady.

'Not exactly this, but it seemed sensible to take precautions.'

She mopped her wet face and tried to sound as if the outburst of a moment ago hadn't happened. 'Your visitor wasn't Roberto himself – I met him going back to San Vicenzo; but he sent the man who came here. He almost as good as said so, but I expect you'll tell me again that we can't *prove* it.'

'I expect I shall,' he agreed with a faint smile.

'Oxford logic – how I hate it!'

'I know.' He stood up and moved away across the room, not seeming to notice the tide of torn paper flowing round his feet. At a safe distance where he wasn't tempted to reach out and touch her, he was able to go on. 'I shall send Roberto a copy of the published book, suitably inscribed – "inhumanly detached" though I am, I shall enjoy doing that!'

If he hoped to make her look less distraught he was disappointed. She could only see in what he suggested a response that would provoke still more retaliation. It was a pattern of feud and vendetta as old and inevitable as the history of the cities that surrounded them. It was Italy's history writ small.

'Don't ever come back to Poggio,' she burst out suddenly. 'Just stay away from us in future.'

The words fell into a silence that it seemed he might not bother to break. Then at last he spoke.

'Brutally frank. But when have you been anything else?'

The question, lightly asked, needed no answer because it didn't matter to him what she was, but she was incapable of making one anyway. Her only rational thought didn't matter either, but it was all her disordered mind could produce: they must have been destined to be always insanely at odds with each other.

'You won't be here yourself,' he finally remembered to point out. 'You'll be with William.'

It calmed her, as a douche of cold water might have done. She almost smiled as she replied, because the agonising question in her mind had finally been answered.

'Yes . . . I shall be with William.' She got up and walked past him out of the room, and only remembered as she went home through the garden that he might have expected her to stay and help him clear up the mess.

He left for England two days later and when the moment came, by planning of the most careful sort, she was able to leave a brief farewell message for him with her grandmother while she took herself into Florence on some vital errand. He'd gone by the time she got back and, after looking at her pale face, Lucia changed her mind about the reproach she'd been going to make.

Enrico admitted to missing their tenant himself, but finally lost patience with his household's mournful air when Caterina burst into tears one morning over a pair of the professor's battered sandals, overlooked and left behind in the porch. Lucia agreed that they were scarcely worth weeping for, but explained firmly to her husband that shouting at a lovesick adolescent was no way to cure her affliction.

'You and Maria are almost as bad,' he retaliated. 'Anyone would think we were never going to see Adam again – he'll be back as soon as he gets another holiday.'

But, much to his surprise, Lucia shook her head. 'I don't think so, my dear. He'll keep in touch with you of course, but I'm almost certain we shan't have the pleasure of his company again.'

She spoke quietly as usual, but with a conviction that Enrico was bound to heed. 'Because of Caterina's foolishness?' he enquired. 'Adam knows how to deal with that. If he doesn't come Alessio will be upset – he asks me almost every day when his professor will be back.'

Lucia gave a little shrug and abandoned the subject for one that weighed on her more heavily – between now and Christmas Georgina must be stopped from working too hard out in the gardens by herself every day.

'I don't stand over her with a whip, *tesoro*,' Enrico protested. 'She's determined that before she leaves everywhere will be ready to look beautiful by next spring. It's for *your* benefit – she knows how you love flowers.'

'Of course I do, but I love her more, and I can't bear to see her come in so tired that she refuses all Filippo's invitations.'

Unwilling to admit that he could never see a way of influencing his granddaughter in any direction whatsoever, Enrico pulled on his cap and went into the soft, damp morning for his customary inspection with Tommaso. With the arrival of the late-autumn rain, they must press on now with the work that would make all the difference between success and failure next year – there were exhausted vines to grub up, healthy ones to be thoroughly pruned, and new stock to be planted wherever gaps were left. When he went outside Tommaso was already at work, training Franco in the delicate task of burying vine runners so that they would root themselves and spring into fresh growth. The two of them acknowledged the *padrone*'s arrival, but went on with the task in hand, and Enrico sauntered on along the terraced rows, wondering yet again how he could have survived the loss of Poggio. But, remembering his conversation indoors, he returned by way of the vegetable garden, and found Georgina there, turning soil with the economical flick of the wrist that spoke of much practice. She straightened up and smiled at her grandfather.

'Next spring's early broad beans need planting, and it's perfect damp weather for the job.'

He agreed, looking round the neatly tended plot. She was as much an expert as he was himself or Tommaso, and the knowledge gave him pleasure. Richard Hadley's daughter she might be, clever and sophisticated; but she was a chip off the Casali block as well, and the future had to be thought of whether *she* would be here or not. In fairness, though, he felt obliged to air Lucia's concern.

'Your grandmother blames *me* for all the hours you spend out here – she thinks you ought to be with young people, enjoying yourself.'

'This *is* where I enjoy myself,' she answered. 'Tell Granny to stop worrying about me. I love what I do, and I'm thoroughly content.'

This was sufficiently true for her to be able to look her grandfather in the eye. The strangest part of the truth was that, in moving into the farmhouse rooms she'd laid claim to, she'd found a quite unexpected comfort. Some imprint of the professor, some friendly ghost she could almost feel, seemed to keep her company, warding off both present loneliness and doubt about the future. She'd be able to manage; she was becoming more and more sure of it.

Enrico smiled, relieved that he would be able to give Lucia a cheerful report. 'The new plantings are looking good – I think Tommaso talks to them every day, to explain that we require them to prosper!'

'Perhaps we should get Father Anselmo to bless them?' Georgina suggested half seriously.

'Why not? God knows we must give them all the help we can; they're Poggio's future.'

She stared at his face, still brown from the summer beneath the thatch of thick white hair. The anxieties of the past year had changed him; he was wiser now, humbled by having come close to disaster. No longer with the unquestioning devotion of childhood, she still loved him very much, perhaps even more now.

'Gramps, are we trying to do the impossible?' she suddenly asked. 'Roberto kept suggesting that. He said we wanted to make time stand still here when it won't anywhere else.'

He didn't misunderstand her question or, as she expected, try to evade answering it. 'You mean can we survive in today's world – against competition that rips the heart out of land in the name of a quick profit, against men who rely on chemicals to boost yields and machines to do the hard work? I think we can, *tesoro*; in fact, we *must*. We inherited this Tuscan landscape – beautiful beyond description simply because it *has* always been tended by hand. It mustn't be lost now through *us* betraying it to the barbarians. People are beginning to understand what matters now. Years back they were abandoning the countryside in search of an easier living, but polluted, crime-ridden cities will eventually drive them back

196

again – look at young Franco. We've got Tommaso, thank God, and Alessio when the time comes. Not to mention my own great-grandchildren, I hope!'

She leaned forward to kiss his cheek, not sure whether the wetness her mouth touched was rain or her own tears. 'You're right – of course you are; but concentrate on Alessio, please. I think that would be safer.'

Chapter 20

The olive harvest, last important event of the year, was traditionally a job for women, and during the month of December they moved about the district, stripping each orchard in turn. Cloths were spread below any branches that could be shaken; otherwise the fruit was picked by hand and gathered in small baskets that the women strapped to their waists. Speed was vital once the olives were ready, but the hard work was no bar to shared talk and laughter, and no one would have dreamed of missing it.

At Poggio, Tommaso was in charge in the *cantina*, supervising the all-important first, cold pressing of the fruit. From this came the pure, green oil of the finest quality and flavour, and bowls of it were always set aside when ready, to be ritually tasted on small chunks of bread. Then heat was used to extract the rest, and finally the mush of stalks and skins went back into the ground as compost – nothing was wasted in the life-cycle of this most vital of mediterranean trees.

Georgina joined in the harvesting, not sorry for the excuse it gave her to refuse Filippo's invitations. But when he reproached her one day for becoming obsessed with saving Poggio, she was obliged to acknowledge the hurt she heard beneath his banter.

'I don't mean to sound ungrateful,' she said contritely. 'You're kindness itself to go on bothering with me. But I just want to get as much accomplished as possible before I return to England. I suppose the truth is that I feel guilty about going at all! Gramps picked up the reins again partly because he thought I'd always be here.'

She smiled as she spoke, but Filippo had a sensitive ear and heard the faint tremor in her voice.

'A Puritan conscience is a terrible handicap to a carefree life,' he pointed out almost severely. 'You've already done more for Enrico than half a dozen normal granddaughters. William's being remarkably patient if you ask me.' He hesitated for a moment, then asked a question she hadn't prepared herself for.

'Do you hear from Adam Fleming? I assume he still takes an interest in what he invested in.'

She managed a creditably careless shrug – perhaps she should have become an actress instead of a horticulturalist? 'I don't enquire about the professor, not wanting to remind my grandfather of the loan that still hangs over us. I expect Adam is too busy with his own affairs to give much thought to it either. He bit my head off one day when I said we felt obliged to feel grateful!' She was pleased with herself for sounding casual, and even managed to touch up the picture of indifference a little more. 'Lucia thinks he won't come back, and I expect she's right; she usually is.' Filippo accepted it with a nod, and changed the subject again.

'We'll make do with you and William, if you can drag him away now and again from that funny-sounding place he seems to adore.'

She agreed that she would do her best, and managed to keep smiling until Filippo had kissed her affectionately and roared away.

But, alone again, she was unable to shut out the memory of the man her cousin had called to mind. By now the Oxford term would have ended; she could no longer imagine him walking across a green quadrangle to work in some remote corner of an ancient building, or sharing in the arcane rituals of dinner at high table. The air of courteous attention with which he'd do that, and the smile he'd offer the diner next to him – these were things she *could* visualise easily enough. But she had no idea how his Christmas vacation would be spent, knew almost nothing about him except that, having loved a woman who'd died cruelly young, he wasn't minded to even consider looking for anyone to take her place. She prayed that one day she would regret that only for his sake; being contented herself, she would want *him* to know contentment as well.

Unaware for a moment of anything but that urgent plea to God Almighty, she scarcely heard Alessio's voice beside her.

'It's nearly *Natale*, Gina. No more school for days and days – *bellissima, non è vero*; at least, it would be if you weren't going to leave afterwards with Signor William.'

'Well, *bellissima*, anyway,' she was able to agree.

'I'm allowed to choose one of Mamma's geese for our Christmas dinner,' Alessio went on. 'Signora Lucia says it's an honour for the one chosen, but I'm not sure the *povero* I pick will think that's true.' Then an entrancing smile lifted the frown from his face. 'Do you remember how all the silly creatures used to run behind the professor whenever he crossed the garden?'

'Yes, I remember,' she murmured. 'The poor things reckoned they'd be safe with him.'

Alessio nodded, thinking it likely – his friend *had* seemed to make everyone feel safe and happy. The truth was that they hadn't quite got used to being without him, and England did seem so very far away. Georgina waited for Alessio to suggest that not only William but the professor as well should be joining them for Christmas, but if he'd been about to say that he changed his mind.

'I've been sent out now to pick greenery,' he said instead, 'and I suppose I'd better get on with it, because the signora and Mamma and Caterina are setting up the *presepio*. Does that happen in England, too?'

'In churches, of course; perhaps not so much in people's homes as here.' She anticipated his next question and managed to answer it calmly. 'I doubt if the professor at this moment is constructing a manger and a crib; the *presepio* needs a family, but I think he lives alone.'

Alessio agreed also that this was so, and wandered away at last in search of the branches of pine and spruce and cypress that he'd been instructed to find.

There *was* no crib being prepared in Adam's house on the outskirts of North Oxford, for the good reason that he wasn't there. He'd been summoned to London to escort his mother to spend Christmas with Amanda and her family.

The ferry-crossing was extremely rough, but having insisted on it herself rather than submit to travelling beneath the Channel waters, Alicia Fleming managed not to complain. Only when Adam confessed, on the train-journey to Paris, that he wasn't going to stay there more than a few days, did she allow herself to protest.

'My dear, how can you *not* stay? Even if Amanda and Jean-Paul don't mind, which they will, the boys will be heartbroken. In any case, what are you going to do instead? See the New Year in somewhere on your own?'

If she hoped to hear him say that he'd got plans – a group of pleasant friends to meet or, better still, a sole companion whose company he craved – she was deeply disappointed. He merely smiled and admitted that he hadn't quite decided where to go. But his mother's hurt expression made him say more than he'd intended to.

'Forgive me, please. Amanda will be her usual lovely welcoming self, and I'm very fond of her husband and her sons; but the truth is I'm looking forward to a little escape from being sociable! After a year's sabbatical I've found it harder than I expected to get back into harness again.'

He smiled as he spoke, but she sensed in him some weariness and strain that couldn't be argued with. She might have suggested that it was the sabbatical itself he needed to recover from, because he'd spoken about it so little; but gentle though he always was with her, she knew she had no licence to delve into what he preferred to keep to himself.

Eventually ensconced in the Blanchards' comfortable apartment overlooking the Bois de Boulogne, she did, however, bewail to her daughter Adam's determination to remain a solitary man.

'It's not natural,' she insisted mournfully. 'How long ago did Elizabeth die? Five years? I don't expect him to marry again if one marriage was enough, and Heaven knows I don't want him embroiled instead with some designing minx of a student half his age; but someone to think about, take care of, even *worry* over again . . . that he *does* need. Otherwise he'll grow into the sort of selfish, eccentric academic that Oxford seems to breed like flies!'

Amanda grinned at the visions conjured up by her mother's plaintive cry, but knew that she was right – there *was* something seriously amiss with Adam. He was having to try so hard this time to enjoy their rumbustious family life that it would have been unkind to talk him into staying longer.

'You'll be back to take Mother home?' she merely asked when he was getting ready to leave as soon as Christmas was over.

'Of course.' He stuffed another sweater in the bag he was packing, then smiled at his sister. 'You're making such heroic efforts not to ask questions that I'm inclined to beg you to fire away before you burst!'

'All right – I'll ask one at least. Where will you go? I know you love walking in the mountains, but they're deep in snow and skiing parties at the moment.'

'*Not* the mountains,' he agreed. 'I think I might make for Venice. Midwinter isn't the ideal time to search cold, dark churches for treasures the custodians scarcely remember they've got, but at least I shall be able to see them without a horde of tourists getting in the way.'

Amanda examined his face, then risked another question. 'Will you stop off at Poggio?'

'No – and nor would I do that even if it were anywhere near the line I shall be travelling on. The very last thing I want is for Enrico Casali to think I'm breathing down his neck, and waiting to see my money back.'

'My impression was that they'd always be overjoyed to see you,' she insisted stubbornly. 'What's more, Adam, you seemed to be happier there than I've ever known you – you loved that Poggio adventure.'

He wanted, suddenly, to shout at her, deny what she said, but it wouldn't have been fair. She spoke the simple truth and he knew it very well.

'That's what it was,' he agreed at last, 'but adventures are like love-affairs, best not repeated.'

The note of finality in his voice warned her to change tack. 'I've written to Georgina about a visit here. If horticulturalists aren't allowed time off in the winter, when do they ever go away?'

He had no answer to that and she was obliged to persevere. 'I'm not saying Poggio isn't absolutely beautiful but a change of scene would be good for her. I thought she looked sad – incomplete somehow – when we said goodbye.'

Adam carefully rolled up a pair of socks, then unrolled them again as if he'd forgotten what he was doing with them. 'Woman's intuition is letting you down, I'm afraid, if that was a hint in my direction; Georgina and I did very little but quarrel. She fell in love with a remarkably handsome villain, and her self-confidence took a knock over that. But she had a bolt-hole waiting for her in London; in fact, she might even be there already. A very nice man called William was patiently waiting for her to get to the point where she thought she could safely leave Poggio. He came out for the *vendemmia*, and a blind man couldn't have missed their affection for each other.'

Amanda gave up with a small gesture of defeat. 'Go and look at your gloomy Venetian churches if you must, but it isn't the jolliest way of seeing in a New Year.' She smiled lovingly at him, but thought of a parting shot as she went out of the room. 'Georgina's still at Poggio, by the way; her card said that *she*'d be there for Christmas, but it didn't mention a William.'

An hour later he was watching the lights of Paris disappear into the darkness as the night-express gathered speed. His sleeping-berth looked comfortable, and he always enjoyed train journeys. At the end of this one the water-cradled city he loved would be waiting for him – so there was only pleasure in view all round. But for once contentment didn't come, and nor did sleep when he finally turned out the light; instead, Amanda's last remark kept beating in his brain, and the click-clack of the train wheels added its own derisive accompaniment.

It wasn't the time to be pruning roses, but the turn-of-the-year weather had become unusually mild and damp, and there'd been more urgent tasks to see to in the autumn. Finally driven indoors by the falling dusk, Georgina went to invite herself and William to supper with her grandparents. For

once, instead of reading the daily chapter of a Jane Austen novel that
Lucia struggled with for the good of her English, she sat with the book
unopened in her lap.

'I was coming out to find you,' she said, forgetting to enquire about the
roses. 'I've just had a telephone call . . . from Adam.'

'New Year greetings from England?' Georgina managed to ask after a
moment's silence.

'No, from Florence – that's where he is. He suggested that we dine
with him there this evening. I wanted him to come here, of course, but
Adam has no car – he came from Paris on his way to Venice by train.'

Never one to consider how one got from A to B, even her grandmother,
Georgina thought, ought to see something odd in a rail journey from Paris
to Venice that took in Florence as well.

'The small boy who likes trains must still lurk inside the professor!'
she suggested calmly. 'Enjoy your outing, *cara*; William and I will eat at
home when he gets back with Gramps from San Vicenzo, and I've had a
long, hot soak in the bath – it's been miserable outside all day.'

Lucia's voice halted her before she reached the door. 'I hope you're off
to change into something more attractive than those dungarees – all four
of us are dining with Adam this evening – I told him William was with
us.' She saw instant refusal in the face opposite her and spoke again,
sharply for once. 'You *must* come, my dear. I accepted for all of us, and
Adam doesn't deserve to be hurt, just because you dislike being under an
obligation to him.'

Her steady gaze demanded agreement, and Georgina finally gave
in. 'All right – we'll come if you insist, but only so that *I* or William
can drive us home and Gramps can enjoy more than one glass of
wine.'

Lucia nodded, deciding not to mention for the time being that their
host for the evening would also be able to drive them home, since she'd
insisted on him coming back to Poggio afterwards.

Enrico and William returned from their errand in town, to be greeted
with the news that they must soon set off again. Georgina replaced her
working clothes with a fine wool skirt and jade-green cashmere sweater,
but made a point of not dressing up. It was enough that two of them should
be overdressed, she suggested, for the pizzeria that Adam probably
intended to take them to. William, comfortable in battered tweeds, merely
grinned at the sharpness, but Enrico took exception to it.

'Scarcely a pizzeria,' he corrected her firmly. 'I gather our host
suggested the Cantinetta Antinori – a fifteenth-century *palazzo* and some

of the finest food and wine in Italy! It seems to me that deserves a little dressing-up for.'

Adam was already there, waiting for them at the restaurant – taller than most of those around him, and also set apart by his straw-coloured hair. Lucia was kissed warmly and he offered William a friendly handshake, but he hesitated about how to greet his other female guest, and she retreated to safety with a cool '*buona sera, professore*' before they sat down.

The restaurant was all that Enrico had claimed – the service a miracle of quiet attentiveness, the *prosciutto*, lobster, and out-of-season white peaches delicious, the Brunello wine alone worth a journey and to be relished sip by sip; but Georgina knew that what she would remember the evening for would be none of those things. Instead, memory would hold only a picture of her companions – Lucia sparkling in the knowledge that all three men she was with loved her and rightly found her beautiful; Enrico trying to mute the operatic richness of his voice in public but frequently forgetting; William rather quiet, but that was how he usually enjoyed himself; and Adam, treating her grandparents with the teasing grace and affection that were his special gift. What had he been like, she wondered, before the death of his wife had made him choose to be a solitary man? Like this, of course, but with some added private warmth that only she would ever have known about.

Accepting the truth of it, she felt the knot of angry resistance with which she'd begun the evening finally subside. She couldn't be anything but glad he was there, briefly lighting up their lives again. Pain would come later, but she'd deal with that when she had to.

When the evening ended William was allowed to drive the car home, Enrico sat with him in the front, and Adam installed himself between the ladies in the back. Georgina left her grandmother to talk to him, only able to remember another car-ride shared with him – a rainy journey into Florence, prelude to a day that remained nevertheless golden in her memory. It seemed a long time ago, and the future that now stretched in front of her looked interminable; but she stared at the familiar shape of William's head in front of her, and pretended that she couldn't even feel the warmth of Adam Fleming's shoulder touching hers in the moments when the movement of the car threw them together.

Chapter 21

At Poggio, exhausted by the evening's strain, Georgina said an abrupt goodnight, leaving her grandmother to explain to Adam that she now used what had been his rooms. Having also told him where he'd be sleeping in the house, Lucia kissed him and William and retired to bed herself. Enrico lingered long enough to pour them a nightcap of brandy – William, he said, having abstained from most of the evening's wine.

Left alone with Adam, William nursed his glass, wondering how to begin a conversation he saw as necessary. But the professor found something to say first.

'With Christmas over, I suppose you and Georgina will soon be going home?'

'That's the plan,' William agreed unemphatically. Then he stared at his glass, trying to decide whether the brandy which he didn't like would be better disposed of in small sips or downed in one huge gulp.

'I imagined you might both be at Kew already,' Adam struggled politely on, 'until my sister mentioned that Georgina was still here. I didn't intend stopping off at Poggio but, once I was in Italy, it seemed a pity not to drop in on Lucia and Enrico.' He thought he was talking too much, chattering like a fool. His glance skimmed the bearded face of William Bird, fearing it might say what the man himself wouldn't put into words – that Professor Fleming was not only a fool but a liar as well. But William had a different comment to make.

'I don't blame you for wanting to come back – this would still be a lovely place even without Georgina, and it's going to be able to manage now, whether she's here or not. She had to be sure of that – now she is, I think.'

'So all I have to do,' said Adam with heroic cheerfulness, 'is wish you both every happiness, and resume my interrupted journey to Venice in the morning. It's been good to see you again but now I shall follow our hosts' example and go to bed.'

But William still had something more to say. 'Nice of you to include me in this evening's party; I doubt if you were expecting me when you telephoned Lucia.'

His quiet voice still laid no particular stress on what he'd just said, but there was something in his expression that suddenly obliged Adam to lay pretence aside and acknowledge the issue between them. 'We should be circling one another like fighting cocks, you realise! But the truth is that Georgina's got a good bargain this time – she needed it after Roberto Artom. I'm grateful to know you'll take the care of her that I would myself.'

His faint, sweet smile shone for a moment, then he put down his glass and walked out of the room. William remained where he was for a long time; then with something resolved at last, he switched off the lamps and went upstairs himself.

For Georgina, in the farmhouse across the courtyard, it seemed a never-ending night. But she slept at last and woke late, with the headache always brought on by restless dozing. Still in dressing-gown and slippers, she was in the kitchen making tea when a knock sounded at the door. The temptation to ignore it was strong, but whoever stood outside would have seen the lighted room. She found Lucia waiting there, looking as if she'd been up and dressed for hours.

'Sorry, Gran, come in. You seem to have managed Antinori's rich food better than I did! Will you share my reviving pot of tea, or have you already breakfasted?'

'I've drunk my coffee, *cara*. No tea, thank you.' Lucia's eyes examined the pale, heavy-eyed face in front of her while she decided how to go on. 'Adam is out with your grandfather, inspecting the new vines.'

'And I expect William is hobnobbing with Tommaso in the *cantina* as usual.'

There was a small, deliberate pause before Lucia spoke again. 'My dear, William isn't here – he asked Tommaso to drive him to Florence, to catch the express to Calais; they left very early this morning.'

'It's not possible!' White to the lips now, Georgina barely muttered the words. 'I don't believe it – he wouldn't have gone without telling me.' She ducked her head under a wave of faintness, and felt the warmth of her grandmother's arms enfolding her while she recovered from it.

'William left me a note,' Lucia explained quietly, 'such a loving note, *tesoro*. He hasn't gone away angry, if that's what you're afraid of.'

'But *why*? Why has he gone at all without me? We were going to drive back together.'

Lucia answered the desperate question by pulling an envelope out of her pocket. 'There was a note for you as well. Shall I go away while you read it?'

Georgina merely shook her head, unfolding the single sheet the envelope had contained. William wrote short letters, it seemed, to match his very economical conversations.

Dearest girl,

It was a sudden change of plan to push off on my own, but I had the feeling last night that it would be the best thing to do, in case you needed some thinking time on your own. If I've got it wrong, forgive me and come home soon. But if our plan was the mistake, I won't have you sticking to it buckle and thong just because you reckon you're obliged to. There's no dishonour in admitting to an error – only false pride in not doing so.

It was the best Christmas I can remember, I've told Lucia that, but I didn't quite have the nerve to mention that I love her nearly as much as I love you. I always shall, whatever happens: it's my special privilege, I reckon.

Yours,
William.

'I'm to tell you that he loves you very much,' Georgina unsteadily informed her grandmother. 'I'm still not sure why he's gone, except that last night seems to have made a difference of some kind. I don't know what he means by that.'

'Nor I, my dear, but he *is* a very observant man,' Lucia pointed out gently. 'What are you to do now?'

'Think, apparently! It's silly, of course, but my dear William wants to be sure I haven't made another mistake.' She made a brave attempt at a smile. 'I don't think *he's* trying to get rid of me!'

Lucia's sharp gesture dismissed the idea out of hand. 'Do your thinking then, *tesoro*, as William asks. I shall be indoors if you need me.'

She kissed her granddaughter and went away, and without her the room seemed suddenly very empty. Life itself seemed empty now because William, instead of being there, was already on his long, lonely journey across Europe. She was beyond the relief of tears or of any belief that what happened to Georgina Hadley mattered in the scheme of things. It was only William's unhappiness that seamed unbearable.

At last she forced her stiff, unwilling legs to move again, showered and dressed, and automatically began to put the room to rights in a desperate pretence that the day was in some way normal. When another knock came at the door she'd just picked up a small wooden carving of the Madonna – her lovely Christmas present from Maria and the children. She was still holding it when she opened the door and found Adam waiting on the step. With no free hand to close it again, she could only *sound* unwelcoming.

'You're supposed to be going to Venice – shouldn't you be on your way?'

'When I've talked to you. Let me come in, please.'

She gave a little shrug, and left him to close the door. He glanced round the remembered room – tidier than when he'd been there, and full of grace notes that only a woman's occupancy seemed able to provide. Then he looked at her, pale and strained, and clearly anxious for him not to be there at all. She waited for some question about William that she wouldn't know how to answer, but what he actually asked took her by surprise.

'What did Amanda tell you about my wife?'

'Very little. Just that Elizabeth had been an old family friend and that she'd . . . she'd died very young.'

'She was your age – twenty-six; we'd been married for three years.'

'I'm sorry,' Georgina muttered helplessly. 'It must have seemed a terrible, senseless waste.'

His reply after a moment was even more disturbing than his question had been. 'Yes, certainly a waste. But the truth is that I felt as much relief as grief.'

She could only stare at him, shocked and disbelieving, and the expression on her face prompted him to a small rueful smile.

'That must have sounded even worse than I expected. It's a shameful confession – not one I've ever made before, even to my mother or to Amanda.'

'Why tell *me*?' she asked baldly.

'Because you once said something about understanding me better for knowing that I'd loved and lost a wife. I had the feeling that what you were more probably doing was *mis*understanding me.'

Georgina watched him as if mesmerised by the need not to make another mistake. 'Caterina said you'd spoken of a woman in England who filled your heart. I didn't know then that she was dead; when I did know, it seemed to explain the self-sufficient air you have about you. You'd known and lost happiness, and it wasn't any use searching for it again with someone else. *That's* what I thought I understood.'

'Then I'd better try to explain. We were a bit like you and Roberto – growing up in the knowledge that we and everyone else took our marriage for granted. In the end it was impossible to do anything *but* marry; it was simply expected of us. Elizabeth was delicately beautiful, a fairy creature not quite of this world, who seemed to ask to be taken care of. There wasn't any problem for me about that; I was happy to know I could look after her. You discovered your mistake with Roberto in time. I had married Elizabeth before I found that the gentle girl had become a relentlessly possessive wife, jealous of any woman I met, determined that my every thought and moment must be devoted to her. Even children were to be ruled out as a possible threat. Love has to struggle not to be stifled to death in such an atmosphere; in the end I was defeated.'

'Perhaps she knew instinctively that she was to be given very little time and couldn't spare you to anyone else,' Georgina suggested quietly.

'I've sometimes thought that was the reason – hoped it was, in fact, because then I could more easily forgive her. But I decided afterwards that I'd rather go lonely in future than find myself someone else's only hold on life. Now do you understand?'

She nodded, then smiled faintly. 'For a man who doesn't want to get too involved with people, you have an unfortunate knack of making them cleave to you! Leaving aside the distaff half of this household, even its menfolk still miss you as well – Nero included!'

'My fatal charm! Still, at least *you* seem to have remained immune.'

She thought that she would be calmly able to agree – would frame the right words to convince him of how beautifully immune she was; but at that precise moment they were both aware of a strange squeaking noise beginning to make itself heard outside the door. The noise died away, then came again louder than before, and a smile of pure amusement changed Adam's face.

'This is scarcely the moment for it, but would you care to bet that it's not my travelling escort outside the door? They can't bear to be left out of anything.'

She followed him to the door, and peered through the crack when he opened it carefully. Maria's latest batch of turkeys were clustered outside on the step, jostling to be the first to see what was going on. He slammed the door shut and leaned against it, trying in vain not to laugh.

'My next Great Work will be a treatise on the destructive effect of turkeys on the conduct of intimate conversations! I shall definitely advise against—' It was no good; the clamour outside moved into a higher pitch of frustrated curiosity and he couldn't hear himself speak.

Georgina collapsed into a chair, wondering whether the desire to laugh fighting with the need to weep would pitchfork her into full-blown hysteria.

Adam frowned at her. 'I'm going to have to do something about those bloody birds, but you don't look as if you're fit to help me.'

She shook her head, doubting her fitness too.

'You're a broken reed,' he said severely. 'Never mind – I shall open the door, slide round it so that the wretched creatures aren't all over the room, then run like a hare across the garden. They'll follow, because that's what they like doing best of all. At the critical moment, I shall step aside, leaving them to push each other inside their own backyard.'

'The scheme sounds excellent,' she managed to gasp, and then buried her face in her hands.

He shook his head at her but quickly disappeared, and she pulled herself together sufficiently to watch the ridiculous scene from the window. Three minutes later the turkeys were frustrated but secured inside their pen, and she saw Alessio come dancing across the lawn to hurl himself at Adam. She was safe, now, from any more 'intimate' conversations. Knowing that his *caro professore* was there, Alessio would dog his footsteps until he left again.

She watched them walk away together, and then suddenly set out herself in a different direction. Her way led through the olive orchard, and then up the hill to a favourite vantage-point. It overlooked the huddled terracotta roofs of San Vicenzo in the valley below, but otherwise spread out for her Tuscany's landscape as far as the distant, blue hills. This was the place she'd climbed to with her father the morning after Lucia's birthday party. All there'd been to recover from then was her humiliating mistake over Roberto; she had immeasurably more pain and uncertainty to deal with now, but must face both alone, without Richard Hadley's wise and loving presence to help her.

Her grandmother had put her finger on what mattered most, as usual: William had been aware of the effort last night had cost her – perhaps had even felt in the marrow of his own bones her struggle to be merry and to ignore her heart's longing that, like a compass-needle finding north, must always home towards Adam Fleming if he was there. Without seeing him again, she could have managed very well; could have continued to love William in a quiet but contented fashion and make life good for both of them. But with William now knowing what he knew, she could no longer believe that it was possible, and nor did he believe it, either. That was why he'd gone – to give her time to work out the answer for herself. There was no hope now of a future shared with him at Kew. Instead, she must find another job, another home, eventually; but for a little while she would have to stay where she was. It was what she'd originally intended after all – perhaps it had been meant all along; Maria would say that what was meant couldn't be indefinitely disregarded.

The morning was still, and not cold for early January, but even so it was necessary to start moving again. There'd surely been time enough for a man with a tedious journey in front of him to have said his farewells and left Poggio. But even as she stood up, the man himself came towards her, apparently with nothing more urgent on his mind than a leisurely stroll through the countryside. There was a moment in which she could look at him before he closed the gap between them. In the clear morning light he seemed older, more wearily fine-drawn than he'd appeared the previous evening. His summer tan had faded and his skin was pale again; it was easy to remember now that he led a very different life from her own – Oxford's stamp was on him again, and the months of intimacy with Poggio's rustic setting might have been only a dream.

'You've stumbled on one of the loveliest views we have,' she said, determined to sound calm and friendly as he came up to her.

'I didn't stumble on it – your scarlet windcheater wasn't hard to spot from down below.' He smiled at her expression and propped himself comfortably against a small, convenient tree. 'The turkeys interrupted us, if you remember. We hadn't finished our conversation.'

She remembered all too well, but decided suddenly that she could shadow-box with him no longer – the time for pretence was over, even though the whole truth was something she must still somehow keep to herself.

'I expect you know that William's gone home earlier than we planned. He hates to be away for long; something might die that he can't spare.'

'I doubt if he can spare you, either,' Adam commented quietly, 'but you don't need me to tell you that.'

She had a moment's vision of the man they were talking about – not smiling all the way to Calais this time, or telling his fellow-passengers about the girl he was going to marry. The pain of it was a stab at her heart, scarcely to be borne without whimpering like a stricken animal. She didn't cry out but, as her grandmother had done, Adam simply wrapped his arms about her, and she couldn't help burying her face against him for a

213

moment's comfort. Then she pulled herself away and managed a smile that went slightly awry.

'Sorry. For a man who doesn't like to get involved with other people you find yourself in some trying situations!'

He brushed back her tousled hair as if this, too, was a service he was sometimes obliged to render. 'Shall we admit the truth now? William didn't rush home to check up on his seedlings. I gave myself away last night though, God knows, I tried not to, and he must have thought he guessed something about you as well. Hard though it is to believe, was he right?'

The quietly insistent question had to be answered honestly but, lodged like a fishbone in her throat, was the memory of what he'd said before – that after Elizabeth he refused to put his life into the demanding hands of any other woman.

'I wasn't "immune" after all,' she admitted with a mad kind of gaiety. 'Wasn't allowed to be. Granny and Maria insisted that we must *all* adore the professor! But it's a pleasurable condition – not life-threatening at all!'

As if she hadn't just managed to explain that she was merely attached to him to the extent that everyone else was, he followed some train of thought of his own. 'I'm supposed to be on my way to Venice. Will you come with me, or would you rather we stayed here?'

She stared at him with sombre eyes, aware of the strangeness of the moment she was caught in. Instead of delight at what he seemed to be saying, she felt only sadness and loss.

'You don't listen, or you don't understand,' she said quietly. 'I won't have you think you must be responsible next for me; I can manage on my own. All that grieves me is hurting William. There's no joy in loving you, because although he probably won't believe it now, I love him as well. That's why it seemed all right to go on with our plan, even after I understood that . . . that immunity to the professor had broken down.'

Adam decided that the little outcrop of rock she'd been sitting on must hold them both, and gently pulled her down beside him.

'I *was* listening, sweetheart, but I should have realised you'd still be thinking of William. Forgive me for the stupid Venice idea.' He felt her shiver, and offered the warmth of his arm across her shoulders. 'I don't know William very well but I'd swear that he loves you as unselfishly as any man can. It's *your* happiness he's concerned about, not his own.'

She thought it was true, but her other crucial anxiety remained. 'I still

214

refuse to be propped up, Adam. I shall do very well on my own, here or back in England.'

His free hand covered and stilled her agitated fingers. 'I'm sure you will, my love, but I'm afraid I shan't manage at all. The past term back at Oxford has been the worst time of my life. I could see easily enough why you'd chosen William, but all along I'd had the conviction that the misunderstandings we were bedevilled by from the beginning weren't important. It was a facer when I finally had to accept that you didn't share my conviction at all. In fact, you seemed determined to show me that if Artom had tried to get Poggio thrown in with you, I needn't expect to get you thrown in with Poggio! Even when I occasionally got a glimpse of you, you melted into thin air if I so much as moved a step in your direction.'

'That was largely for Caterina's benefit,' she was obliged to admit. 'She even begrudged the cross words we occasionally exchanged. Franco's been making progress with her recently, but your arrival will have upset things again.' She was silent for a moment, then went on more gravely. 'It's upset everything, of course. I realised that day your papers were destroyed what I'd been running away from, but I'd given my promise to William by then. I didn't mind not being in love with him – Roberto had cured me of that; I just believed we could be happy together. But it's not possible now that he knows about you.' Her voice faded into silence and it was a moment or two before Adam spoke again.

'I came because Amanda told me you were still here, and your Christmas card didn't make any mention of William. It seemed my only chance to tell you the truth – that I love you more than life itself, and shall do until I die. If that sounds as if I see you as a tiresome burden I feel obliged to shoulder, then my usual way with words has deserted me just when I need it most. I hope you'll go on loving William, but *not* go on feeling guilty about him; I shall continue loving the girl Elizabeth was a long time ago, and try not to feel guilty that I *stopped* loving her.'

He turned towards Georgina, cupping her face in his hands. His mouth found her own, and there was no barrier she could erect against him, no denial she could make of the sweet delight that flooded her body. Breathless himself when he released her, he asked unevenly, 'Are you sure there can't be any joy for us?'

Joy looked entirely certain but she was unable to speak, and Adam had to go on himself.

'I know it's too soon – you need time to talk to William – but, when you're ready, *will* you live with me and be my love, for ever and ever?'

215

She nodded gravely, unable to say that any other future now seemed possible. 'My father will be pleased, but you'll have to give Olivia time to get used to the idea! She did so want me to choose an Italian – the idea being, I think, that in the fullness of time we should *all* be back in Italy for good.'

'Which brings us to Poggio, and the present,' Adam had to remind them. 'Can you really bear to leave it? Even more to the point, perhaps, do you feel that you dare leave it? Having *you* here is what has really put fresh heart into Enrico and restored Lucia; God knows you're entitled to a life of your own, but without you might they not fall into despair again?'

After a moment's thought Georgina shook her head. 'I don't believe so. It's Tommaso who's the essential one now, and he looks set to stay for the rest of his life. In any case, we can keep nipping back during those long, long vacations!'

'So we can. Presumably your parents will be settled here by the time Enrico and Lucia are ready to take things easy, and when Richard and Olivia have earned armchairs on the terrace, *we* shall be able to carry on. I can see it now – I shall let you and Tommaso run things while I sample the vintage and write the occasional scholarly monograph on some artist no one's ever heard of . . . What a blessedly lovely life! Until then, though, can you make do with a Victorian-Gothic villa and an unruly garden on the fringes of North Oxford?' He looked down at her, waiting for the smile that lit her face to beauty. 'You look pensive, sweetheart. Is it asking more than you can bear?'

'I could probably bear the Gobi Desert with you! I was just thinking about the muddle I've been in, the mistakes I've made. The day I met Roberto in the lane he blamed *me*, for not sharing his vision of the future. William is too kind to burden me with blame, but I shall always know he deserved loving in a way I couldn't manage. But I love *you* in every way there is; I know that now, and it's like walking out of darkness into golden Tuscan sunlight.' She fell silent again, and then frowned over someone else's happiness that couldn't be forgotten. 'There's still Caterina to worry about – she's been her old friendly self lately, but that won't last now; she'll hate me all over again.'

'I shall beg Maria to hint at an ulterior motive – "my well beloved hath a vineyard in a very fruitful hill", as Solomon neatly puts it! And if I also hint at my age and declining powers she'll think more kindly still of Franco.'

But he kissed his well beloved again in case she feared his powers had declined too far, and then said regretfully that he was committed to collecting his mother in Paris for the journey home.

'I'd give a great deal to take you with us, but I'm afraid you'll say it's too soon. Besides William, there are other people to consider – a wedding must wait for the presence of your parents, and living together before wedlock is something I think you would probably reject – am I right?'

She smiled ruefully. 'Quite right – I expect it's Lucia's fault. *She* taught me to have no truck with society's contempt for the holiness of marriage; but I agree with her.' She fell silent for a moment, then began again.

'Adam, *you* spoke a moment ago about succeeding generations following one another here into their armchairs on the terrace. Do you mind having the future laid out for you like that . . . Poggio's future? You probably had a different vision. You love teaching – you said so once – but I shall be saddling you in the end with a life you wouldn't have chosen, just because I passionately want *this* way of life to continue.'

He shook his head reprovingly at her. 'If you remembered half of what I've said to you, you'd recall something else – that you worry too much. If I yearn to teach above all else, I can find children to teach here; but I doubt if there'll be time. Loving you and keeping barbarians like Roberto Artom at bay – that will keep me busy enough.'

'You *sound* happy about it.'

'My darling one, I'm so happy about it that I'm inclined to burst into song again, which you'll have to learn is the way happiness often takes me.'

'More of dear old W S Gilbert?' she enquired suspiciously.

'No, certainly not . . . Robert Burns is the man for a love-song. Listen:

> As fair art thou, my bonnie lass,
> So deep in luve am I:
> And I will luve thee still, my dear,
> Till a' the seas gang dry.

The clear, sweet sounds faded on the still air as he looked at her. 'Sweetheart, I didn't mean to reduce you to tears; I'd better not render the rest of it, lovely though the words are.'

'It's only because you sing so beautifully,' she insisted between sniffs. 'I suppose you're going to tell me next that you were a boy-chorister when you weren't riding bareback on the downs.'

'All-round versatility,' he apologised. 'I did mention it once before—'

'The Oxford way, in fact – I dare say I shall get used to that as well.' She smiled suddenly, caught between tears, laughter and delight, because

217

already the day had held too much emotion. 'I'm not sure what Granny's going to make of my next piece of news, but we'd better go and find out.'

'I doubt if she'll mind having me in the family,' Adam said as modestly as he could. 'She's known for a long time that it's where I belong.'

Smiling at the idea, they went hand in hand down the hill, and crossed the garden, unsurprised to find that Maria's livestock had decided to accompany them like a joyous wedding-procession.

218